FRANCESCA THE FLORENTINE

Francesca The Florentine

by

Sandra Shulman

Dales Large Print Books
Long Preston, North Yorkshire,
BD23 4ND, England.

British Library Cataloguing in Publication Data.

Shulman, Sandra
Francesca the florentine.

A catalogue record of this book is
available from the British Library

ISBN 978-1-84262-599-6 pbk

First published in Great Britain 1971
by New English Library Ltd.

Published in Large Print 2008 by arrangement with
Sandra Shulman, care of Watson, Little Ltd.

Dales Large Print is an imprint of Library Magna Books Ltd.

Printed and bound in Great Britain by
T.J. (International) Ltd., Cornwall, PL28 8RW

FOR MY PARENTS
WITH GRATITUDE

BOOK I

'Yesterday's Child'

Francesca

It was Franca's favourite hour: the hour before sunset, when evening seemed to creep up beneath the sun. Though the brazen disc was still high in the cloudless blue, a misty lilac light suffused the hills beneath and gave distance the darker tones of twilight.

She looked down across the groves of craggy-trunked, silvery-leaved olive trees into the valley of the Arno. The river was a shining pewter snake, and the city, bathed in shadow, was already part of evening. Only Brunelleschi's great dome of Santa Maria Fiore, and Giotto's Campanile were distinct above the huddle of tiled roofs and enclosing walls, as if they sought the light while its source hung in the heavens.

Cicadas filled the lonely place with their incessant scraping. Above her, swallows wheeled, dived and chattered, full of the feverish activity with which they always greeted oncoming night. Against pale, dry grass their shadows were myriad whirling leaves … a portent of autumn.

The tall cypresses were intensely black on the golden hills surrounding Fiesole, and the distant buildings bathed in russet light.

The world was a still, warm place. The deep shadows cast by the trees were as soft and comfortable as bed on a cold, dark morning.

For miles around, vineyards, orchards, streams, farms, wayside inns ... their produce, animals and game belonged to the Narnis of Castelfiore. They were among the oldest Florentine families, descended from the magnati, who had been deprived of their oligarchical rule in the city when all the nobles' proud, watchful and advantageous towers had been truncated to no more than fifty brachia as a reminder that no one could rule over his fellows merely by virtue of an old title.

Franca threw open her arms to embrace the sweet air, perfumed with an abundance of wild thyme ... the drowsy haunt of murmuring bees. She licked her lips, savouring the taste of herbs implanted by the caressing breeze. That summer, around her thirteenth birthday, Franca had grown almost agonisingly aware of her senses: of colour, of texture, of smell, of sound...

She was glad to have the beauty all to herself. Who could tell how she would feel after the betrothal? With the registering of her dowry, and the exchange of rings, the future would be prescribed, and no longer full of infinite mysteries like an unexplored continent. Now, she must imbibe the glowing ripeness as if it was the final draught of wine. Indeed, Franca felt as lightheaded as if she had drunk too freely of undiluted Trebbiano.

At least the marriage itself was five years off. 'Thank all the saints for that,' she breathed. Something exciting must happen in all those days and months.

Absently she stroked her smooth, golden cheeks. Surely one day a beard would sprout, her voice become manlike, and she would not have to turn into a helpless female, forced to submit to her husband's will in all matters, condemned to sit by the hearth, quiet the children, and watch over the servants, while the men explored the world's wonders.

Franca had prayed ardently at the Badia Fiesolane that the baby growing inside her mother would be a girl. It was impossible being the only daughter in a household of men. Like some curse. If the new baby should be a girl then some of the burden of unwanted femininity could be temporarily shed. Someone else would be forbidden to roam the countryside ... sit astride the spirited Narni horses ... climb trees or the backs of oxen. Oh yes, the child must be a girl. That too would prove the validity of prayer.

Yet, living on the farm had taught her without subtlety the precise differences between male and female, and their respective roles. She knew there was no escaping her womanhood no matter how much she might fume at its limitations. Her mother and her nurse, Gostanza, had warned her she could not avoid destiny: to become a woman, a wife, and bear children.

'It is the duty allotted by God Himself,' Madonna Ginevra explained, 'and if the Holy Virgin did not protest at such a life then my daughter must not complain.'

'Aye,' Gostanza muttered out of her mistress's hearing, 'and sometimes motherhood precedes a marriage which then does not take place. May the blessed Virgin intercede for all our female weaknesses in the face of soft-talking rogues of men.'

Franca had a notion that her words had something to do with the unhappy cripple, Taddeo. The stable boys threw stones at him, while all other people crossed themselves whenever he appeared ... especially pregnant women. He was said to be half-witted because he mumbled to himself. Like some grisly carnival mask a livid purple mark stained his upper face.

Berto Spenozzi hated him. Whenever Taddeo glanced at Franca, he would drag her away. 'It's a vile sin,' he declared passionately, 'that such a fiend should be allowed to live and look on beauty ... as if the inmates of hell peeped through the windows of Paradise.'

Franca was not quite sure how long she had known Taddeo was Gostanza's son, but it never surprised her to see the nurse creep out to give the stunted creature scraps from her own platter. Although Madonna Ginevra was pious and kind, she did not encourage beggars to crowd her doors: for that would mean she was a wasteful housekeeper. Besides she was appalled by her maidservant's lapse, and doubted whether Franca should be cared for by such a woman. Yet Gostanza had begged so hard to stay with the Narni's beautiful baby girl, swearing by all that was sacred never to go with another man, nor have anything further to do with her miserable sin-made-flesh, that Madonna Ginevra had relented.

Gostanza did not know that Franca often talked with Taddeo. She did not fear him, and knew the dribbling mouth talked sense, and that he only muttered to himself through loneliness. Taddeo showed her the first wild strawberries … the hares dancing on spring mornings … he let her hold the tiny fox cubs he reared because their own mother had been slain. His home was a cave near the charcoal burners' clearing deep in the upper forest. They paid him little attention, fearing intruders from the outside world more than winter wolves or outcasts and vagrants seeking refuge in their trackless territory.

Franca rolled back on the ground, relishing her freedom and isolation, pointing her narrow feet towards the sun. There was no Madonna Ginevra to scold on the folly of idleness, and lolling with her skirts anyhow. 'If only you would train yourself, Francesca, then in time to behave like a perfect lady, the future wife of an important man, would be no effort, but second nature…'

'One day,' Franca vowed, yawning luxuriously and scratching flea bites, 'I'll do it, but not just yet. Life is too sweet to waste sitting upright, sewing, praying, and learning.'

There was no grumbling Gostanza either to warn her that acting like a hoyden could never tempt a fine rich gentleman to be a husband. Certainly not if she spent time in the company of Giovanni Spenozzi's boy.

'And getting up to Lord knows what,' her nurse added darkly, 'though the blessed saints know you're but a child, yet there's plenty of strange men who prefer their fruit unripe. Berto may be only fifteen but the Spenozzis were always a curious secret lot. His grandmother was a witch from Norcia – well, they're all witches there … and the boy has an evil name. Just keep out of his way.'

Franca had carefully ignored Gostanza's warning for at least six years, and knew Berto as well as any of her own brothers. If he had not been among the crowds bringing in the harvest, he would have insisted they spend this last golden hour in their spasmodic pursuit of a wily carp, that lived deep in the dark lake.

Berto was the only son of a tenant farmer who worked a few fields on the Narni estate. The one-roomed stone hovel had smoke-blackened walls, and housed the family, an emaciated goat, and some scraggy chickens. They ate plain pasta most of the time unless Berto or his father snared some wild creature in the woods, or caught a fish. Franca never considered the differences in their lives … only bemoaning the fact that she was a girl and couldn't run as fast as Berto. Maria Spenozzi's hands were rough and red, but she was always mutely amiable to the lord of Castelfiore's daughter, even allowing her to roll out the greyish dough for macaroni. Giovanni hardly ever spoke to anyone. It was impossible to tell if he minded Franca's occasional visits.

All the women around Castelfiore considered the Spenozzis undesirable, and Berto the worst of the lot. A by-blow of Satan, for surely his mother had danced naked with the witches, and then copulated with the devil's cold, scaley horn. One of these fine days Berto would end on the gallows, so they warned their sons, but more particularly their daughters to keep away from him.

He was tall, dark and well made. The forbidden reputation made his unsmiling features attractive to the girls, who gave him soft, sideways glances with their liquid, knowing eyes. The boys thought him a real lad; always ready with his fists, strong enough to knock down a grown man, and with enough manhood in his loins to father a legion of sons.

Slow-thinking and taciturn, Berto did not deny the tales spread about him, so they grew. Indeed he was indifferent to the rumours. This increased his notoriety as a vicious, godless creature, who would violate any woman he encountered … be she nun or grandmother.

Franca de' Narni was the one member of the entire female species he had any time for. The others were good for only one thing, though naturally they feigned unwillingness, even when their eyes said 'yes' … so that, afterwards, he suspected, they could declare themselves ravished virgins, even if their maidenhead had vanished years before.

Not that he had been with any woman. All he knew was from listening to wineshop and stable gossip and from what he'd seen in the woods when the couples thought they had the secret places to themselves. He knew just how the giggling, sighs and foolery ended: ailing, unhealthy babes; the pretty wench suddenly an old nagging drab; and the man tied all the stronger to his master's land, out of necessity of feeding a new mouth every year. Freedom lost because the Spring had entered the blood, and a man acted out of instinct with an eager girl.

Surely there was another life for a man: else a peasant was no more than one of the beasts he tended. Yet, when the awakening of masculinity set his body afire and quivering, he feared that one day, he too would be caught in that sweet brief snare which lead to eternal captivity, and turned the dreams of youth into the sterile dust of discontented age.

Franca had inspired his restlessness: she was entirely outside his knowledge of females. Unlike the rest of 'em, she didn't weep all the time, not even when she cut her knee badly. She didn't make sheep's eyes at him, or chatter about love … or run to her mother with false tales of how he had pulled her hair, tried to lift her skirts, or used a bad word. She did not look for holy relics or miracles behind each bush, as his own sisters had done before they were pinned down to reality with babes in their bellies, and unwilling husbands to wait on.

'So now folks are saying it wasn't religion Tessa and Gina found in the forest.' Berto growled to Franca one day in disgust and shame.

According to Gostanza the Spenozzi sisters were harlots: they lay with any man for the joy of it, and a crust of bread – so it was no miracle how their belies had been filled.

Franca demanded in her usual direct manner: 'If they are so poor and hungry, how can we blame them seeking pleasure?'

'Don't ever let me hear you say that.' Gostanza's own fall made her stern and unforgiving. 'Death is better than to lie with a man without a wedding ring.'

'So the giving of a ring makes the same thing good that was bad without it.' Her small charge added thoughtfully.

'It is a sacrament.' Gostanza crossed herself, thanked God that Madonna Ginevra was not around, and wished she hadn't plunged into such deep waters.

Berto loved to hear Franca talk in that strange husky voice ... a voice that did not quite belong to childhood. It could crackle like crisp autumn leaves, and then slide away as dreamy as the sweep of birds' wings on still air. It was none of your usual girls' daft chatter. She told him all she knew of the places beyond Florence ... even across the seas: of the dread and godless Turk who had wrested Constantinople from the Christians twenty-four years before ... of ivory, gems, monkeys, ginger and cloves that the merchants brought back from trading with the east. Strange words described goods unlike anything the itinerant pedlars displayed in the villages on feast days.

She told him all she read in her father's famed collection of manuscripts and new printed books: the sad and bawdy tales from Boccaccio's Decameron, the dread images of hell in Dante's own words, Petrarch's Italian poetry, and the wonders from Ptolemy's Geographia. The more tantalised he was by these fragments from an unattainable world the more he brooded about his own lot.

Sometimes Franca spoke of her dream to sail far away and discover some uncharted world which she and Berto could rule. His unimaginative, hungry soul believed it would happen. He sat with mouth open, and hands idle, as she recounted the preparations for her brother's great journey in the russet-sailed carrack, San Miniato from Maremma. Her father had poured a fortune into Raffaello's expedition to find trade with Naples, Sicily, Greece and Spain. Although the youngest son, he was more practical than the others, and longed for travel.

He had departed just before the storms. It would be a year or more till his return. If the voyage proved a success then Raffaello would bring back fifty to a hundred times what had been invested. Besides the lure of wealth, the Florentine spirit of gambling found this kind of risky venture irresistible. As well as the natural hazard of storm and shipwreck, there were the pirates working for their own gain, or in the pay of rival kingdoms … and of course the Moors with their fast, light craft whose fight against the Christian was holy.

Raffaello might be murdered, or tortured, or sold into slavery, or forced to abjure his faith. Franca spun a great story about his adventures until sometimes her tears would flow at the privations her mind imagined he was enduring. Then she would laugh at her fancies … like sunlight bursting through a storm. The sudden change of mood reminded the stolid Berto of the kingfisher on his brilliant flight among the reeds … flashing with colour, alighting in tremulous beauty, until the watcher cannot believe his eyes … only that he must be dreaming of this swift lovely vision.

There was another talent Franca possessed that only Berto had really noticed. With her thin child's hands she could fashion out of mud or clay dogs, birds, soldiers, and ships. With a twig or a feather dipped in dye from petals, or juice from berries, Franca made pictures from her mind: battles, castles, streets, ugly and beautiful faces on some smooth white stones. She could not explain how she did these things, except that they seemed to spring from her finger tips as the brain visualised them.

Berto marvelled that such magic could be

wrought, and feared it. Yet when he was with Franca he believed she could do anything she chose. She was a fairy child who wove an enchanted ring around them where they could play and dream, and in which he could forget the outside world, its indignities and injustices.

Trudging through the densest parts of the forest in their land of make-believe they looked typical peasant children. The tall silent boy in coarse ragged clothes with calloused dirty feet, followed by a slender volatile girl in a gown as torn and soiled as Berto's tunic … but the fine bone structure proclaimed her forebears were not peasant stock.

Franca did not believe there could ever come a time when the two of them would not wander the countryside.

'And when I'm bigger,' she said confidently, 'we shall walk further. Over the hills to Pistoia, where they make those fine daggers.'

She did not understand the impotent misery and anger in Berto's black eyes.

Neither talked of their friendship. Franca was forbidden the company of boys, or even to play outdoors without the attendance of nurse or tutor: a rule which had proved unenforceable. Berto knew his relationship with her would have been the subject of coarse jests over the whole area. He didn't want Franca's name linked with his. Other people would not understand, and only besmirch everything with their foul lies.

It just wasn't fair that soon she would grow up. Then their disparity of rank would be irrevocably apparent to her. He could no longer be the playmate who took out splinters and stings, buttoned her gown, or tidied her hair so that her appearance would not provoke too much curiosity when she arrived home late. As a man he would merely be a boorish unlettered peasant, who she would not even care to bid good day. His little Franca would be an exquisite gifted lady – the finest in the whole of Florence … or anywhere else he didn't doubt, and wife to some knight, worthy of a king.

When Berto thought of that inevitable marriage he was consumed by such fury he battered his fists against a tree trunk until blood ran down his arms, but pain did not drown the knowledge that the future must lead them along divergent roads, and that the slowly developing body could not become woman in his arms. He would no more have touched her carnally than he would have spat on a statue of the Holy Virgin. It would have profaned his deepest faith.

Franca knew nothing of his torment, and found him neither wicked nor fierce … only superstitious and silent compared with the voluble, questioning Narnis. But then she saw a side to his character no one dreamed existed. Anyhow she preferred to do all the talking.

She admired the fluent and obscene streams of abuse Berto could produce without any hesitation ... and the music he played on a reed pipe which he cut for himself while they waited for the fish to bite. Then he was a gentle creature who reminded Franca of the Fioretti of San Francesco, especially when the birds flew down to perch on nearby branches and listen to the pipe's tremulous notes welling amid the green woods.

Her education owed as much to Berto's rough influence as to Ser Agnolo, who had been her brother's tutor, and was now, in his own often expressed opinion, working off days in Purgatory, by attempting to teach the Narni girl.

Franca squinted up through the interlacing of leafy boughs, and began to giggle at the memory of poor Ser Agnolo's scandalised face when she told him her own forthright views on Paradise. The pale lean features seemed to grow even narrower, until she thought his face would disappear, and the long unhappy nose glowed red with indignation.

'...and if it's not like endless summer, singing among our lovely hills with fegatelli for dinner,' she was strung to insist, 'then I don't intend going there. I shall seek out those ancient gods, who the Greeks and Romans wrote about as having a very good time.'

'My little pagan!' Vincenzo de' Narni exclaimed with amused affection, avoiding his wife's horrified gaze. 'Our ancestors' crusades to the Holy Land did nothing to erase the blood left by Etruscan forefathers.'

Madonna Ginevra crossed herself, and automatically began to tell her beads. Of course, Franca was a foolish child. Yet, she had spoken heresy and blasphemy. The sin could not go unpunished on earth in case a higher authority demanded greater punishment. In order to drive these unholy concepts out of her daughter's rebellious head she had forced her to kneel in prayer in the musty chapel one glorious afternoon when Franca and Berto had planned to catch trout. That evening, a wooden bucket appeared containing three fat fish. Franca understood Berto didn't blame her for not keeping their appointment ... something which troubled her all afternoon, and caused the acutely penitent expression.

Madonna Ginevra also hung a great topaz set in a golden claw about the girl's slender neck on a gold chain. The stone ensured its wearer's chastity. Franca loved jewellery: her mother could not really be so angry if she gave her such a pretty trinket – one she had worn as a girl.

She reached inside the wool-embroidered bodice of her linen gown, and drew out the jewel. Against the light it was a mass of crystallised sunshine. Flashes of gold radiated from the many surfaces. Her eyes fixed on it until she felt drawn right into its yellow depths.

The golden trance broke as the advent of evening was emphasised by the chimes for vespers ringing out from San Francesco. Almost immediately the call was taken up by bells pealing throughout the valley. Then came the sonorous tones of the great bell in Castelfiore's tower, summoning the household to the evening meal. The labourers in the fields knew that the long working day was over.

Carts, loaded with mountains of hay like plaited gold, and huge panniers spilling forth masses of jade and amethyst grapes, trundled along the rough tracks, churning up clouds of pale dust which inflamed the eyes, and further whetted the thirsts of the harvesters trudging behind. Pairs of snowy oxen swung heavily towards the farms, as dignified as the white-haired grand-sires in the market place. From every side came the plaintive lowing of heavy-uddered, little cows going home to be milked. The cooling air was full of chatter, laughter and snatches of song, as if the whole world was suddenly happy to be released from its toil. Franca blithely joined in the refrain of a ballad.

'An hundred, and yet one, are we;
In heart and will we're all united,
Let every dancer jump for glee,
And he who will not be blighted!...'

Hunger yawning in her stomach drove Franca homeward like a spiked goat ... although part of her longed to stay out among the deepening shadows to watch the new sickle of golden moon drift over the city, and the sparkling stars peer down through the olive trees like jewels mislaid amid the branches.

The memory of Tullia's words made her race down the steep hill towards Castelfiore. That morning while Madonna Ginevra was at Mass, Franca had crept down to the vast kitchen. It was hot, steaming and dark but for the glare of the enormous enclosed cooking range. Always full of noise and movement, it was affectionately named by Tullia Maestro Dante's Inferno to the amusement of everyone save her mistress.

The gigantic and all-powerful cook was tyrant in this underground kingdom. She whacked maids, kitchen lads and flies with a wooden ladle used for tasting everything from broth to sweet batter ... and screamed like a wounded boar if anyone annoyed her, or too many rats scampered in her territory.

Only the sight of Franca softened the woman's glowering expression. To the girl it seemed incredible that this mammoth creature had once been the most popular strumpet in the San Spirito quarter of the city. Madonna Ginevra had taken Tullia into the Narni household to reform her, and the slender temptress became the largest and best cook for miles around; sacrificing one fleshly pleasure for another.

Tullia had beamed greasily and crowed like a furious cockerel: 'For my little darling I've made fegatelli in case none of the special dishes are to your liking.' She smacked her lips resoundingly. 'Such beautiful calves' liver, so tender so tasty, they deserve a sonnet in their honour. They will make a dish fit for my princess, although…' Tullia frowned terribly and reminded Franca of an angry red moon, 'there's some fools who consider fegatelli only belongs on peasants' tables.'

'As for the rest,' the cook began counting on her bulbous fingers, 'there's the sweetest melon cooling in the well, and my finest Berlingozza, as light as a virgin's first kiss.'

This large cake of flour, sugar and eggs was a speciality at wealthy men's tables, but the Narni version was regarded as supreme. In Franca's honest opinion, it didn't compare with everyday pasta fried and flavoured with garlic and cheese, but she would certainly have a large slice of it after the melon.

'…and my famous sausages, and plump capons, and tender veal stewed with rosemary, raisins, wine and spice, and young kid with almonds, and delicious lampreys … oh, and a few trout…' Tullia continued her litany to the belly, 'they're for the finicky, or those whose heads are overcome from too much Trebbiano. There's some fine ripe cheeses, and fruit … and those saffron jellies you love, shaped into men, animals and fishes. Just you wait till you see the palace of marzipan. No one will go to bed hungry tonight. I, Tullia, swear that.'

She thumped her massive bosom as if it was a drum. Madonna Ginevra left the task of upholding the high reputation of Castelfiore's table to her cook, whenever there were guests: for she was more taken up with praying and fasting for the good of her everlasting soul than eating for the pleasure of her life on earth. Tullia considered this a blasphemy, but it did give her the opportunity to be munificent with her ingredients.

'You, my little beauty, like to eat. God be praised. That's on the side of life. One day you will be ripe for love and bear fine sons. And, your big brother, Andrea, that wicked scamp…' she rocked with laughter so that all her fat chins quivered like a dish of saffron jellies. 'Holy Mother, how he likes to eat, and needs it to pursue his amorous sport...'

The appearance of Madonna Ginevra curtailed Tullia's rich remarks about Andrea's flagrant pursuit of Lucrezia Bonati, Lorenzo de' Medici's titular and virtuous mistress.

Poor Mamma, Franca thought kindly. She really believes I don't know what our dearest Andrea does with the lovely ladies in the city.

Castelfiore

The farm buildings were grouped around the ancient castle to form a great square. Granaries, barns, stables, and cow byres occupied the lower storey. Above dwelt the labourers, and their families, who tended the home farm.

Franca ran through the archway into the inner court. A flock of doves rose from the cote ... white feathers gold-tipped, their soft voices as much part of Castelfiore as each one of its worn stones. The birds drifted down to mingle with the painted frescoes on the inner curves of the colonnades, or range themselves like sentries on the four outside stairways which lead to the upper floors of the great house.

Momentarily, she pressed her face against a golden stone wall, feeling and smelling the warmth it had absorbed from a long summer. Castelfiore's unhurried seasonal life was as permanent and secure as sunrise and sunset, and Franca loved it wholeheartedly.

She gazed at the brilliant frescoes which never failed to entrance her. How proud she had been the day her father had allowed her to help mix the colours when he refurbished them. Then she had understood just how complicated it was to produce the new damp 'buon fresco' which lasted so well, and couldn't scale, because the colours seeped right into the walls. Both Gostanza and Madonna Ginevra had been appalled by her stained fingers and insisted she'd be better occupied at real lessons. Painting could never be the province of women, but Franca had remained in silent disagreement.

These frescoes lived in her mind. She had studied them minutely since her eyes first grew aware of sight. The lion, who had miraculously failed to devour Daniel had a friendly, doggish face like old Cassio. The Red Sea that Moses divided for the Israelites contained some dumpy cross-eyed fishes. The wedding at Cana was lightened by an old man asleep in a corner unaware of the festivity or the great miracle.

More than anything Franca preferred the tournament scenes ... so vivid and brave that sometimes she listened for the crash of arms, the snort of horses, the cheers, the screams. All the sounds she could remember from that glorious tournament held two years before in honour of the exquisite Simonetta, Giuliano de' Medici's mistress. Her flame of beauty had already been extinguished by consumption, but Sandro Botticelli's miraculous art had made her and himself immortal with the painting of the Primavera.

It was then that Andrea, looking like the god Apollo, all gold and white, and wearing some un-named lady's favour, overcame the eldest son of the Pitti, Salviati, and Pazzi clans in chivalrous combat. The delighted crowds had been swift to note that the sweet Lucrezia Donati had bestowed her gentle smile on Andrea de' Narni, so that many wondered if hers was the glove pinned to the handsome youth's sleeve ... and it was said that Lorenzo's eyes were narrow with resentment. The family had little time to enjoy Andrea's popularity for Umberto had contracted the plague while watching the tilting ... and the sunlit glory of a battle game became entwined with the reality of death. Vincenzo de' Narni had nursed his youngest boy without fear of catching the disease, but the plague reaped its unripe harvest. To Franca it seemed Umberto had gone on a long visit, so that when she thought of him it was to wonder if he would return grown taller. Death had not yet proved itself to be any great tragedy. It was, after all, as normal as birth.

The light in the empty court was red, and made the intricate patterns on the flag-stones appear freshly painted. Like some glowing beacon the rounded time tower was wreathed in fiery creeper. Vermilion leaves nodded about the sundial, and the clockface, and whispered that they did not care for time.

The place was completely deserted. Even the dogs were at their food. There was no chance to make herself tidy. No doubt Gostanza would be cross, for she had laid out the new green and yellow shot taffeta. Hastily Franca smoothed down the rough skirt, recalling the blissful softness of that other gown in her chamber ... but the tantalising aromas of food chased out vanity.

She did not bother to look into the familiar white chamber with its dark wooden supports making curving elegant patterns on walls and ceiling, where the family generally ate, talked, and played games and music in the summer. Tonight they were dining in the great hall so that the guests could admire the costly new wainscotting. Each time she saw it, Franca marvelled that wood could be carved to make flat surfaces appear like chairs, a desk, and cupboards full of books and musical instruments.

She pushed her way among the serving men and women. Candles had not yet been lit in the vast chamber. The long table was illuminated by the last soft light of day. The high ceiling and distant corners were already in darkness so that the company grouped about the table seemed to be under a golden halo. Through the open shutters, the outside world was tranquil beneath the new moon.

The place was warm and alive with the throb of chatter and bursts of masculine laughter. The best of the Narni silver and gold chinked musically against the majolica dishes. The few rare pieces of Venetian glass sparkled like rubies. The air smelt of good food and wine. The Berlingozza rapidly disappeared amid enthusiastic praise.

Despite his wife's unspoken disapproval Vincenzo de' Narni never allowed meal-times to be formal, and insisted that child-ren, dogs, and their tame goose, Bicci, were part of the company. Those who wished could talk. Those who desired to make music could sing and play for their own and others' delight. All he required – and Franca had learned this as a baby – was that anyone who spoke, or played, or sang should do his best. He was not content with prattle, or false notes. Talk should be witty or inform-ative, music tuneful.

Beside the empty hearth with the Castel-fiore emblem of two towers set inside a ring of lilies carved on the immense triangular chimney piece, the newest member of the family, Franca's nephew, Christofero de' Domenico Narni, aged five months, gurgled in his basket, a splash of milk on his fat chin. Madonna Isabetta smiled down at him, while she laced her tawny velvet bodice. Her cheeks were plump and glowing, her round blue eyes were proud and content.

Domenico took her hand and lead her to table. He looked upon his wife and firstborn with extreme tenderness, and the same keen interest he gave to all life on the estate. Domenico was happy to have married Isabetta, who had been his childhood sweetheart; although she came from a very ordinary family who owned only two farms, and had no business connections in the city. Other girls had been offered to him, with greater dowries and noble relatives, but he had been obdurate. Isabetta came from good stock, and would produce lusty children without any too finely-bred airs, and he wanted to wed young. Now she had proved herself to them by bearing his son. This new mantle of motherhood gave the plain, good-tempered girl the assurance and dignity of more than seventeen years and an uneducated background.

Franca loved Isabetta, who uncritically mended her gowns to prevent Gostanza's wrath. She was as predictable and stolid as her husband, and neither of them minded being teased about their rustic life. They waited comfortably for the next baby, secure in the knowledge that harvest must follow seed time ... and they intended to live out their days as part of that great cycle.

Franca missed Raffaello, so conspicuous by his absence, since wherever he was arguments and fights abounded: Castelfiore had never known such peace as during the last two months. He was as sharp and questioning as the other Narnis, but without the sweetening of his mother's nature, or his father's lazy good humour: the dash of pepper in the Narni dish. Raffaello reminded Franca of an aggressive little bull: shorter and stockier than his brothers, but with hair just as red, his face forever irascibly flushed, and eyes a scorching blue like the core of a candle flame.

Standing in the shadows Franca was a spectator on this vivid tableau, enjoying the few seconds before stepping into the scene to take up her role. She was safe, content, hungry ... and close to nearly all her dear ones. It was truly raining caresses, to use one of her father's favourite quotations. Paradoxically, she felt cheated that such a perfect moment could not be held forever.

Even now as I think, she mused, time is passing. With bewildering clarity the girl perceived that everything was in a state of perpetual change. There could be no finite except death ... or to try to transcribe the scene into words, or paint, or bronze. Yet the most perfect representation by the most skilled hand could be no more than an approximation to the reality as felt.

So there was no forever. It was a momentous recognition. Soon, she was to thank her mind for revealing this truth ahead of maturity. At present, she mourned for the happiness which like some delicious sweetmeat melted away even as she relished it.

Is that what always troubles my mother? she wondered, studying the woman who sat on the left of Vincenzo de' Narni, and in the old-fashioned manner shared his platter. The quiet brown eyes were so often glazed with unshed tears … the hands always folded in a beseeching attitude as if begging life to treat her gently. The bronze velvet houpelade trimmed with sable, the heavy golden necklace, shoulder ornaments, bracelets and earrings, studded with large amethyst, seemed a burden rather than a decoration. Beneath the golden gauze butterfly, Madonna Ginevra's face was drawn and weary. The sockets round her eyes were full of shadow, and the lines at the corner of her mouth gave it a sad downward droop.

She reminded Franca of the Mother in a Pieta. The girl felt guilty. What right had she to feel such compassion for her own mother? Yet, it always seemed that Madonna Ginevra was never at ease in the rambling castle, with her noisy children and smiling, thoughtful husband. She seemed an alien … a visitor to her own family, who would prefer to live in their elegant palazzo down in the White Lion district of the Santa Maria Novella quarter. Unlike the heads of other prominent families, Vincenzo de' Narni preferred to reside in the country for most of the year, instead of merely during the hottest, disease-ridden months.

Ginevra de' Narni glanced down at her beringed hands, clasped over her swelling belly. This was her fifteenth pregnancy. She had done her duty to Vincenzo, and borne him four living sons, and a daughter who promised to be a great beauty. She thanked the Virgin for blessing her so much more than many women. Though she could not understand her children's tempestuous natures, at least they were healthy and well-formed. Thus, it did not seem a sin to pray earnestly in the darkness of the great marriage bed that this would be her last confinement. She was very tired, and her head and back ached. It would be bad to miscarry now. How the men talked ... but it was their world, and had always been so ... she could barely understand one word in ten.

Her upbringing had been founded on extreme piety and modesty, and she had been taught to converse only with other women. To express an opinion on anything beyond housekeeping and children still seemed to Ginevra, even after twenty-three years of marriage, indelicate and unchaste.

Vincenzo considered such ideas archaic. She had reluctantly yielded to him on the matter of Franca's education, and knew her daughter would grow into one of the sophisticated breed of Florentine women who were intellectually equal to their husbands, could converse widely and wisely, and draw the great thinkers and artists to their tables. Yet, what did it profit them? Still their role was to conceive, bear and rear a child. All the Latin, Greek, logic and geometry in the world could not alter that fact or make nine months but five minutes.

The learning had only enabled Franca to read her father's manuscripts … all of which, except the religious writings, were unsuitable.

If the girl had to be educated beyond housewifely duties Ginevra would have preferred to send her to a convent where all knowledge would have true Christian foundations, and not be tainted with this Humanism her husband so admired, which impiously questioned all that had been accepted for centuries.

Perhaps – though she secretly doubted it – these classical teachings were all right for men, but where could it take a girl, whose sole duty was to become a good wife? Allowing Franca to think of other possibilities might only make her discontented, and that could lead anywhere: the first footsteps on the road to damnation.

Ginevra's eyes were tender as she looked on her second son. At twenty-one, Nofri was respected by older men. At the University of Padua his opinions as a physician were sought and acclaimed … ah, Maestro Nofri was something to be proud of.

If only … and her eyes darted to Andrea's empty chair … her first born could be guided by his equally subtle brain rather than his senses, he could have done so much better with their great silk business. He needed to settle down, marry a good woman, and so be thoroughly anchored in the merchant life of the city.

She glanced at Carlotta Corbizzi … so beauiful, virtuous, and well-brought up. The poor girl looked sad, and no wonder with Andrea – when he bothered to come home – treating this distant cousin paying Castelfiore such a long visit as a cross between an angel and a sister. That wasn't what had been intended.

At least Domenico had settled down. Ginevra sighed. Then she heard the baby mumbling to himself, and smiled. Her first grandson made her feel more like the mother of a family than her own children. Isabetta was a good wife, housekeeper and mother, and though she did little to gild the Narni name she would never disgrace it. Ginevra made the best of this alliance with the comforting thought that a fashionable young lady would be bored by her third son's complete preoccupation with farming, and might look for diversion among shameful and scandalous paths…

Then she noticed her daughter. Franca's gown was creased and stained from moss. Blackberry juice had turned her lips dark crimson. Wilting honeysuckle was tangled among her thick curls, for she had woven a chaplet of the sweet-scented blooms and then admired the effect so much in the surface of a pool she had quite forgotten to throw it away.

'Francesca Lauretta de' Narni, where have you been?' Madonna Ginevra shook her head so that the gauze butterfly fluttered like a shimmering cloud. 'You're so late, and how untidy. Pay your respects to your father's guests, and sit down.'

All heads turned to the girl. Carlotta blew her a kiss. Isabetta removed the tired honeysuckle. Franca turned laughing eyes to the company, made a graceful curtsy, and then grinned unrepentantly at her father.

Madonna Ginevra bit her lips crossly, but her husband held out his arms to their daughter. The girl would never learn discipline from him. He was always saying childhood endured so briefly that he wanted his children to be free to enjoy it.

Franca threw her arms around him, and kissed his mouth. She loved to see his face close, with its strange tawny eyebrows which seemed to leap about above pale green eyes that lived in deep lines forged by constant good-humour. His unruly russet hair had a streak of grey, and he, too, had failed to change into the fine clothes his wife preferred him to wear. The ragged sleeves of his dark green everyday robe were stained and spotted with paint and powders: evidence of this two over-mastering pursuits – painting and chemistry.

'My bad girl,' he said affectionately, 'what will our guests think of me for allowing you to be so wild?'

Franca peeped at the stranger next to her father, and saw two long black eyes studying her with unwavering attention.

'Eat,' Vincenzo patted her shoulder, 'you must be hungry.'

She slid into her chair, and with more zeal than grace dipped her grimy hands into the bowl of lavender-scented water her father's page, her cousin, Lionello, handed her. They eyed each other without comment, as if they had not fought that morning … after he'd pulled her hair, and said that girls should not be running and jumping as they were so bad at it. They should sit and sew, and pray for a husband, like his sister Nannina. Franca had immediately challenged him to a race, and then beaten him by a whole bracchia, so he had to swallow his words.

She dried her hands vigorously, and handed him the fringed towel. As he took it, Franca made a face, crossing her eyes and screwing up her nose. Lionello hurried away in case he was drawn into another scene which would damage his pride and reputation. Franca noticed that the stranger had silently observed these actions. To cover her faint confusion she winked at Nofri across a wedge of yellow melon.

'You look very fine and learned, Maestro brother.'

His serious features were parchment compared with the sun-touched skins of his relatives. Yet when he grinned his greenish eyes were gay with Narni laughter, and the thin straight hair was bright red though it already receded from his over-high forehead. The deep purple gown was costly and trimmed with lustrous fox, a heavy gold chain hung about his neck, and many rings adorned the thin nervous fingers.

'While you, little sister, resemble a shepherdess in one of Lorenzo de' Medici's poems in praise of rusticity. Don't you remember any of our guests?'

Franca smiled in recognition at an elderly man with a full grey beard and deeply-set brown eyes. 'It is the gentleman of the sweet spices!' she exclaimed.

The company laughed. Paolo del Toscanelli could often be found in the spice merchant's warehouse of the San Spirito quarter, which belonged to his nephews, but he was famed near and far as physician and astronomer. The doughty navigator, Christopher Columbus, had sought his sea charts and advice to seek out routes to new lands full of wonders and riches. Toscanelli also owned a magnificent library of scientific works, where artists and scholars came to browse. Franca had heard that he was among those who considered the world to be round like a China orange. She had spent some time trying to convince Berto without being too sure of her facts. 'But if it is,' she'd declared triumphantly, 'we can sail round it!'

'And I recall,' Toscanelli said gravely, 'a certain little lady who came into the warehouse with her father, and whose pretty but inquisitive nose could not be kept out of sacks, vats, and bins. One far too curious a sniff ended in a fit of sneezing which shook the bats out of the rafters, and sent the 'prentices running as if the earth quaked!'

Franca laughed. She had not realised how strong peppercorns were.

'For the very reason you like to breathe sweet aromas I have brought you a gift.' He dug into the pouch suspended from a jewelled belt at his waist, and produced a fine gold chain on which hung a tiny pierced orb. 'Here, my little dove.'

Franca inhaled deeply, closed her eyes, and murmured: 'Ah, so sweet. What is it, Maestro Paolo?'

'Cloves, cardamon, coriander and nutmeg.' The very words had a magical ring to them. 'When you visit the city use this pomander against the foul odours rising from the river, and in the narrow streets when there has been no rain. The evil miasma is full of infection.'

'Thank you, my doctor of spice.' She kissed him, and called to her mother. 'Would you like to smell this pretty thing?'

Madonna Ginevra held out her hand, but Isabetta intervened. 'Nay, Franca, your mother must not inhale anything which might irritate her nose. To sneeze is bad when you are carrying. God!' she added merrily, 'what trouble we had to stop me sneezing while Christofero was on the way.'

'And do you advocate such beliefs, Nofri?' Vincenzo demanded. 'I'm all for destroying old myths and letting new ideas take their place. Yet, the ladies, bless them,' he smiled indulgently at his wife, 'cling to their grandmothers' advice.'

Nofri said gravely: 'I think the ladies are right in this instance, sir. A sudden jolt disturbs the child, and might produce a miscarriage or misplacement which would make the birth hazardous. This is woman's province though, kept near as secret as the ancient Bacchic rites. Mainly we are forbidden to attend confinements, and still don't know enough to help mothers and save babies.'

Toscanelli nodded. 'Your son is right. The Church prevents genuine doctors from discovering so much, although I realise many of our profession are naught but mountebanks and rogues, doctoring with simples concocted of cabbage leaves.'

There was great laughter. It was the current city joke that any cabbage patch contained all the nostrums .. and a cuckold's garden held a deal of parsley.

'We are gradually gaining more respect,' Nofri added. 'Sometimes I wonder whether we should follow ancient Galen's teachings quite so blindly. It is almost medical blasphemy to ask this: but are his discoveries made some 1200 years ago really the final words on anatomy and medicine. We have borrowed much valuable knowledge from the Arabs...'

'Surely,' Madonna Ginevra interrupted timidly, 'the Infidel knows nothing of value, and I believe our doctors must work best in conjunction with holy relics.'

Franca stared openly at the man with the glittering black eyes whose soft tones might have sounded well on the lips of the serpent in the Garden of Eden, and seemed to make the very shadows leap with astonishment as he spoke now. His beard was an unusual feature on so young a man, but it was trimmed and pointed. Above the amused mouth a fine dark moustache gave him a sardonic air. 'Madonna Ginevra, during my travels throughout Europe and to Jerusalem, I have seen wondrous things, and also many foolish ones. The Infidel has plenty of wise notions that have not been constrained by the Holy Father in Rome, and can follow paths of thought, which are not open to our learned men on the grounds of heresy, and the terror of being accused of witchcraft. Knowledge should not wear blinkers, even if it sometimes confounds all we have held true and sacred for centuries. Let us question everything afresh, and learn to be wise.'

Madonna Ginevra's gasp of horror made Franca start. What right has this man to disturb my mother, she thought furiously?

'The churches over all Christendom are full of relics,' he continued ruthlessly, 'how many phials of the Virgin's milk, how many heads of saints this or that, and so many splinters of the true cross that I verily believe our Lord was crucified in a whole forest! Nay, Madonna, I tell you truly – and though you may doubt that I am a Catholic – sometimes I am ashamed our religion can be so ridiculed, and that the priests will buy up such relics from Infidels, often knowing themselves to be duped in order to have glory attached to their churches…'

Vincenzo nodded vigorously. 'I am sure Messer Ridolfo speaks sense.'

Franca stole a glance at her mother, and

saw the brown eyes were glowing with angry tears, and that she twisted the crucifix hanging on a finger ring. Meekness did not permit her to argue with any man, and since Messer Ridolfo di Salvestro was a guest she owed him politeness.

'You only underline what I have always thought of priests,' Vincenzo went on, glad to have such a well-informed ally. 'I would not let any of my children enter religious orders which have become so corrupt. I believe it is the greater evil to take vows and forswear them with rich clothes, and every kind of fleshly indulgence than to be a sinner in the world outside. I would not have my girl taught by the nuns either,' he added with unusual vehemence, 'for I am all in favour of worldly education, but not when it is given with sly winks and nods. I would not have the Narnis sin against the light they have sworn to keep burning...'

The arrival of plates of meat halted conversation. The fegatelli dish beside Franca emptied rapidly. Now and then she found the bearded stranger watching her with amusement, but she threw back her hair and continued eating. I do not like that man, she thought, he makes everyone feel uncomfortable and enjoys it. Yet her eyes often returned to his compelling figure.

One guest ate more ravenously than anybody, and as usual his untidy beard was scorched. The blue eyes reflected fire red from the wine in his silver cup. Between great mouthfuls of stewed kid he explained: 'I am working on some new designs, but though I badly need the florins that work pays me, it uses up so much valuable time…'

'My friend Cosimo,' Nofri spoke with mock severity, 'you are foolish to spend your talented time, and money on alchemy. You are nearly ruined.'

Franca's eyes opened wide with wonder. They said Cosimo Rosselli was a magician, but he looked starved rather than terrifying.

'I don't think Maestro Cosimo has found the Philosopher's Stone yet,' she piped.

'Little Franca has a sharp eye,' he grinned, 'you're noticing my garments, eh.'

His velvet gown was worn and rubbed, and the stockings so often darned they seemed patterned. He was bereft of jewellery except one thin silver ring, and his gaunt restless hands were stained and burned from his experiments.

'We artists have our weaknesses,' he murmured, smiling dreamily at Franca. 'Perhaps that is the way our God forces us to realise we're merely human beings when our fellow men tell us we have the divine spark at our finger tips. Sandro Botticelli dotes on his wine and girlfriends. The sweet Filippino's late father, Fra Filippo Lippi adored lovely ladies to the point of idiocy. Your brilliant friend Leonardo, Maestro Paulo, is always bursting with marvellous and impossible schemes, but fresh ideas frequently force him to leave old ones incomplete. My own weakness might at least bring me a fortune.

'Last week I vow I was so close. I had just reached the Yellow, which as Vincenzo knows, is the stage of Separation. It is not easy to get thus far...'

Franca's father leaned forward, nodded expectantly.

'At any moment the final step would be in my grasp. I am sure I should have created the Stone that would give me gold, and the secret of life...'

The company ceased eating, held by the artist's words. 'Then my neighbour's wretched, flea-bitten mongrel ran in. Seeing the steaming pot, he overturned everything and ruined the experiment ... all because I had once been foolish enough to feed him a mutton bone. He thought I must be preparing one for him again...'

Even Madonna Ginevra laughed at this tale, and silver cups of wine were raised in tribute to Rosselli's sweet-humour. He did not seem embittered, even though he'd lost an eyebrow in the explosion.

'Did you know, Vincenzo, that San Ambrogiano is being renovated at long last?' Rosselli's voice was distorted by the leg of capon he gnawed. 'Mino da Fiesole is producing the tabernacle, and the della Robbias the two angels. It's decided I shall paint the transubstantiation, and a picture of our Lady with the saints. How I should love to use your wife's head,' he smiled kindly at his hostess, 'she has just the features I bear in mind when I paint God's Mother.'

Ginevra coloured. Her eyes smiled. Franca was happy that the ill-clad, comic figure had soothed the hurt the elegant worldly stranger had caused.

'Tell me, Rosselli,' his insidious voice demanded, 'do you also use astrology…'

Franca did not listen to the reply, for she knew that Rosselli like her father consulted the planets' movements to discover propitious times for his experiments.

'Who is he?' she whispered to Domenico, who was stolidly chewing his way through a mountain of sausages, and taking no part in the conversation. (Mealtimes, he insisted, were for eating. 'I open my mouth to put in food. There's too much idle talk about.')

He swallowed a whole sausage and murmured behind his greasy fingers. 'He's someone important from Milan. Supposed to be in the service of Duchess Bona. She's the French king's sister-in-law. Nofri told me privately that this Ridolfo clandestinely visited Pisa where…' Domenico looked round furtively, 'his close friend, Lodovico

Sforza lives in exile. He's the brother of the late, and from all accounts unpleasant Duke Galeazzo. Note how Ridolfo wears only mulberry coloured clothes – a subtle announcement of his real allegiance since it's a pun on Lodovico's nickname. Il Moro, which derives from one of his names Mauro. The widow Bona is reputedly stupid and obstinate, but she won't have Cardinal Ascanio or Lodovico in Milan in case her wily brothers-in-law seize the power she ineffectually holds in trust for her young son, Duke Gian Galeazzo.

'Ridolfo is very rich, and a great patron of the arts. Those with little sense claim he's an astrologer and magician. Our Nofri met him at Padua where he was studying law and medicine. Besides all this learning, he's said to be a first rate soldier. Looks a shrewd devil, doesn't he? Mark my words, little sister, he's not taking a holiday in Florence...'

Gostanza and Lionello brought in the candles. Their winking flames made Ridolfo di Salvestro's slim figure glow like the interior of a goldsmith's shop on the Ponte Vecchio. His clothes were of the richest material, heavy with gold thread. Around his neck was a magnificent collar of rubies. Several precious rings embraced each finger. The cabochon ruby on his right thumb was engraved with a lion grasping a man in its jaws. Messer Ridolfo gave the impression of darkest night with his smooth sable hair and swarthy skin. The strong white teeth reminded Franca of some ferocious animal devouring its prey. He ate his food with one of those new forks – the first she had ever seen. It seemed a strangely graceful action for such a man, as if he attempted to conceal his power under delicate trappings, which he might suddenly cast aside to reveal a full and dread strength.

It was the first time Franca feared someone without any apparent reason. Whenever Messer Ridolfo looked at her, she longed to stretch out two fingers in 'cornu' to ward off the evil eye. Catching her glance, he smiled and bowed, then whispered something to Vincenzo de' Narni.

Vincenzo laughed heartily. 'Franca, my love, come here. Our illustrious guest has asked me if you are already betrothed.'

She stood between the two men. Her father held her close so that she felt secure though she was very near the prince of darkness.

'For if you are not, Madonna Francesa,' the soft voice contained intensity, 'I shall be glad to wait until you are of an age to marry. My eyes tell me of your beauty. Your father and brothers tell me of your wisdom, and I have observed you have wit. In five years I shall be under thirty, which is not old. I promise you a fascinating life, and unquenchable love. What do you say?'

Franca could not decide if he jested, but she would not be discomfited, and run away like a silly, giggling child. His mention of love made her skin feel strange as if it replied to some question she neither heard nor understood.

She curtsied. 'May I thank you for your offer, Messer. I am indeed honoured above all ladies, but unable to consider it, for I am to be betrothed to Messer Lambarda della Sera's son, Daniello.'

'The Medici's favourites, eh?' he chewed his lip. 'I can't yet compete with such an influential family. To show you bear me no grudge for putting such a bold question in public, will you share this peach?' He cut a lush globe of juice in two, and handed her half on the little golden fork.

Franca recalled Berto's warning about witchcraft: if he is indeed a streghone, as he seems, and I accept something from him he will gain power over me. Then she gave a soft laugh, and bit into the fruit, watching him eat the other half. There can be no bond, her mind said, unless I agree to it. The black eyes regarded her fixedly.

'Your daughter is born under the sun, in the house of the Lion,' he said quietly.

'How do you know?' Vincenzo was delighted.

'Can you read the future?' Franca burst in excitedly, 'Ser Agnolo has cast my horoscope, but it describes more my nature than my destiny.'

'And she is as wilful as good Ser Agnolo predicted.' Her mother remarked.

The tutor bowed his head in Madonna Ginevra's direction, and Franca noted that the whey cheeks had turned a sore red. He loves her, she thought, like the knights in those old tales – a faithful lover seeking nothing but the right sometimes to speak with her. Franca knew her mother could not be aware of this, for then Ser Agnolo would have been sent away. The thought of a man's love would not quicken Madonna Ginevra's heart. Its shadow would endanger all she held sacred. Franca noticed her father's eyes smile roguishly towards the tutor, and she understood he shared this intuitive knowledge, and was amused and compassionate.

Poor Mamma and poor Ser Agnolo, she thought. If I were married, and a man other than my husband loved me, I should be proud. She smiled at the idea. The smile was returned by Messer Ridolfo. Franca had the uncanny sensation that this stranger knew her thoughts. Her large eyes regarded him fearlessly. 'What can you tell me of the future?'

He took the small sunburned, right hand, and traced the lines on the palm with his flashing fingers. Franca tried to conceal the tremor his touch provoked. The others at the table leaned forward. Isabetta muttered to her husband: 'I fear that man. He has the power.'

'Governed by the sun, fire cannot burn you, but others will be scorched by your bright flame...' he murmured, and then passed a hand across his eyes as if to obliterate whatever his wisdom showed. 'Nay, Francesca,' Ridolfo said soberly, 'I shall not tease you with lies of the future. There is too much shadow in our own times even to know the present with any certainty. Be happy while you may...'

Then, as if she were a great lady, he raised her food-stained fingers to his lips and kissed them.

Franca was disappointed, and her hand felt inflamed as if it had been too close to the fire. No one spoke for a long minute...

The tension around the table was broken by the barking of dogs outside. Old Cassio, Vincenzo's greyhound, rose to his feet, yawned, and growled. Bicci strutted crossly in the shadows, honking warningly...

Storm Clouds

The door was flung open. Candle flames trembled and almost dissolved into darkness. The intruder was clad in the coarse sleeveless garb of a humble labourer belted close about his tall figure. A hood concealed his hair and shadowed his face.

Without hesitation, Franca ran straight to the stranger. He threw her high in the air. The hood fell back to reveal long curling red hair.

'Andrea! My sweet brother!' she clung to him, kissing his lips, 'what has happened to your poor face?'

He smiled, but one eyelid was puffy and bruised, nearly concealing the eye beneath, although the other was as green and merry as ever. A wide gash on his smooth forehead was crusted with dried blood.

Ignoring all questions and greetings, Andrea moved to his mother, and knelt at her side. He took one of her frail hands in both of his and kissed it with genuine devotion and love. 'Madonna, Mother mine, forgive me for my unkempt appearance and tardiness…'

Ginevra placed her free hand on the thick

hair so bright it seemed to emanate warmth. The Narni torch casting gaiety and light, friends said. With cunning to match a fox's brush, muttered others. She loved her first born intensely, yet he troubled her. How could this wild and sensual man have once been the tiny baby who had sucked the milk from her breasts so that she knew fierce joy and pain? She still recalled the pride of giving her husband a strong son as their first child…

'Aie … aie…' she sighed as if in travail, 'Andrea, my son, why must it always be so? Fights and secrets. Why not settle with a good and sweet girl?' her eyes strayed to Carlotta, who was watching Andrea with anguished adoring eyes, 'then there will be no need for brawls and disguises.'

Andrea looked up at his mother with the same rapt expression he gave to the elevation of the Host. 'Madonna, I am not good enough to be your son.'

'Go now and eat.'

As she spoke, a tear fell on his forehead. For a second it pained Andrea more than the cuts and bruises. He rose to his feet, blinking as if dazzled by candlelight.

'You need food, Andrea,' Vincenzo called, smiling and understanding. 'Afterwards you might care to give some account of how you earned your wounds, and why you are wearing such plain garb when I know, to my cost, just how much you spend on finery.'

Andrea grinned and bowed to the guests. He began to eat with ravenous concentration, and Franca, sitting beside him, kept adding more food to his plate. She adored him, and as a very tiny girl had been heartbroken to learn that he could never be her husband. All she could hope for was one almost as perfect. Her eldest brother laughed at all laws, and saw life as an unending sunny day ... and loved his sister as much as that life ... and quite as much as she loved him.

'My own little sweetheart,' he whispered, 'surely there is no lady in Florence as beautiful and kind.'

'You would certainly know, eh, Brother?' Domenico asked with sly good humour. 'How you eat!' He closed one eye in a slow wink, and then asked seriously: 'Nofri, don't you think our good Andrea resembles Papa's horse, Scipio?'

Nofri considered, and then gave a staccato burst of laughter. Andrea joined in, and the three brothers, alike in colouring, yet so different in temperament and interests, were linked. Franca also laughed, although the jest was not meant for her ears or understanding.

As all the farm hands knew, the stallion liked nothing better than serving mares. Afterwards he would eat and eat. Many times Franca had witnessed Scipio's prowess, even joining in the burst of ribald cheering which the horse seemed to accept as his due.

She looked around the table. A great love welled within her embracing everyone from unborn babe to aged dog. Without doubt to be a member of the Narnis of Castelfiore was the most blessed fate in the world.

Vincenzo pretended not to understand his children's mirth, though he knew his horse's and his eldest son's appetites. Gazing at his daughter, he momentarily glimpsed how she would look when grown: a beautiful alluring woman, but what deadly clarity sparkled in those eyes … eyes that usually reminded him of the new violets found in the deepest part of spring woods, dew-glossed and peeping from under dark green leaves. For the span of a breath Franca's gaze held what he would have her ignorant of: complete knowledge of the world. Vincenzo wanted to throw up his arms and plead with fate, or the saints, or whatever power controlled their future: his little girl must not be corrupted, or suffer. It was written that she was to be wed, the mistress of a vast household and know only beauty and peace. Whatever unhappiness Messer Ridolfo had read in her palm he would prevent.

Despite teasing and entreaty, Andrea would say no more about his disguise than it had been part of a wager to go around without any of his friends recognising him near the Mercato Vecchio.

'As for these wounds, they're nothing.' He jerked his head as Nofri's fingers probed the cuts, and applied a honey-based salve. 'Ouch! That stings worse than a dagger thrust. I was thirsty so I went to the Snail. The Vernaccia is always good to drink there, although the inn is in a cursed dark alley. When I came out some ruffians took exception to my face. It's often the way in big cities.'

'Weren't those ruffians wearing some distinguishing badge?' Ridolfo di Salvestro demanded.

Andrea looked astonished, and held the dark gaze. 'They say you have magical powers of acquiring knowledge, Messer Ridolfo. You know as much about our city as you do of Milan,' and he added significantly, 'or Pisa. What are you suggesting?'

Ridolfo's smile made Franca uneasy, but his voice remained as gentle as the brush of taffeta. 'And you, Andrea, appear to know a lot about my business. Yet, I do not fear your tongue, because the name Narni carries honour, and no deceit.'

Andrea bowed his head as if accepting a rebuke, and the guest continued: 'Their clothes bore the Palle device.'

The company stirred without speaking, for Messer Ridolfo had mentioned the golden pills – the round and unmistakable emblem of the Medici's.

'How did you know?' Andrea whispered.

'Why does the Narni heir involve himself with the ruler of the city of the Red Lily? Better pursue some other treasure than one already publicly prized by so noble and powerful a being.'

Andrea's tanned skin darkened as the blood surged near its surface. 'It's all rumour. Nothing more.'

'Rumours flying provoke daggers as much as plain truth,' Toscanelli remarked. 'Be advised, Andrea. Admire the lady from a good distance.'

'Both ladies,' Ridolfo breathed.

Andrea reacted sharply. 'You are the very devil with knowledge, Messer.' Then he laughed. Sunlight poured over dark clouds. Franca's tension dissolved. 'I broke at least three heads. They were forced to retreat. All because I wrote some pleasant verses in honour of a fair lady.'

Vincenzo shook his head ruefully. He knew that at least two golden-haired toddlers on the estate owed their existence to his son's charming audacity. Girls just melted before his warmth. Andrea was kind and generous to the mothers of his love children, and never avoided his responsibility, even if lately he rarely visited them. Lucrezia Donati, if that was really the quarry, was not a simple wench to be pursued, wooed, and won away from another man … not when the other man was Lorenzo de' Medici.

Gazing at Andrea, Franca was convinced that any woman must prefer him to the ruler of Florence.

At last, only flagons of wine, dishes of fruit and nuts, and Tullia's exquisite marzipan confection remained on the table. The men pushed back their chairs, and some loosened their belts. The ladies brought forward the embroidery frames to work at the altar cloth Madonna Ginevra had promised to the convent of San Francesco. Blushing a little at the enthusiastic masculine praise for their intricate and fine sewing, the three ladies started to sew, only stopping to compare threads or stitches in faint whispers.

From the safety of her father's feet, Franca prayed Gostanza would not suddenly appear with that wretched piece of needlework she was always endeavouring to mislay. 'Your grandchildren will finish it for you at the rate you sew,' Gostanza used to chide, 'and those butterflies will turn back into caterpillars…'

Oblivious of conversation, Domenico began to mend a saddle. Nofri and Ser Agnolo returned to the chess board to continue the game they had started before the meal. While Rosselli sketched the sleeping Christo, Toscanelli and di Salvestro examined their host's latest acquisition from Vespiano Bisticci's bookshop, a handsomely illuminated copy of the Aeniad. They took it in turns to declaim their favourite passages. Franca found it difficult not to join in. It was her father's fond boast that she knew this work by heart. It wasn't surprising: Ser Agnolo's choice punishment was to set her to learn screeds of Latin, and translate them into everyday Italian.

She noted with contemptuous amusement that Lionello was ostentatiously reading from the Dialogue of Santa Caterina of Siena, slyly looking up to see if anyone observed his piety in the midst of so much irreligious entertainment. Just like his awful father, the boy was always trying to win the attention of any important personage who might recall him favourably at some later date.

Andrea had said: 'Uncle Weasel…' they all called Maximo di Aquia that for obvious reasons, '…would crawl on his belly to any man's tune. He's afraid to fart in case it's against the wishes of some potential patron. It seems a shame that at fourteen Lionello has acquired a similar trait!'

Uncle Weasel volubly disapproved of the Narni attitude to life and politics. He had only married into the family for the generous dowry, but was never adverse to using the name Narni when his own more meagre one failed to open the right doors.

'Your father must have choked swallowing

such a lump of pride,' Andrea had observed when Lionello first arrived, 'actually sending his beloved son to act as page at Castelfiore, but I suppose he can bend his anti-magnati principles as the Narnis often entertain renowned folk!'

Although Ginevra complained about her children's recklessness, she was dismayed by her nephew's orderliness and constant displays of piety. Though practised silently they seemed to be accompanied by a fanfare of trumpets blaring: 'Look at the good and clever Lionello di Maximo Aquia!...'

'It's not normal in a child,' she confided to her husband in their bed.

Vincenzo grinned, and patted the soft face close to his own. 'That young scamp is as two-faced as Janus. He doesn't fight, but he's always sneaking about bearing tales, and causing other people to fall out. I don't like him now. Can you imagine how he'll be when he's a man? Poor Riccarda is too weak to have any influence over him.'

He often sighed remembering his sister's plight. She had never seemed more than a chattel to be disposed of by their autocratic father, Messer Riccardo di Narni, and she had never known how to do anything but bow down to the rule of all men. Vincenzo could not bear to visit the di Aquia residence in the city, for he was sickened by the sight of his sister – a pale shadow constantly in terror that her slightest glance, because of its Narni origins, might bring disgrace to her husband's noble profession as lawyer…

Vincenzo despised only lack of nobility of soul. 'It is better to be a pauper with dignity and honour,' he instructed his children, 'than cast in the mould of that Maximo, who cannot even be loyal to himself.' And he quoted Petrarch to remind them that they must not think to rely on their ancient name: 'One is not born noble, one becomes noble.'

'What do you think of the Medici?' Messer Ridolfo asked, putting aside the book, and breaking off a piece of marzipan. 'I am to visit him soon, and would know the manner of man I'm to deal with.'

Vincenzo cracked walnuts and fed them to Franca. 'A noble patron of the arts, always surrounded by poets and philosophers. A lover of beauty and gaiety, and much liked by ordinary folk for the wonderful spectacles he arranges on feast days. Truly he is not called The Magnificent without reason…' he added guardedly: 'I have no quarrel with the Medici family, but it pays to be among their close friends especially in times of rigorous taxation – which is ever – and to be favoured by Lorenzo often means total tax-exemption…'

'He is assiduous in scotching the faintest of plots against him,' Toscanelli interposed.

'Exile, assassination, or execution take care of any potential rivals. Thankfully, he is not among those blood-crazed rulers who employ cruelty for the love of it.

'With subtle, almost invisible power, Lorenzo controls Florence by withholding civic offices from the magnati unless he personally trusts any particular family. He ensures the Signoria – our governing body – is composed of men without great names, or wealth, and whose loyalty is secure because they dread the return of the ancient families…'

Vincenzo glanced at Andrea who stood staring into the evening, uninterested in the conversation, and sighed: 'Personally, Messer Ridolfo, I should advise every citizen to be loyal to the Medici, and try not to provoke his enmity, even if they don't crave his favour…'

He stroked Franca's cheek, and said soberly: 'We shouldn't complain. The Medicis keep their enormous banking concerns safe by controlling our state, and they wish to make Florence rich rather than embroil her in costly wars which only damage trade. Prosperity cannot flourish in the midst of turmoil. Alas, past attempts at so called democracy led to nothing but squabbling factions in the commune. Perhaps men will never be able to rule themselves. The increasing gulf in learning standards ensures that a favoured, highly-educated minority must always gain control, because only they can understand the world and its complexities.'

'Philosophers for rulers,' Ridolfo said bitterly, 'with hired soldiers to put right errors of thinking by the sword!'

Vincenzo frowned. 'Each state wishes to be superior, and so all rulers fight and scheme for advantage.'

'None more so than His Holiness.' Ridolfo spoke out sharply. 'Examine most plots these days, and the villain is that bad-tempered, one-time fisherman from Savona, Pope Sixtus. His desire to increase papal domains is only exceeded by his incredible nepotism.'

Madonna Ginevra's eyes were sad but she could not dispute this fact. Rumours of the life at the papal court sounded very like the debaucheries of ancient Rome. She had been shocked when the extravagant, extremely carnal and cruel Pietro Riario had been made a cardinal. Nominally he was Sixtus' nephew but everyone knew he was really the Pope's son. Still, dissipation, or God's judgment, had killed the young cardinal within three years of him receiving his hat!

'Our present unrest is the fault of that ex-customs clerk, who used to sell oranges in the streets of Genoa,' Vincenzo's voice contained a dose of venom. 'Another of the Pope's favourite *nephews:* Giralomo Riario.'

His sons laughed. Vincenzo and half

Florence blamed young Riario and his Holy Father when anything went wrong … even if it rained for the Palio.

'He's come a long way that one,' Vincenzo continued, 'Captain General of the Church, and Commander of Castel Sant' Angelo. Serve His Holiness right the day dear Giralomo has to do any serious fighting. They say he's the biggest coward and military fool in Christendom. He's also Count of Bosco, and the Pope giving him control of Forli and Imola caused all our problems.'

'Giralomo is universally loathed in Rome,' Ridolfo commented. 'He's fat, lazy and cruel, and dare not walk abroad without a guard because of the many murders he's said to have committed. I attended the celebrations when he wedded our Caterina Sforza, the late duke's natural daughter. She's rich, lovely, courageous and brilliant … and now pregnant I hear. How she endures her boorish husband I don't know, but his new titles probably compensate for his character. The young lady of Forli is an arrogant and forthright girl…'

She's only two years older than me, Franca mused, and Ser Agnolo claims I almost rival her in learning when he's in a good mood. Yet she has had to marry a vile and despised creature for political reasons. She shivered and thought of her own betrothal.

'My darling girl is cold,' Vincenzo said

with gentle concern.

Andrea lit a heap of pine cones in the grate. Soon the evening chill was banished by a soft warmth and the scent of woodlands. The flickering light made Franca sleepy, yet she did not wish to go to bed. It was pleasant to dwell in this circle, and listen to the men talk of great events which could not affect her life.

'Yet Florentine problems go back further than young Riario, my friend.' Messer Ridolfo spoke earnestly, and Franca leaned forward to watch him. 'Just look at the geography of politics.'

With the point of a splendid jewelled dagger, he drew a rough map in the dust of the hearth. 'Your territory,' he marked it with circles to emphasise the Medici's control, 'is bounded on three sides by petty states, nominally papal in allegiance', he marked these with crosses, 'but they look to the city of the Red Lily because of its greater trading power…'

He smiled at Franca's serious face. 'Besides your ruler has always been clever in taking their sides in disputes against other petty states, just as long as they were far away from your borders. It's easy to look brave by sending out a band of condottieri. Rome could equally claim such actions were subtle attempts to extend Florentine influence.

'We are all agreed that Sixtus is ever-desirous of expanding his territory … not in a necessarily holy manner. It was no wonder he thought to secure Imola and Forli by making Riario their ruler. Look at their position in the plain of Romagna, just at the foot of the Tuscan appenines…'

'Messer Ridolfo, you must allow that Lorenzo could not permit the little upstart to control these towns without some struggle,' Andrea interrupted. 'No one with half an eye would look away from Sixtus extending his power. Where will it end? None of us are safe. Milan and Venice are just as anxious as Florence about Rome's ambitions.'

Nofri spoke quietly: 'All the same, Lorenzo went about matters badly. The pact made in November 1474 with Venice and Milan nominally to safeguard the peace of the peninsula, but actually to curb Sixtus' spreading power has proved a great error.'

'Why so?' Narrow dark eyes studied the speaker.

'It's simple, Ridolfo. In the past, Milan, Florence and Naples were allies. Only after everything was arranged with this new pact did Lorenzo invite Naples … oh and of course the Papal States, merely for the look of the thing, to join the alliance. Even a child would take offence at such a piece of trickery. Would any of us join a pact after three other people had secretly conspired to form it without our knowledge, especially if we'd always considered we were all friends? That old treaty with Naples had existed since the Magnificent's grandfather's days. Poor old Cosimo must be turning in his grave. So now we have pushed cunning King Ferrante of Naples into the eager arms of Rome. Lorenzo sometimes spoils his game with speed.'

'It's a matter of personalities,' Toscanelli remarked shrewdly. 'Sixtus and Lorenzo are both strong men. When either makes a mistake he knows it all right, but pride does not allow retraction. Each only gets deeper entrenched determined to prove himself right.'

Domenico who hardly ever spoke unless it was about pigs or the price of maize astonished his father by saying: 'The final straw for Sixtus came when Lorenzo sided with the Vitelli family when they took Citta di Castella. From then onwards the Pope was obviously determined to hit out openly and secretly at our state. It has become like some mad game of chess. Can anyone know what or where His Holiness will strike next?'

'And what a hornets' nest the Pope stirred up,' Roselli observed, accepting the hot spiced wine Lionello offered round, 'when he appointed Francesco Salviati as Archbishop of Pisa in place of a Medici. The Salviati clan are Lorenzo's arch-enemies in

Florence, and they have ever hated the Medici upstarts – as they think of the ruling family.'

'It's not only that the Pope nominated a Salviati,' Toscanelli said wisely. 'Remember, His Holiness had given the Medici a solemn undertaking not to appoint bishops or archbishops in Tuscany without consulting the Signoria. Lorenzo could not be other than furious at this slight.'

Andrea gave a shout of laughter. 'Angry! That he is. So's Salviati and his entire family. The Medici has them looking like fools. For the past three years Lorenzo has used condottieri to prevent the archbishop entering Pisa...'

'My good Andrea, it's not funny except in a comic poem,' Ridolfo spoke cold reality. 'These are not petty farmers squabbling over a prize sow. I am to talk with Lorenzo very soon because he wants to know Milan's exact strength in any alliance. Alas we are greatly weakened after the murder of Duke Galeazzo by the wretched Lampugnano...'

'That was a dreadful business,' Vincenzo said fearfully, 'to kill a man on Santo Stefano at High Mass in the Duomo... I hear the assassins were only prevented from fleeing by the ladies' skirts. Galeazzo was in some respects a bad man, but...'

A bad man, Vincenzo mused silently. He could not say how wicked before the ladies.

Galeazzo had relished the refinements of murder and torture … he had delighted in raping the ladies of his court, and even forced some victims into prostitution. Could an assassin's dagger really be an instrument of divine justice?

'Is it true that Duchess Bona asked Sixtus to ensure her husband escaped purgatory?' Madonna Ginevra asked curiously.

Messer Ridolfo bit his lips to hide amusement. 'Aye, for a deal of money Sixtus agreed. The only endearing streak in Bona's crass stupidity is that she did love Galeazzo while acknowledging his gruesome sins. I imagine the Medica fears our weak and foolish administration, but let me speak bluntly … as I shall to him. In our turn we fear that Florence, despite her tremendous wealth, is being undermined by all enemies Lorenzo has made, either by imperious actions, or through the violent hatred of the magnati…'

'Who hates the Magnificent besides the Salviatis?' Carlotta ventured a question, and her face was a blush rose. She rarely spoke to any man outside the family, but gradually her needle travelled slowly until it remained poised in her fingers, and she listened openly to the conversation.

Ridolfo, looking at the smooth oval of Carlotta's face, thought that her beauty belonged to a purer world: a gentle unearthly being who made men remember virtue and attempt to lead a better life.

'You, Madonna, are of an old honourable family,' he said gently, 'who share the Narnis' view of the world. They do not crave power or position simply because of their noble past. Yet there are others who believe that a glorious family tree entitles them to great things in the present. After the Imola business Sixtus found a practical way of attacking the Medicis. He took away the hefty papal account from their bank and placed it with the Roman branch of the Pazzi bank. The Pazzis are magnati, but in Cosimo's time they were removed from that damning list which prevents nobles from rising to high office. Therefore quite legally the family can look for greater power, but not while Lorenzo holds the reins.'

Ginevra pursed her lips. 'You are saying in a somewhat oblique way, Messer Ridolfo, that the Medici should beware because the Pazzi family might attempt to usurp the Magnificent's rule. Don't you realise Lorenzo's sister, Bianca, is married to Guigliamo Pazzi? She's a fine girl...' she added, 'not just at her books, for she manages her household very well...'

Ridolfo raised his wine cup to his hostess. 'Madonna, I bow to your superior knowledge on womanly matters. You may be right that the Pazzis really do love the Medicis because of this family connection. However,

I shall urge Lorenzo, and his advisers, to study that rival banking firm…'

'I, too, fear things are coming to some climax,' Nofri murmured. 'From a distance Florence is not the calm trading city, we Florentines insist it must be. There are enemies inside and out. If real trouble arose it is not easy to guess which way the people would turn. Then I think…' and his wise eyes sought his father, 'we shall be asked to state our true colours. There will be no place for those who try to remain outside the argument.'

'May heaven forbid that your beautiful city becomes as Milan,' Ridolfo said quietly. 'Pray for the long rule of Lorenzo whatever his faults. Where there is weakness too many men seek to seize power. In their fight so many perish. The order and peace painfully won are easily lost, and it takes a long time to rebuild a strong state…'

'Enough of this gloomy talk,' Isabetta cried, as the men's faces settled into grim and thoughtful lines. 'Thank God, we live in the country away from all those problems. We are surrounded by new life, so we have no need to think of destruction and conflict.' She smiled tenderly at her mother-in-law, then picked up her own child and clasped him to her breast. 'Cannot one of you learned gentlemen cheer us with a song?' She stood close to her husband, who slipped his arm around her waist until a big calloused hand lightly caressed their baby's golden head.

Still leaning against her father's knee, Franca let her eyes wander around the company. Their faces seemed remote and unreal in the firelight. Ser Agnolo picked up a viol, while Andrea plucked at the lute strings and began to sing softly. All the Narnis loved music, and were gifted in this art, but Andrea had the greatest talent.

More white than mother's milk are you,
More red than dragon's blood your hue,
When at your casement you appear,
The sun is risen we declare.
The sun is rising, the moon sinks lower
Say good morn to your lover.
The sun has risen, the moonlight goes.
Say good even to your rose…'

There was something intensely moving about the handsome man with the bruised face singing so passionately. Nobody could doubt he was in love. Carlotta's heart throbbed. Messer Ridolfo read her expression and shook his head sadly.

Gostanza invaded Franca's haven. Her rough hands and scolding voice dragged the child to the normality of bedtime. She scarcely had time to make a faint curtsy to the company. Messer Ridolfo kissed his sparkling fingers towards her.

'I hope, little lady,' he called out, and his voice seemed to follow her from the room into the shadows of her own chamber, 'that we shall meet quite soon. It is already written that the great magician must bring us together...'

Her last glimpse of that stranger whose words and eyes disturbed her, was a face etched against fire, which caught at the gems on his person. He was the master of the inferno.

Gostanza grumbled and questioned all the while she undressed the child, but Franca was too tired to reply. She was asleep by the time the woman climbed into their high curtained bed, still scolding the darkness and life in general...

Betrothal

Franca had vehemently objected to her hair being washed. After all it wasn't a Saturday: the customary time for women to wash their heads in preparation for Sunday's blessed joy. Saturdays always saw meatless fare: you couldn't rely on any complicated dishes with most of the womenfolk washing, drying, curling, or colouring their tresses.

'If only the sun wasn't shining I shouldn't mind staying indoors.' Franca moaned, kneeling on a cushion-covered chest in the deep window embrasure. Warm gold countryside beckoned her through the open shutters.

'I never met a maid so unwilling to face her betrothal unless of course she was set on becoming a nun, which you show little signs of,' Gostanza retorted. 'Think, how fortunate you are. Many a girl is forced into a convent because her family don't want to find a suitable dowry. What's the world coming to? In the city marriages are going out of fashion. Men and women actually live together without sharing a bed. They call it spiritual marriage. I call it plain stupid. At this rate human beings will come to an end.'

At intervals she held up the soft curling skeins on the teeth of a double-sided carved ivory comb so that the morning sun glowed through a rippling brazen veil, and then let the hair drift back to envelop the child's nakedness.

The chamber was full of the sweet-scented warmth of the walled herb garden. Camomile flowers and verbena had been steeped overnight in rainwater to rinse Franca's hair the required thirty times to keep it bright and perfumed. The unemptied bath still smelt wonderfully of roses, even though the water was cooling and cloudy.

Bathing and clean underlinen were daily rituals enforced by Madonna Ginevra's gentle rule. She insisted that a real lady was always fresh and sweet, no matter how she felt, and Franca looked on the custom as a pleasure rather than a chore. She relished splashing about in the great wooden tub even in winter when it was drawn close to the fire in her parents' tapestried bedroom ... though Gostanza kept muttering that all this washing was unhealthy and only fit for dirty folk.

'Come then, my love,' the nurse coaxed, kissing the girl's cheek. She slipped a new silk camisia over Franca's head, which temporarily stifled the protests, and then lifted the gown from the bed. Myriad Castelfiore emblems embroidered in golden threads and tiny pearls decorated the filmy white robe which peeped through the opening of the violet silk overskirts, and at the top of the low square bodice.

Franca found it impossible to maintain a mutinous expression as soft cloth caressed her flesh, and perfume teased her nose. Whenever she moved silks whispered, jewels rang like distant church bells. Her lips relaxed, and her eyes dreamed, as Gostanza plaited a lock of hair with a string of pearls to form a bandeau which held back the cascade of curls.

The woman's normally harsh face softened. Her eyes misted. 'Thank the sweet Virgin I have been spared to see you this day. May I live to dress you on your wedding day, and help put you to bed beside your own dear lord. Look on your beauty, my little madonna.'

She held out a Venetian mirror in a frame of golden seashells. Franca could not associate the reflection with herself. A dainty creature of gold, violet and snow, glinting whenever a mote of light caught the jewels at ears, throat, or on wrists impossibly fragile beneath the trailing sleeves lined with white lawn. The flame of hair tamed, the perfect face painted with a serene smile and faint flush; the long sweep of dark lashes gold-tipped shadowing eyes that exactly matched the silk's hue and texture; the hair-fine brows arched against a broad creamy brow. All this belonged not to wild little Franca de' Narni but to a miniature Florentine beauty.

'Perhaps it will not be hard to behave like a lady dressed so,' she murmured, kissing her fingertips at the reflection who returned the homage. 'Dearest, sweetest Gostanza,' she entreated, 'just let me go down into the court to dry my hair completely.'

Franca turned her face upwards, and the nurse was reminded of a pale rose opening its petals to the sun.

She scrubbed at her eyes. 'When you look so I can't refuse you anything. I vow when you are full grown your sweet lord, and all other men will give way before such magic. Aye, Franca, you will always have your heart's dream – that is the reward of such special beauty.'

Franca walked out into the pillared upper loggia, and descended the staircase, demurely holding her skirts to display the dainty white and gold slippers, embroidered with pearls, that scarcely pinched toes so unusually constrained. Ordinarily she went barefoot, loving the soft moss or damp earth which squidged under her feet. Consciously, she ignored the admiring whispers of loitering serving women, and the approving whistles and catcalls of the stableboys. Then, the old and familiar Gostanza reached her ears.

'You listen to me, Franca,' she screamed, 'don't go getting your gown soiled, or your hair untidy, or running like a wild thing. Remember that young lady betrothed to a duke: she danced so boisterously she broke her leg. Then of course her noble suitor wouldn't marry her. Think of the shame...'

Franca's laughter mingled with the calling doves. Life was as usual despite the day and her finery. Since her first unsteady steps Madonna Ginevra and Gostanza had cautioned her with that story ... no doubt they would be saying the identical thing on her wedding day.

She managed to escape from the inner court without attracting Gostanza's infuriated yell. In the distance Berto's familiar figure shambled along, a heavy sack on his shoulders. Franca picked up her skirts, and ran towards him.

'Berto! Look at me!'

There was no recognition in his eyes. 'Madonna.' He touched his forehead in brief salute.

'Don't be silly.' Franca began laughing. 'Fine clothes don't alter me that much, you melon head! You know who I am! Shall we go fishing tomorrow?'

His gaze was hostile. 'That gown tells me who you are indeed,' he agreed slowly. 'Good day Madonna Francesca Lauretta de' Vincenzo Narni. Pray excuse me from coming out fishing with you. I have to help bring in the harvest which buys you some fine name as a bedfellow.'

She caught his arm. Coarse cloth burned fingers suddenly accustomed to silks. 'Don't you like my gown?' she demanded. 'Today is my betrothal day. I must look fine. Tomorrow will be different, you know.'

'Tomorrow will be very different. So you're to be wed to some young lord without his wits, and a strange taste for embracing boys … or to an old man with rotten teeth, stinking breath, and limbs twisted from gout, who only needs your warmth in his bed against the winter chill. You will turn to heat yourself against the loins of some worthless gallant decked in pretty ribbons, while your old husband mutely wears horns gilded with your dowry. Be happy, Madonna, for that is what tomorrow brings.'

Berto swung away. She started after him, understanding his words, but not the change in attitude. She wished for her old gown. Then she'd chase and punch that Berto into some good sense. 'Just you wait,' she muttered, looking down at the purple silk which had become a sudden burden.

Franca began walking back to the house with unwilling feet. It was colder. Clouds massed between her and the sun. Summer was waning swiftly now. A bevy of unfamiliar servants in the distinctive della Sera dark blue and gold livery crowded the court.

Soon, she thought fearfully, I shall know if Berto is right. Franca sought the chapel, and lit one taper before the laughing Virgin. She sank down and buried her face in her hands.

'Holy Mother, let fate be kind … please, please.'

Yet, a sober mature streak in her mind could say: it is already completed. No prayer can alter the age or disposition of Daniello della Lambarda Sera…

The carved and gilded cassone was decorated with a lordly hunting scene. It stood open in the wainscotted hall, overflowing with the rich items which were the smallest part of the dowry, for the bridal chest could never contain all that Vincenzo de' Narni would be giving by putting his name and seal to the marriage contract.

The cloud-decked sky poured pewter light on the pearls, the ropes of jewels, the rings, the bracelets, the pins … the rare porcelain, the crystal and golden goblets and plates, the majolica tableware, the gem-studded Book of Hours, the collection of gold medallions and engraved jewels, the exotic bolts of silks, velvets and brocades, heavily encrusted with pure silver and gold thread, and turquoises, emeralds and diamonds…

With the eager eyes of a hunting dog, the Sensale, Roberto di Bini read aloud the details of the dowry, and tried to keep the excitement out of his dry lawyer's voice. It had been unusually interesting acting as the go-between in these marriage arrangements. Certainly, the owner of Castelfiore was a generous father, but then his ambition for his daughter was as high-flying as any Gothic steeple, and could only be attained at extravagant cost.

The dowry was almost worthy of a foreign princess, but how else could anyone marry into a family elevated by the Magnificent's affection? 80,000 golden florins in cash: none of the customary practice with Florentine dowries which meant waiting for the official Monte to pay out part, or all the amount from interest accrued on an investment made fifteen years before any actual wedding. The scheme was a good one to ensure a bride brought a suitable dowry, but lately the Monte was getting more than a little backward in its repayments. Fortunately – from the point of view of Florentine revenues – many a girl died or decided to become a nun before her wedding day, so the original investment became the rightful property of the State.

Besides the lengthy inventory of small but valuable items similar to those displayed in the cassone, the girl was to receive a country house on the edge of Castelfiore which had been designed by Michelozzi; two farms, vineyards and olive groves; a prosperous inn, 'The Golden Grasshopper', just outside Fiesole; a goodly share of the annual profits from the Freddiano Lucca silk business in the city; and naturally part of the tremendous potential riches which might spring from young Raffaello de' Narni's expedition.

For once Vincenzo looked the wealthy man he was, arrayed in splendid velvet and dark ermine, a heavy gold and jewelled collar about his neck, and each finger seemed to droop under the weight of so many costly rings. His smile was ironic but he kept silent. Franca was fit for a king with her beauty, education and noble ancestry, but he knew it was only the abundance of the dowry that had tempted the wildly extravagant della Seras into marriage with any family so undistinguished and unfashionable as the Narnis.

With the completion of the contract a great piece of life would be settled. Every day the times seemed more uncertain and hazardous, but whatever happened Franca would be secure under the Medici aegis. Vincenzo knew he was right to tie up so much wealth in this match. His sons would have plenty anyway, and might yet make the name Narni famous and respected in modern Florence. He doubted it though: they were too learned, too bold, or too contented. His certain stake in the future was the beautiful girl who would become Madonna Francesca della Sera.

With reasoned detachment Vincenzo saw that this alliance might also cause the name Narni to be struck off that all-prohibiting Magnati list, so that one or another of his sons could become eligible for the Signoria.

For once sweet Ginevra need not be disappointed with her husband's planning. Poor lady, he thought with tenderness. They had never really loved or understood each other, and yet the marriage had been quite happy ... in fact better than most. He had reason to be grateful to her as a virtuous wife, a good mother, and an excellent housekeeper. He had never loved another woman – the pursuit of ever elusive wisdom was his true mistress.

Vincenzo smiled across at her. The brown eyes were not sad. Their gleam of triumph inspired by Franca's prospects competed with her jewels, and she resembled her shrewd father, the late Paulo di Freddiano Lucca. Despite wealth, high position in the Arte de Sette, and frequent important offices in the Signoria, that merchant had longed to link his self-made fortune with the name of a noble family. For him that was the secret accolade of success.

Messer Riccardo de' Narni had permitted Vincenzo to wed Ginevra partly because of the enormous dowry, but mainly in the hope that marriage into the merchant class would outweigh the magnati stigma, so that his only son could aspire to high position in the city.

Both fathers, and the gentle Ginevra, had been frustrated in their ambitions, because they had misjudged Vincenzo's character. He was content to emulate the ideal life as set down by his Humanist hero, Alberti. What else did a man need if he had a home filled with beautiful treasures, the love and laughter of his children, conversation with wise and witty friends, good music, books, and frequent opportunities to sit in the sun and drink the wine of his own estate?

He scorned all those who connived to gain power in the city. 'Like so many maggots crawling over a dead carcass!' he'd declared passionately, when Ginevra timidly suggested he try to become one of the four gonfalionere who represented the Santa Maria Novella quarter for a period of two months. It only needed a word here, some money paid there, and these things could be arranged. 'What do they do but sit and argue through day and night, and never decide, while the Medici controls everything anyway. There may be certain advantages, but being in the public eye is liable to win you as much enmity as honour. I don't want to end up exiled for some genuine or concocted misdemeanour because I spoke out of turn, nor do I want to have to reside in the Palazzo della Signoria for two whole months with a pack of argumentative Florentines… No, my dear love, let us be content in our rustic tranquillity, and leave power to those who hunger for it…'

He signed his name, and then looked towards the man sitting beside the window. There was a satisfied smile on the heavy lip, and he nodded: 'My dear Vincenzo, welcome into our family.'

Vincenzo de' Narni bowed, and poured Trebbiano into four silver cups.

'Now, it's all settled,' the Sensale rubbed his hands, and accepted the wine. 'Legal work is thirsty business. Let's drink to the young people's health. Can we meet the little lady?'

'I shall bring her.' Madonna Ginevra prayed Franca would still be tidy.

The sun emerged from behind a swollen storm cloud as the door opened to re-admit mother and daughter. The three men blinked at the sight of the figure standing in the blinding light, for Franca sparkled like one of the ornaments in her dowry. She curtsied low, and then smiled up at her father who kissed her brow.

'Allow us to congratulate you, Franca. You and Daniello are now betrothed.'

Roberto di Bini forgot about money and

property, and remembered his own granddaughter, and smiled kindly.

'Where are the della Seras?' Franca demanded. 'I've seen their attendants...'

She gazed round the chamber. The smile on her lips stiffened, and then faded. The man who had risen to his feet wore magnificent clothes and jewels. He had heavy blonde hair, but was only a little taller than herself, and appeared ill-balanced because of his massive shoulders. Fine crimson and gold brocade did not disguise his slightly hunched back. Prayer had not altered anything. Franca knew despair.

She looked accusingly at her father, but he said in a level voice: 'Franca, this gentleman is Matteo della Sera, Daniello's uncle.'

Her smile was bright with relief, the curtsy deep and grateful, for it was directed towards the Virgin. The low-statured man raised her, and kissed her cheek.

'Had you thought that your beauty was to be mated with my ugliness, little Madonna?' his questions contained amused bitterness. 'Remember this one day when you are old enough to understand: a man is still a man even if his body is not fit for Adonis. Sometimes a handsome face and figure offer no real manhood.'

'It's not that!' Franca cried, anxious to soothe the hurt she understood her expression had caused. 'You are so much older than I had imagined Daniello to be. I feared I had nothing wise to say to you, and I shouldn't like to bore my husband.'

'Bravely said.' Matteo glanced at her father. 'She has a swift mind and the rarest beauty. Allow me to explain, Francesca: I represent the della Seras who alas are unable to come here for this greatest of all days. They ask me to beg the Narnis' forgiveness, but it turns out that the Medici brothers are hunting close to our Buonventura estate, and so the family must be at home to receive them.'

Vincenzo avoided his wife's hurt eyes, and did not speak his thoughts out loud: they had secured the dowry. What else mattered? This uncle was saying as much. The Narni wealth was required to entertain the Medicis. 'That's the way of the world,' he commented acidly, and Franca started to laugh in quick understanding.

She knew disappointment and a sense of relief. The Sensale beckoned her towards his chair.

'They tell me you can recite whole works in Greek and Latin; that you know logic and geometry; that you can converse learnedly on Plato and Socrates; that you compose sonnets and play the lute, the viol and the flute; that you sing like a choir of nightingales; that you dance like a summer butterfly; that you sew and cipher and cook and weave.

But, Francesca, don't you ever play at ball like other little girls?'

To her mother's chagrin and her father's amusement, Franca launched herself on to the old man's knee. 'I'm not always this good,' she confided with a sideways glance at Madonna Ginevra. 'Sometimes I climb trees, and I adore riding and hunting ... only,' and she put a finger to her lips, and eyed Matteo della Sera with some doubt, 'perhaps you should not mention those things to Daniello. He night not want such an unruly wife.'

'If he saw you now,' Roberto di Bini spoke with doting admiration, 'I believe it wouldn't matter if you chose to ride through the streets in the Palio.'

The uncle shook his head. 'No, Francesca, our Daniello worships beauty, so you would be permitted to do what you chose.' He drew a tiny silk purse out of the pouch at his belt, and emptied a small ring into his palm. 'This is for you. It is called a gimmal ring, and always worn by the young lady betrothed to the eldest della Sera.'

Franca examined the slender gold ring that ended in a delicately-formed hand; each finger nail a perfect diamond.

'From this day onwards,' Matteo della Sera explained, 'Daniello wears its twin. The two hands clasp to form a single ring which after your marriage you will wear to show you are a wife.' He glanced expectantly towards her father.

'Franca, my dove, in your turn you must give Daniello a ring.' Vincenzo handed her a thick gold band heavy with intaglio work, and set with one fine bluish diamond.

She watched Matteo della Sera smile as he weighed it on his hand. 'Daniello will treasure this token of your affection, little Madonna. It is worthy of a prince. Come, allow me to put his ring on your finger.'

Franca held out her hand, and admired the small glinting stranger. 'See, Mamma,' she called, 'now I am a betrothed lady.'

'Only if you behave like one,' Madonna Ginevra replied promptly. 'Remember this, Francesca, you must not put your future husband's ring to shame by playing the hoyden.'

Franca lowered solemn eyes, and thought: this betrothal business is going to prove an awful nuisance sometimes.

Vincenzo read her expression, and stifled his laughter in an orange sleeve.

'Now would you like to see your husband?' the Sensale asked.

She looked hesitantly towards the door.

'No,' said Roberto di Bini. 'You will not meet him until you are grown up, but here is something for you from Maestro Verrochio's workshop.'

He produced a small painting of a golden

youth in exquisite clothes and jewels. He was tall and well formed. Long curls gathered about his beautiful dreaming face as if they wanted to kiss the soft flesh. A cheetah with a jewelled collar looked up at him, but the man's eyes only saw the rose marking the page of the book he was holding. Behind him the Tuscan hills reached towards a morning sky.

'Ah, sweet Virgin,' Franca gasped enchanted. 'What a glorious youth. His perfect hands … and what a wonderful painting.'

'That is Daniello della Lambarda Sera,' Matteo said simply. 'Your reaction speaks of your pleasure, and I am glad for you.'

'Then I am to wed a man even more handsome than Andrea,' she breathed. 'How good the saints are to me.' Abruptly her eyes narrowed with suspicion and she demanded:

'Is he truly like this painting, or did Maestro Verrocchio make a pretty picture for many florins to please Messer Lambarda della Sera rather than describe the truth? It would not be difficult for an artist of his worth to transform Vulcan into Apollo.'

Vincenzo hastily swallowed some wine. Ginevra's voice was shocked. 'Franca, apologise. What a wicked thought!'

The Sensale laughed delightedly, and kissed her cheek. Matteo della Sera's worldly eyes creased with merriment.

'Franca, you have a wise head, which is better than being beautiful, and rarer in one so young. Many a maid has been duped into marrying some fellow ... like my ugly self ... with a pretty painting. Just as Sandro Botticelli painted your likeness for us to marvel at, so this is a true representation of Daniello. Neither artist have painted as truthfully as they should ... but they haven't that much talent: for you are more beautiful than your painting, and Daniello handsomer than this portrait. He is gentle and agreeable, loves to ride, to run, to play tennis, but best of all he prefers music, dancing and to sit in a lovely garden and tell stories. His many friends are a proof of his pleasant disposition. I don't believe I've heard him utter an angry word to a dog or a servant.'

With happy eyes, Franca could almost see the future. She stroked the betrothal ring with a gentle finger. They would have a blissful life. It would all be like some perfect story ... yes, just like the fair men and maidens in the Decameron who escaped the plague-ridden city to dwell in idyllic surroundings and recount tales, sing, dance and talk of love...

'Now I shall not mind when the years have passed. In fact I shall welcome my wedding day with song and delight,' Franca said softly. 'Marriage to such a glorious youth must bring great happiness.'

Madonna Ginevra's lips smiled, but her eyes were forlorn and frightened. Pray God, she entreated silently, that it will be as she sees it. Vincenzo rubbed his eyes against his sleeve.

The Sensale was delighted to join the boisterous Narnis at their table, and admired everything from the food to the baby. Matteo della Sera was silent and obviously ill-at-ease. He slipped away before he had sampled more than one of Tullia's festive dishes, and it was fortunate she was not around else he'd have been forced to remain at table and taste everything … or face her wrath. The family sat in uncomfortable and unusual silence as the company of horsemen faded into the evening.

In an effort to dispel the grief in Madonna Ginevra's features, Ser Agnolo began to tell a story.

'A foolish young man who had sampled too much cervisia and Chianti fell into a drunken sleep. When he awoke, this melon head could not remember anything. He stumbled to the closet, opened the doors, and seeing it was so dark, went back to bed.' The tutor stared in red-faced triumph at the astonished Narnis, 'You see, he thought he was opening the shutters!'

It was so unusual for Ser Agnolo to relate a comic tale that the brothers and sister laughed more than the joke deserved. He was well rewarded with one of Madonna Ginevra's gentle smiles, and Vincenzo poured him another cupful of wine.

When their mirth had subsided a little, Andrea gasped: 'Perhaps Matteo della Sera was scared we'd poison him. These great families are brought up on such terrors. Probably because their cooks are so bad.'

'Andrea!' his mother reproved trying to hide her smile. 'He is most likely a busy man.'

'No,' Franca said, smiling at Isabetta and Carlotta, who were trying to mask their sympathetic concern with merry looks. 'He has what he came for. Why should he stay? If he hurries he'll be in time to sit down and eat with the Medicis. Now you wouldn't expect him to miss that.'

She glanced at the gimmal ring and grinned wickedly.

'But, they're bound to come to the actual wedding. I don't think they can avoid it.'

Franca's dry humour caused further mirth, but the women wept as they laughed. Vincenzo lifted his wine cup, and looked tenderly at his beautiful child, whose glowing hair had come unbound, so that she resembled a wood nymph. Naturally his sons were often wild – that was how it should be – but his girl had a streak of more than wildness: fine, burning and devilish. God help and bless the man who loves her, he breathed, and then aloud: 'For my part I'm not too worried. Let young Daniello see our Franca but once, and he is bound to love her as we do. The Narnis are all here, save one, who I know would share our feelings, so it doesn't matter who else is absent. We can drink to the betrothed's happiness.'

The cups were raised in Franca's direction. Outside voices sang lustily, for Vincenzo de' Narni had supplied all his tenants and workers with good wine so they could pledge his daughter's health.

Everyone was smiling. Even Ser Agnolo. Gostanza, Tullia, and the other house servants crowded at the open doors laughing, crying and calling out God's blessing on their little Madonna.

Franca felt the great love which enfolded her…

Departures

Franca wandered the orchards, sliding her feet through the crackling russet carpet. The last leaves were golden coins hanging on the denuded darkening branches. Her breath clouded on crisp air scented with fruit and woodsmoke.

Now Berto shunned her company she felt lonely, but still preferred the empty fading countryside to the noise, warmth and order prevailing in the house. Often she pondered why the time after her betrothal seemed tedious. Life continued as before. Only her ability to enjoy it had somehow altered. It was foolish of course to expect the exchange of rings could turn each fresh day into some magnificent adventure.

The crunch of other footsteps made her turn to see Lionello di Aquia.

'Good day, cousin,' she smiled and invited his presence. Even to talk with him would be better than dwelling in her own thoughts. 'I'd have imagined you'd be indoors at your books. You don't enjoy fresh air on the finest summer days.'

'We all need a change. You're alone and far from the house.' Lionello grinned, and added slyly: 'I suppose you're out seeking your rustic swain. I've seen you two together often enough when you thought no one observed your antics in the greenwoods.'

Franca knew a swift pull of anger. So this creature spied on her. 'I hope you saw it as your proper duty to inform my parents,' she retorted coldly.

'How could I tell my poor aunt and uncle I'd glimpsed their virtuous daughter "putting the devil in hell" with a lout who is only just above a farmyard animal. Perhaps that ruttishness is what appeals to you.'

He laughed in a hot breathless way. His usually pale pinched cheeks had a touch of carmine below the eye sockets. More than ever he resembled his weasel-like father. Franca felt scared as when some incomprehensible dream left her melancholy and nauseated.

'There are evil thoughts in your mind,' she snapped. 'So you read the Decameron privately as well as holy books when there are people watching. Don't cloak your lewd lies in Boccaccio's choice expressions.'

'If you can give so much of yourself to that Spenozzi beast,' Lionello put his thin face close to hers and she could smell his onion-tainted breath, 'then for the sake of your fair reputation, little cousin, with the della Seras you can give me one kiss.'

Whatever reaction he had anticipated,

Lionello did not expect the burst of derisive laughter. Franca threw back the cloud of hair and laughed until her eyes overflowed, and her arms and legs felt weak. With a helpless finger she pointed at him, and mocked: 'Oh upright young Lionello, is this the way you intend to win kisses when you're a man?'

'I am already a man,' and his voice was feverish. He seized Franca by the shoulders so that her slight body was pressed against him, and he sank his open mouth on to the still laughing lips.

Her eyes were wild. Kissing her kindred had never been like this ... or so unpleasant. She wrenched her face from that loathsome embrace, jerked her knee upwards catching him in the groin, and was aware that his tensile condition was very similar to the dogs roaming the farmyards when any bitch came into season. Anger rather than revulsion kindled her senses: to be spied upon, insulted, and then handled by this snivelling little weasel was not to be supported.

'This is something that Berto did show me in the woods,' she shouted, jabbing at his nose, eyes, and mouth with her bony fists. The gimmal ring caught his cheek and left a jagged crimson tear.

'Vixen! Bitch! Strumpet!...' Lionello screamed.

Franca smiled through her dishevelled

hair. 'Uncle Maximo would be astonished by his son's concealed vocabulary...'

'Enough. Madonna, leave him be.' Berto stood close by watching the panting children. He seemed much older and taller, and in control of the situation. 'You have blood on your lip, Franca.' He added 'wipe it off.'

'Ah, here comes my cousin's gallant paramour. Perhaps I have prevented some passionate embraces.' Lionello sneered.

Berto put a thumb to his nose. It was a challenge no grown man would ever ignore.

'Me fight with you?' Lionello said with indignant surprise. 'You're nothing but farmyard dung. You can kiss my arse!'

'The language of a gentleman,' Berto observed slowly. 'It matters little what you think of me or whether you fight. I'm going to thrash you, master Lionello di Aquia, and you will never again dare lay your lying, prating lips on Madonna Francesca's beauty and innocence.'

'Haven't you laid more than lips on her?' Lionello was frightened, but his poison couldn't be confined.

Franca stood by quite expressionless as Berto beat her cousin. He struck him again and again with deliberately aimed blows of his huge hands, without any fury, and the blood streamed from Lionello's nose and mouth.

'No more now, Berto,' Franca commanded

quietly. 'If you kill him, you'll be the one who suffers.'

Berto ceased immediately, and he gasped for breath. They both stared down at the sobbing, bloody face. 'Swear never to touch Madonna Francesca again, or utter foul lies about her.'

'You go to your father the devil!' Lionello attempted defiance. 'And take that accursed little witch with you!'

Berto shrugged, and looked around the orchard. Close by stood a stone trough for watering the cattle. He picked up Lionello as if he was a fragment of chaff and dumped him into the dank cold water.

'I hope it doesn't poison the poor beasts who drink there,' he commented. 'Good day Madonna, you had best go straight home.'

Lionello di Aquia did not appear at dinner, and departed hurriedly next morning to the delight of the whole household. Rumour reached Franca that Giovanni Spenozzi had thrashed his son senseless for no very good reason as far as any of the gossips knew … just to drive some of the evil out of him, they concluded, and good job too!

Vincenzo de' Narni found Franca wandering in the courtyard. He walked beside her, a hand resting on the soft little shoulder.

At last he spoke: 'I know some of the tale.'

She looked up with unhappy eyes.

'Your mother knows not a word of it, and I don't want her to. The miscreants are being punished. From all accounts, the Spenozzi boy can take another beating, and his father did not have to know a good reason to obey my order. I am content that Maximo di Aquia's son has left my house for good. His punishment is being himself, and having such a father as Uncle Weasel.'

He smiled at his daughter. 'This is probably the first of many instances when men will fight over you, my angel. Always remember a man can redeem his honour with heroics, but alas a woman never can, and her virtue is a bright jewel treasured by all those who love her best. Those who bid her cast it aside, or wrest it from her care nothing for the lady.'

'Babbo ... babbo...' Franca used the babyhood word for father in her misery and anxiety. Her cheeks flamed. 'Whatever he said about me and Berto isn't true. I will swear it on the Holy Sacrament itself...'

'Hush, my lamb. I never doubted your honour, any more than I doubt my own. Young Lionello never finished his sly tale.' Vincenzo grinned, and reminded his daughter very much of a fox. 'Because I'm ashamed to admit I hit him in the mouth.'

She had never known him to strike anyone. That was not the way he had trained his children, his servants, or his horses. Franca was bitterly ashamed she had caused this gentle man to act with violence.

'Forgive me, babbo.' She clung to his arm in great distress.

'There is nothing to forgive, my own Franca.' Vincenzo knelt on the paving stones so that their eyes were level, and she could see his were smiling. 'All I beg is that you beware of your own beauty. It has such power over other people. You can't help it. Don't fret that the Aquias will traduce your reputation. I expect the old Weasel is most impressed by your betrothal, and looks to make revenue out of his distant kinship with the Magnificent's favourites. He'll be lauding the name Narni instead of cursing it. Most likely he'll beat his repellent son for leaving Castelfiore under a cloud.

'Come, my dove, let us laugh at them, and their nastiness. If you are too solemn, people around will begin to seek for reasons. I don't want that. Whatever occurred was none of your making.'

Franca threw herself against his padded gown in a storm of weeping. He held her close, shaken at this grief. It was very unlike the mischievous girl he knew, but Vincenzo understood that the years were drawing her towards womanhood.

'Oh Papa, I feel dirty, as if I've fallen down in the midden. Why is it?'

He stroked the quivering shoulders and sighed. 'I wish I knew how to turn all life into a splendid silken carpet for your dainty feet to dance upon, but I haven't that power. You are growing out of childhood, little daughter. Every day you will learn that your knowledge is never great enough for the situations you encounter. But, you cannot be dirty or defiled, because others are vile. Keep the memory of this business in some part of your mind as a lesson acquired without much hurt, except to your pride. In time perhaps you will even understand Lionello and young Spenozzi...'

The second departure from Castelfiore caused genuine grief. Carlotta Corbizzi decided to return to her parents.

'Stay with us through Christmas,' Franca entreated. 'What a feast Tullia will prepare – better than the end of Lent ... and then the new baby will be born. We all love you so, Carlotta. You are as much part of our family as Isabetta.'

'And you, Franca, seem more like my own sister than the two I have down in the city. Yet I doubt we shall ever be true sisters now.' The pale cheeks glistened with tears, but Carlotta's beauty was enhanced rather than dimmed by sadness. 'He does not care for me. I fear too my presence drives him from home, because he feels forced to be kind to a lady not of his own choosing.'

Certainly Andrea's unexplained absences had become even more frequent. Yet it was rumoured he no longer paid open court to Lucrezia Donati. When he was at Castelfiore everyone sensed his heart and mind were elsewhere.

'Definitely not in the silk business,' Vincenzo de' Narni commented bluntly to his wife. 'Young Raffaello will be needed there when he returns.'

'When you are in the city,' Franca insisted, 'you will be nearer Andrea, and he can visit your family. Perhaps that's better, because you will then seem much less like his sister … or so I heard Mamma say … and she understands such matters.'

'Oh Franca, can that be?' Carlotta clasped the girl to her breast. 'Do you understand how much I love him? It hurts my heart.' The damp cheeks became pink. 'Even if it is immodest to say so.'

'Then he cannot help but return your love.' Franca decided aloud. 'For, Carlotta, you are the kindest, sweetest, most beautiful young lady in Florence. If a lady loves a man then it is only correct that he loves her too. I am determined that is how it will be with *my* Daniello…' Carlotta hid a smile at Franca's proprietorial tone, 'because, you see, I love him already.'

'I don't doubt *you'll* succeed,' the young woman agreed.

The whole household assembled to say farewell to Carlotta, who inspired everyone's affection. Even Tullia excused her small appetite by saying: 'Angels don't require too much victuals...' Gostanza worshipped her. 'If you would only model yourself on that perfect lady,' she spoke crossly to Franca to hide her real sadness, 'we'd all have a much quieter life. Whatever is that dough-head, Andrea, thinking of?'

Vincenzo de' Narni was accompanying Carlotta to the city for he was anxious to oversee details in the Freddiano Lucca warehouse that Andrea had overlooked, and also he wanted news of the San Miniato.

'At least she has him with her on the journey, for he has to go with your father,' Isabetta whispered to Franca.

Andrea lifted Carlotta on to a white horse. Only a blind man could have missed the glow which shone from her lovely face.

'Can't he see how she feels?' Franca demanded of her sister-in-law. 'Any man would be honoured by such adoration.'

'You've a lot to learn little sister,' Domenico said soberly from Isabetta's side. 'I hope you never have to learn this: that when a man is dazzled by the woman he loves, he sees nothing of other people's love, or the whole world; its beauty and danger pass him by unremarked. Oh, my Isabetta, weren't we fortunate to be in love with each other. Unrequited passion is the saddest of all feelings I'd imagine.' He gave her a boisterous kiss, and she grinned happily.

The cavalcade moved down the winding muddy track, and were soon obscured by distance. Madonna Ginevra put an arm around her daughter. Her face was exhausted in the pale morning light. 'We shall miss her, my Franca, let us pray that soon she will have cause to live with us permanently…'

Nativity

The week before Christmas a flurry of snow brushed the hills. Rain soon washed away the frosting. Damp mist concealed the city and the river. The dun-coloured land was sodden. A chill wind keened through trees bowed in grief.

Franca wondered if she would ever be warm again. Her hands were red and itchy from crouching by the fire, which made writing, sewing and playing music painful. Even indoors breath condensed in small clouds of vapour. Food was as monotonous as the weather. Summer seemed to have departed taking with her everything that made life pleasant. Winter was worse than Lent. The Christmas feast would make an ambrosial change, but Tullia was always so furious while she prepared the special delights that not even Franca dared approach the kitchen.

It seemed very lonely in the great house with her father and Andrea still in Florence, and Nofri back at Padua. Domenico had taken Isabetta and Christo to visit her family in the Mugnone. They were all due back for Christmas, but in the meantime the world was a flat dull place. Winter days disappeared in the blink of an eye. Morning was always dark, and evening seemed to chase away noon…

Franca first knew something was wrong when she found Ser Agnolo missing from the winter parlour where he gave her lessons. Papers, pens and books were scattered about. The unusual disarray suggested something very amiss.

The great house was ominously quiet for that time of the morning. Her mother's women hurried about the upper floor with chalk grim faces which had not known sleep. Gostanza passed carrying a bundle of coarse linen, and Franca caught her skirt.

'What's wrong?' she demanded.

'Your mother's pains started in the night, and there's a show of blood,' she muttered. Beneath the brown hood her face was grey and tired, and the whites of her eyes threaded with red. She looked twenty years older than usual. 'The baby seems to be coming much earlier than expected. I've sent a man for the midwife. Pray God, they are quick in this weather. Normally, she would come to live here at least three weeks before Madonna Ginevra was brought to bed.'

'Did you send Ser Agnolo?'

'Him!' Gostanza's lips pinched with contempt. 'I told him our lady was in labour, and that this time it would be difficult. All he did was to begin to tremble. His short-sighted eyes filled with tears as if he was having her pains. That Agnolo is only fit for reading verse, and mooning around with his music and books. No doubt he's praying for your mother's soul, the poor fool. He's not a real man. Carlo from the stables has taken the master's fastest horse Fulmine. They're both good enough for the Palio, and God knows this is a more important race. How I wish the master was at home.'

Franca wandered down to the chapel. It was cold and damp, and smelt of mice, candlewax and stale incense. Fresh candles had been lit on the altar, and stars of winter jasmine were clustered in a silver vase before the statue. The mother and baby had always been Franca's favourites: they resembled Isabetta and Christo – so plump, comfortable and happy.

Before the brightly painted and gilded figures knelt her tutor in an attitude of abject despair, his face buried on his arms. Grief seemed incongruous beside those carved smiling figures.

'Why, oh why must she suffer so? My poor dear lady,' he moaned. 'She has had enough pain in her life.' Agnolo's voice contained infinite sorrow.

Franca sensed he would hate her for witnessing his agony. She curtsied briefly before the altar and slipped away.

The wind blew shining diagonal needles of

rain across the sullen sky, and the courtyard was filled with cold emptiness. She crept up an outside stairway, uneasy in the troubled atmosphere pervading Castelfiore.

Generally, her mother's quiet but firm rule kept the vast place running smoothly. Each servant knew his or her duty according to the hours of the day. No maid dared stand in idle chatter, or call down to the men working outdoors. To earn Madonna Ginevra's calm rebuke was far worse than facing Tullia in one of her volcanic rages. Now, the women clustered together, talking in whispers. At intervals, a farmhand would run upstairs – something totally forbidden – to ask if there was any news. All eyes strained to skim the mist from the distance and see if the midwife was approaching.

Franca ran along the terrace, dodging between the painted pillars, towards her parents' chamber, but no one heeded the girl. She felt unimportant, isolated, and utterly useless.

Despite its enormous size the bedroom was stifling hot. The shutters were tightly closed, and covered by tapestries. A fire roared in the vast grate. Gusts of wind wailed down the chimney and sent the flames swirling and sparking. There were only six women in attendance, yet the chamber seemed crowded, for each draught sent the shadows cast by candle flames pursuing each other across the hangings which had been among Madonna Ginevra's dowry.

Whenever Franca had been ill she was put to sleep in her parents' bed, which novelty relieved the dismal imprisonment ... so the designs on the tapestries were old friends. Each marvellously worked panel depicted the story of the Creation – the last one being the expulsion from the Garden of Eden. In the shadows the serpent always appeared to sway, as if preparing itself to descend into the world and lead her into temptation. The first time Franca saw it she had screamed in horror, and her father had sketched an angel with a fiery sword, so his little daughter could use it to frighten away the snake!

Madonna Ginevra lay propped up in that great curtained bed. Her face, as tiny as a child's, was yellow and sheened with sweat. It seemed impossible that the ungainly bump under the fur-trimmed coverlid was any part of the frail figure. The long brown hair, always so neatly bound, was loose and flowed heavily over the thin shoulders and small breasts. The coral necklace Gostanza had fastened about her mistress's neck to facilitate the labour was a touch of bright colour.

Franca expected to be sent away, but Ginevra managed a gentle smile, and beckoned her to the bedside. Even as she approached the child saw the calm, familiar face contract, and heard the faint cry. Teeth clenched on the lower lip. Small garnets of blood gleamed in the light. Franca took her mother's cold moist hand, and did not pull away as the fingernails bit into her own flesh. Tenderly, Gostanza wiped away the blood and sweat with a linen cloth steeped in vinegar.

The tide of pain receded, and Madonna Ginevra said unsteadily: 'You really should not be here, Franca, but it does me good to see you. If only Vincenzo was at home. I'm so lonely.'

It was the first time Franca had heard an adult admit to a feeling she imagined only belonged to the uncertain realms of childhood.

'I shan't leave you, Mamma,' she said calmly, and she was deeply afraid, understanding that at this time she had to be stronger than her mother by pretending to have no fears or doubts.

'Go then, and sit by the fire where your mother can see you,' Gostanza commanded. 'And keep quiet, and out of everyone's way … no matter what happens. Now, Madonna…' her voice pretended a brisk cheerfulness, 'do not be as brave as I recall you were when this little maid was born. It is no sin to cry aloud. If only you would scream whenever the pangs come I swear it would ease the birth.'

Ginevra shook her head obstinately, and

Franca thought: she will never cry out even if the pain kills her.

Afterwards she only remembered a procession of unconnected memories, like a wall painting with faded indistinct patches where the paint has worn away.

The stifling heat... The smoky atmosphere... The dull haze of damp covering the unreal world outside whenever she peeped through the shutters... The faint moans from the bed interspersed with long empty silences when her mother lay so still, with her eyes closed, and Franca feared to put her dread into thoughts... The serving women's rising and descending murmurs like the ebb and flow of a troubled sea... The soft opening and closing of doors... Running feet outside in the gallery... The hiss of rain falling down into the hearth... Cassio, his old eyes partly filmed with blindness, prowling about the room, or sprawling at her feet.

Now and then Gostanza moistened her mistress's lips with hippocras from the desco da parto. The birth tray, heavily laden with sweetmeats and spices, awaited the time when the ordeal would be over, and the mother could be plied with every kind of delicacy to restore her strength and spirits.

Down in the kitchen Tullia lovingly prepared stewed breasts of capon larded with almonds and truffles. As she worked she cursed the anatomy and appetite of men who caused suffering even to the most gentle and virtuous of ladies.

No one thought of Franca. Indeed she forgot herself, not even remembering the need to eat or drink. The only reality was the waiting. Every part of her mind and body attuned itself to this vigil.

It was evening when the midwife arrived. Many more hours elapsed before Madonna Ginevra's women supported her to the birth stool.

The aroma of almond oil the midwife used on her hands and Madonna Ginevra's parts filled the room for a few minutes. Then Franca's most distinct memory that shocked her from a bout of drowsiness was of the pig.

That was the first time she had inhaled the rank hot smell of blood. When they killed the pig. Some of the thick dark clots had splashed on her skirts. Berto had regretted agreeing to take her along. Afterwards she was sick and dizzy, and he had to hold her head while she vomited. Then he'd washed away the stains and bathed her face in cold clear stream water. Franca had known shame and self-contempt.

She couldn't even look at the sausages and puddings which resulted from that pig's slaughter. Tullia had been heartbroken, and feared her darling to be sickening for the plague. No one knew Franca had been at the kill. It would only get Berto a beating, and herself a lecture, and another page of Plato to translate.

Now her mother's chamber, with its smoke shrouded ceiling was full of that bloody stench … her mother who was always so clean and fragrant … who kept her own and the whole household's clothes and linens fresh and sweet by strewing linen bags of dried lavender and rosemary in the cypress wood chests…

Madonna Ginevra squatted upon the birthstool. Gostanza and Violante grasped her shoulders, while the black-garbed midwife crouched before the spread legs, hands reaching beneath the voluminous linen shift. A knife gleamed red from the fire.

Franca believed the midwife to be an evil spirit who had materialised to murder her mother and the unborn babe. Women were sobbing around Castelfiore's mistress, their covered heads like massed clouds in the hazy light.

She wanted to scream to prevent them slaughtering her mother. Her lips opened, but she never knew whether the cry came from her own mouth. Then there was a different sound: a thin wail which broke the spell of silence.

The women at the doorway ran forward with linen strips and ewers of hot water, their faces smiling and relaxed because at last there was something practical they could do. The long waiting was at an end.

A tiny mottled creature with wisps of red hair on its head squirmed in Gostanza's hands, screaming furiously. Cassio wandered close, sniffed at this protesting newcomer, and then loped away as if he had satisfactorily completed the inspection on his master's behalf.

'A real Narni. God be praised.' Gostanza exclaimed joyfully. 'Red haired and bawling for food. Come, Franca, look on this miracle.'

With a sense of wonderment, the girl approached, and watched the child being bathed in a silver basin. Gostanza's face was wet with tears, but she was laughing.

'See, it's another fine man for Castelfiore,' she pointed between the fat, waving legs, and gave a bawdy wink: 'Oh it's not much now, but given the years he'll show the girls some pleasure. After all Domenico started out with one no bigger than this, and look at the fine son he got...'

To Franca the baby's minute sex seemed a sweet and ridiculous proof of her new brother's manhood. Expertly, the nurse began to swaddle him in linen bands.

'So, it's a boy,' the girl's voice contained no discontent ... only relief and a strange respect for some invisible force.

Chattering like happy sparrows, the women put her mother back in the bed, which had been warmed with hot bricks, and removed the bundles of blood-stained linen. Violante, the youngest maid, whose berry-red cheeks and round white neck had won all the farm men's appraising glances, held a silver cup of dark wine to Madonna Ginevra's lips.

'Come, Madonna,' she encouraged, 'Drink it all down. Then you will take a little of Tullia's special dish. Your long struggle has earned you the right to eat and rest. The wet nurse is here to feed the babe, so don't think of him any more. Think of yourself, and getting strong.'

Beside the hearth, a plump peasant girl was already giving the baby her breast. Monna's soft eyes were fixed lovingly on the minute red head nuzzling against the heavy curves of white flesh. Her own first-born had died ten days before in the freezing weather. This flow of milk had been a constant reminder of his loss, now she was content that it could be put to such use. During the cruellest winter months she would live and eat amid such comfort. It would be an affliction not to be allowed even to see Ercole all the time she fed this Narni, but at least the money she was being paid might ensure that their second baby survived. Meanwhile she had as much love as milk to give this young starveling.

'It is the first time I have no milk.' Madonna Ginevra patted her empty breasts with regret and sighed to herself. 'I'm getting old I suppose.'

Franca took her hand, and the woman smiled and smoothed her daughter's tresses. The mother's face was tranquil again, but the eyes were set deep in dark circles as if they peered through tunnels.

'Oh Mamma, it is so wonderful, and so terrible.' Franca's tears flowed for the first time that day.

'No you must not cry, my little daughter, my only girl, really you must not. The pain goes, and think what joy follows. One day you will know it.'

It was to share a secret, Franca thought, a secret that only women could know. Oh yes, it took a man to father a child, she knew that, but for the rest it was all woman's work. What a miracle it was. Someone so frail, so gentle, so calm as her mother could in great torment bring forth a lusty little boy.

'I'm sorry it's a boy,' Madonna Ginevra whispered sleepily, and Franca realised that all these years of secret grudge had been known to her mother.

'It does not matter,' she smiled. 'Suddenly I am glad to be a girl, Mamma. Think how proud, Papa and the boys will be. Another man. Will he be a doctor, a lawyer, or perhaps as great a merchant prince as the Magnificent…'

The mother's eyes closed, and Franca looked with swift fear towards Violante. The young woman shook her head. 'Don't you fret, Franca. She is very tired now, and will sleep. It's normal.'

'I wish Vincenzo would let him go for a priest.' Ginevra murmured, but Franca knew this was something her father would never permit…

It was a perfect Christmas at Castelfiore.

Somehow the new baby united even more an already closely-knit family, and they adored little Benvenuto as if he was the Holy Child, and lavished upon him a love as precious as the gifts brought by the Three Kings.

Franca was much closer to her mother, and the Narni brothers smiled at this sudden change. She was quite happy to sit rocking Benvenuto in his carved cradle, which had once lulled them all in turn, and sing to him in her sweetest voice. All the family and servants competed to nurse the baby who seemed to learn laughter before tears. Even Ser Agnolo's pained features smiled to hear him crow.

'Though, doubtless,' the tutor made a rare joke, 'when I have to teach him the rudiments of Latin he'll prove just as wilful as the rest of the Narni brood.'

'Do you realise,' Franca said to her sister-in-law, as they watched Christo and Benvenuto sleep side by side, 'that they are uncle and nephew.'

Isabetta put a finger to her mouth, which wore a contented smile, to show she shared a secret. 'In six months or so, Benvenuto will have another nephew, fittingly younger.'

Franca smiled and kissed her. 'Perhaps it will be a niece.'

'Oh no!' Isabetta shook her head with certainty. 'Narnis do not have girls.'

'Then despite my hair,' Franca laughed, 'I am a changeling.'

Vincenzo de' Narni treated his wife with even more tenderness than usual, and let her talk to him for hours about their baby's progress, without showing any signs of boredom, or wanting to leave her bedside to find a book. The streak of grey in his hair had widened.

He waited until the Epiphany festivities were ended to tell his family:

'While I was in the city, I received news of the San Miniato,' he pressed Ginevra's shoulder. It was the first day she had been allowed downstairs for a few hours. Wife and children looked towards Vincenzo with sudden fear. 'The ship was attacked by Moors off the Spanish coast. It is likely the entire crew perished.'

He sat down heavily. The deep laughter lines in his unsmiling face made him look haggard and old. Ginevra put her arm gently around his shoulders, and seemed curiously stronger than her husband. 'Let us pray that our dear Raffaello has only been captured,' she whispered. 'I would not have Benvenuto born merely to replace another son.'

Andrea smiled sadly. He was thicker with Raffaello than any of his other brothers, and they had enjoyed many a swaggering, carousing time together down in the city. 'You always said that scamp would set the saints at each other's throats up in Paradise, Papa. If Rafaello is alive, and pray God he is, then the Moor will certainly send him back, just for the sake of a peaceful life...'

It was a noble attempt at a jest, and his father's glance thanked him.

The fortune lost in this tragedy was neither mentioned nor remembered. All eyes rested on Raffaello's empty chair, which always had a place set before it in case of his unannounced return.

Franca found the lump of grief in her throat unbearable, and she was forced to speak aloud with a savage conviction: 'I have a feeling he is not dead. He cannot be. Indeed I know I shall see him again.'

'We can only hope your words are predictive, my dove.' Vincenzo sounded weary. He held his last born in the crook of his right arm. 'There is nothing more precious in life than my children...' and he bent and kissed the baby's puckered face to hide his tears...

The Lovers

No further news of the San Miniato's precise fate reached Castelfiore. Shred by shred hopes for Raffaello's survival were picked away by the passing weeks, leaving a bare carcass of grief.

When the first buds broke to deck the distance in a mantle of faint green gauze, Andrea took his sister riding. He had spent a rare whole week at Castelfiore. His ill-concealed impatience and sadness was replaced by a quickening excitement.

The countryside was alive with the sounds of rebirth. Franca believed she could hear Spring waking ... like a beautiful maiden opening her eyes, stretching her pale limbs, and murmuring to herself before rising to run through the land scattering blossom and the promise of fruitfulness. The lilting music of streams in full spate, and the chorus of birds which increased each dawn were her heralds. Franca felt that if she put her ear to the damp ground she would hear the soil stirring as new shoots sought the returning sun.

She was grateful to Andrea for this outing. The 25th March was after all a highly significant date – the first day of a new year. To spend it uneventfully suggested to Franca that the next twelve months would pass without anything exciting happening. Lately everything had become uninspiring … a long yawn of monotony. The others had a nearer boundary to their expectations: Benvenuto's first tooth, Isabetta's new baby. Anyway the men were free to ride out to claim their own lives. Her own future seemed too far away. Daily life itself was the barrier. Often she woke with a secret prayer: that some message would come from the della Seras, or even that her betrothed, overcome with curiosity about his future wife, would make an unexpected visit. She went to bed angry with herself for being disappointed.

It was obvious this ride served a definite purpose. Andrea had dressed himself very finely indeed. The new green doublet with yellow embroidery, violet hose, soft yellow leather boots, and the sparkling multitude of jewels seemed more suitable for visiting a king than a gallop in the hills with a little sister. There was an earnestness about his beautiful mouth which made her feel he was praying.

Franca was not too surprised when they rode through the gates of a large estate, with a squat red stone castle at is centre.

'Casa Cuono.' Andrea motioned towards it.

'Ugly!' she commented. 'They should have it renovated. It looks like a prison.'

'It guards the most precious treasure in the world.'

'What is *her* name?'

'Madonna Cosima di Vanozzo Cuono.'

'So you do not really pay court to the Donati all these months?' Franca said shrewdly.

'Of course not. She has eyes for no one save Lorenzo. That just served as a device so no one would know where my true feelings belonged. Cosima had been betrothed since her childhood to a knight from Rome. He has died lately: Now we are thinking of some way to persuade her father to permit her to become my wife. She is uncertain of his intentions, so we meet in secret in the city. Sometimes I have to go about disguised as a labourer just to bid her a passing good day. We can't exist without each other,' his voice broke with passion. 'Since her father brought the family out here for a few weeks we have been kept apart, and had to find some chance to be together. My Cosima sent me word that today so many different people are visiting Casa Cuono my presence would be unnoticed. I thank the Blessed Virgin, for I swear to you if I had to spend another week without seeing my beloved I should have gone stark mad.'

'Poor Carlotta,' Franca remarked sadly, at the same time feeling honoured by her brother's confidences.

Andrea looked genuinely astonished. 'What has our cousin to do with this? When you meet Cosima you will understand why I am a captive of love.'

'Was hers the favour you wore two years ago?'

He smiled remembering. 'Aye. She was just fifteen, and bold even then. No one knew but she and I.'

'Couldn't Papa arrange matters so you two may be betrothed, and put an end to all this secrecy?' Franca suggested. 'He will not object if Cosima is neither rich nor well-connected. You know he is only concerned for our happiness, the more so it seems since the loss of Raffaello.'

'Her family are also magnati,' Andrea said proudly, 'Distantly related to the Salviatis. They are wealthy enough to judge by Cosima's and her brother Guido's finery, and their palazzo lies close to the Medici's. My darling fears we shall not get permission from her father, or the Magnificent – you know how he scrutinises magnati alliances – if we reveal our feelings too soon.'

'You could run away.' Franca's eyes shone with delight.

'But I want to live and be happy with my Cosima. She is to be the mother of my sons. I am not going to be a character in one of your sad ballads or tales, who ends up murdered, or castrated … or with his head planted in a pot of basil for his bereaved darling to weep over until she too dies…'

The stableyard was crowded with horses and servants in different liveries which showed there were many other people about besides the di Cuono family, and a young groom took their horses without question.

'If anyone asks your business – though I'm sure they won't enquire such a thing of a little girl in humble attire,' Andrea instructed, 'say you came with someone who is delivering a message.'

'So I am to serve instead of Madonna Lucrezia Donati in the country.' Franca said slyly. 'No man would go clandestinely a-courting his true love accompanied by a grubby young sister, eh? If you had warned me we were visiting somewhere fine I should have dressed more suitably … but perhaps that would not have fitted your purposes as well.'

Andrea became contrite. He put his arms around her, and kissed her lips. 'Are you angry, my little love? But I have to see her, Franca. I adore her. Can you understand? And we have to guard her fair name too. She says her father and brother have murderous rages, so…'

She looked into the anguished familiar eyes, and smiled kindly. 'Save your kisses and protestations for your Cosima.'

'I won't be very long,' he promised. 'Keep to the courtyard and the gardens. If it is at all possible you may meet the most perfect being in this world, and heaven too.'

Franca lingered among the horses for a while, but since no one questioned her presence, she began to wander among the walled courts and gardens surrounding Casa Cuono, each linked to the other by archways. The sun emerged. Its warmth tempted her to loll on a stone seat supported on carved lion's paws, beside a small artificial lake.

She admired the bronze fountain at its centre, and guessed it came from Maestro Verrocchio's workshop. A naked youth struggled to hold a dolphin spewing jets of water into the air. The gentle breeze stirred this sequinned cascade. It wavered from side to side, catching the sunlight that created rainbow strands like crowds of hovering dragonflies.

A boy with a flushed face, and flour dusting his Cuono livery came from the kitchen quarters and crossed the water garden. With one hand he held a huge tray on his head. A spicey aroma made Franca's nostrils quiver greedily. She fixed the lad with her most beguiling smile.

He looked round hastily before grinning. 'I have here cakes for the fine folk who are out riding with Guido di Cuono. The steward has the wine, but they allowed me to carry out our cook's famous delicacy.'

He winked. 'Now if you were to give me a little kiss, sweetheart, in return I'd give you a piece of this beautiful pie, which is never tasted by the likes of you or me.'

Franca considered the bargain, smiling all the while. If Andrea had been around he would have thrashed the imp, but how could this scullion know that she was anything other than a peasant's child in her rust woollen hood and gown.

'Very well,' she agreed, 'but to show you are a true gentleman you must first give me the cake.'

He handed her a large slice with crumbling edges. Franca's teeth crunched ecstatically on almond paste, juicy raisins and Madeira sugar.

'Thank you. It is wonderful,' she called, and darted to the far side of the lake, knowing he wouldn't dare follow in case he dropped his precious burden.

'What about our bargain, you little witch?' he shouted, half in anger, half in jest.

'I forgot,' she mocked, and with a dainty gesture kissed her hand towards him.

'Next time I see you, my fine lady,' he threatened, 'I'll take that kiss. You watch out for Gianni.'

But Franca had slipped through another archway out of his sight. Gianni reminded her of the kitchen boys at Castelfiore.

Though naturally whenever she appeared they ceased their tease-and-kiss games with the maids in case she reported them to Madonna Ginevra.

She picked the last crumbs from her gown and sucked her fingers, anxious not to lose the least delicious morsel, and then regretfully scrubbed the stickiness from her face and hands.

A narrow stairway entwined with ivy wound up the back of the house. Below, the formal walled garden with its many bushes cut to resemble strange birds and beasts, was quite deserted, except for one tame and very timid chamois. Every time Franca approached the creature it fled. At last, with nothing left to do, she began to wonder just where those twisting stairs led. There seemed little harm in finding out.

At the top a long window opened on to a chamber furnished with greater luxury than she had ever seen or imagined. It evidently belonged to a fine lady … if not a queen.

An inlaid table was scattered with alabaster boxes and pots of unguents and cosmetics, vials of perfume, ivory implements for paring and shaping finger nails, carved combs, a mirror in a gold frame set with alexandrites. A tangle of jewels spilled from a silver casket surmounted by an exquisitely fashioned gold and enamel bay tree. The silk wall and bed hangings were thick with golden threads. On a small marquetry table rested Venetian goblets and an elegant silver wine jug with a great topaz set in its lid.

In the centre of the room stood a large bed of inlaid wood. Its open curtains showed embroidered linen sheets, and a coverlid of stranded fur hung with small silver medallions. A few beautiful soft rugs made bright pools of colour on the floor. Over the back of a marquetry chair hung a crimson gown trimmed with dyed-red fur. The gold and jet embroidery on the sleeves formed designs of trailing flambeaux. An open cassone overflowed with other costly vivid gowns.

Franca absorbed all the details with envious wonder: a wolf's head fashioned in gold and crystal to hold candles in its snout and ears ... a carved jasper lion ... the heavily jewelled crucifix above the bed ... a Carrara marble bath tub half concealed behind silk curtains...

When I am wed, she promised herself, I shall have a bedchamber just like this.

The sound of voices made her dart to the side of the window, so that she could observe without being seen by the occupants of that wonderful room.

A girl stepped close to the window. In daylight her pale nakedness was almost translucent. The ebony shadows of hair on loins and underarms emphasised the whiteness of the flesh with its tracery of faint blue veins. Franca was reminded of full moonlight spilling on to a dark woodland.

The young woman was tall and full-bosomed. Her narrow waist flared to a firm belly. Soft rounded hips tapered into long shapely legs, with slim ankles, and small highly-arched feet.

With each movement the dark fall of hair swirled to reveal a lovely arrogant face. Its finely boned features had strength, and a certain completeness rare to find on a young girl. The cheeks were softly pink and shadowed by a long feather of eyelashes. The red mouth was wider than perfect beauty demanded. A sulky lower lip suggested its owner was difficult to please, and accustomed to being obeyed by people who longed to make her smile. Indeed when her mouth relaxed, Franca understood that any man might ruin himself to receive such a smile. Beneath finely-plucked black brows the enormous brown eyes contained golden specks as if they reflected two distant lamps.

Franca regretted her own bright hair and thin body, and was jealous of the exquisite naked girl so openly enraptured with her own beauty. She circled the room, laughing and singing, her rounded arms gracefully spread as if between invisible partners. Occasionally with slow caressing movements she ran her narrow hands over the jutting breasts, whose small dark nipples were tight rosebuds.

An elderly serving woman, puffing with the exertion of following her young mistress, tried in vain to comb the tendrils of dark hair.

'Madonna be still, please,' she begged.

'Have done, old nurse,' the high-pitched imperious voice sounded breathless as if its owner could scarce contain her excitement. 'Am I not beautiful enough?'

'You are too perfect for your own good, but I always knew you would be, right from the day you were born, and I laid you in your lady mother's arms... God rest her sweet soul.'

'My dearest nurse,' the girl laughed and threw her arms about the woman, so that her breasts were crushed against the dull woollen gown. 'Who else could I trust to share my wonderful secret?'

'A secret that will cost me my life if anyone else discovers it,' the woman spoke with genuine terror.

'But nobody will. We have always been very careful.'

Franca grew aware of a man's voice singing within that room. She expected the nurse to cover the beauty with a camisia, and then understood that the lovely creature had been displaying herself for this man's eyes.

'Now, my good Bianca, pour us the wine,

and then go, so I can lock the door after you. If anyone asks I am indisposed ... oh, tell them I have the colic and can't leave my room. Run away. We have so many things to do, eh, my love?' she called towards the shadows.

The woman did as she was bid, curtsied to the unseen man, and then scurried from the chamber. The girl turned the ornate key in the lock, and then flung herself on to the bed, extending her arms as if beseeching an embrace.

From the shadows bounded a naked man. The lean, hard-muscled body was as tall and ideally proportioned as any classical statue, and the perfect partner for that female figure. The locks that curled towards his broad shoulders were the same hue as Franca's own, and she wondered why she was surprised.

So that's the message he had to deliver, she thought, and this lady is his Cosima. Pray heaven she is as kind as she is beautiful for he has a soft heart, and is near-foolish in this passion.

The couple drained the wine goblets ... green and brown eyes laughing across gilded rims. Andrea stood before the bed, gazing down at the girl whose provocative position contained no modesty, and showed that this was not the first occasion they had been together in such intimacy. He knelt and buried his face against the apex of her spread legs.

Cosima laughed: a high, mocking note, and stretched her hand to cover the intumescent passion of his loins. He seized the pale voluptuous body in his arms. She struggled, but only to tantalise him. With fierce hunger, he began to kiss her mouth and breasts, tears coursing from his eyes, although his mouth was laughing. Their breathless utterances of each other's names drifted to Franca's ears. Then Andrea's body covered Cosima.

Franca turned away quickly. The air felt chill on her burning face. She climbed down the stairs leaving the couple to their loving. Although curiosity surged within her, she knew this was a secret thing ... and that she had already witnessed too much even to try to forget it. I should not like to be spied upon, she reflected, when I am grown old enough for such pleasures. People are not animals. It is not like watching Scipio with the mares.

'Oh, Andrea, Andrea,' she whispered, frightened for her brother. 'Where will this folly lead? You are reckless to love your mistress while she is under her father's roof, and your Cosima is crazy to yield her virtue so carelessly ... even to you...'

Franca perceived that love was a madness which swept human beings into a maelstrom without allowing them time to reason. Even if it destroyed its victims there was no controlling this force. She feared and longed to be caught in the flood.

In case her presence in that secluded garden might provoke someone else to mount the stairs to a very personal paradise, Franca hastened back to the main court. A group of men, still on horseback, were drinking wine, and eating the famous cake, while grooms held the reins of restless, sweating horses. Sunlight struck harnesses, spurs, jewels and swords with torches of fire.

One young man seemed to be the centre of attention. The others edged their horses close to his chestnut gelding. It was as if he was a flame, and they merely moths entranced by the light he shed. He was clad in pale blue and gold, and his short blond hair resembled silk. Now and then he bent to soothe a young cheetah with a jewelled collar attached to his wrist by a strong leash. It order to eat a sweetmeat, he removed one blue kid glove with a golden acorn painted on its back.

Franca's heart began to palpitate. For among the many rings which practically hid his fingers was the twin to the gimmal ring on her own hand. The painting had lied. The reality of Daniello was far more beautiful. Beside him in grim contrast sat a humpbacked dwarf, who made her remember

Matteo della Sera as quite a handsome being. Close to the golden angel, this swarthy pock-marked face seemed to belong to a demon.

Daniello's voice reached her ears above the laughter and speech. It was clear and gentle, and suggested an equable nature. 'Thank you, Guido, for a pleasant day. Now I must ride back. We have guests.'

Guido di Cuono inclined his head. Even in the saddle he was tall, and curiously like his sister with fine pale features and shining dark hair. Whereas her colouring suggested vibrant sensual beauty, his had the detached austerity of an aesthete ... as if he could control all emotion to suit action. While other men and women gesticulated to accentuate their mood and words, Guido's white hands remained calmly clasped. Even in the parti-coloured flame and blue finery, Franca found it easy to picture him in the drab robes of some hermit, because of his appearance of immense spirituality.

'Is your little bride visiting you?' the dwarf demanded.

Daniello shook his head, and the blue ostrich plumes on the beaver hat stroked his flushed cheek. He glanced at the betrothal ring before drawing on his glove. 'Not for many a year, Altoviti, thank the Lord. She is still only a child, not ripe for any act of consummation.'

'Our Daniello seeks more immediate

pleasures, eh?' Guido said.

Daniello smiled, and Franca's heart leaped so hard it hurt her faintly swelling chest.

'Of course. Would you have me wait? She brings a vast dowry. Not that it will be so hard for me to accept. Little Francesca Lauretta is damnably lovely. Look – like the dutiful lover I'm supposed to be, I carry her likeness.'

He drew the small picture from a pouch, and Franca crept into the shadows cast by the house. 'In fact the dowry will be very welcome...' he added laughing, and stroking the diamond crucifix on his chest, 'the way our family spends gold. They do say Vincenzo de' Narni dabbles in alchemy, and the family's so rich I'm inclined to believe he's successful at the art, which is more than fortunate...'

The other man examined the picture but Franca did not heed their doubtful jests. Even to hear him speak of the Narni wealth as the sole inducement for their marriage did not diminish his splendour. She recalled Andrea and Cosima. Was it possible that one day she and that remote godlike creature would cling together in naked embrace? She could visualise it as a picture but not infuse the scene with feelings which had not yet been aroused.

'Then stay and dine,' Guido urged. 'If you

haven't the wealthy Narnis to entertain.'

'Really I cannot. Madonna Clarice has been staying at Buonventura with my mother, and Lorenzo and Guiliano are joining her, so that we can celebrate this blessed first day of the year together. They're bound to bring along a host of friends, so I must be at dinner.'

He spoke without any particular pride of his intimacy with the Medicis, but the other men's eyes held mingled respect and envy.

'Then I will not attempt to detain one who basks in the warmth of the Magnificent's love.' Guido di Cuodo said civilly. 'I wish you much pleasure, dear Daniello, and that this year of the Incarnation 1478 brings you and your family God's Grace.' They clasped hands affectionately.

Surrounded by a retinue of servants in the della Sera livery, Daniello rode towards the gates, the lithe cheetah loping alongside. Once he reined in his horse, and turned in the saddle to smile confidently at the group of friends who were still watching after him in silent admiration. He raised his hand in salute. Franca found herself waving at that glorious figure, which was finally lost among the dark evergreens ringing the estate.

A cloud obscured the sun.

The men dismounted and went into the house. Franca felt sleepy and cold. She trailed indoors. Nobody paid any attention to the solitary child, assuming she belonged to one of the many servants. Franca did not remain long in the draughty old-fashioned chambers on the lower floor. Servants hurried back and forth with trays of food and flagons of wine. Everywhere gentlemen were eating, discussing the merits of their falcons, horses and dogs. The hounds prowled about picking up scraps. Gradually the atmosphere reverberated with raucous laughter and ribald song, and the air became stuffy with the smells of food, sweat and leather.

Franca mounted a steep wooden staircase. It led to a gallery. Here in the evenings, concealed by an ornamental wooden latticework, musicians played for the entertainment of the company dining below. At the back of this gallery was a small inner bower for the ladies who wished to retire from male company while continuing to listen to the music.

A worn ledge concealed from all eyes by a wooden pillar made an ideal nook. Franca curled up like a puppy, and tried to sleep. She dozed uneasily on this hard couch, and woke with the sensation of falling from some great height. I must have been dreaming, she thought sleepily, as her heartbeats subsided to their normal rhythm. She stretched her cramped legs, and then became aware of men's voices coming from the bower.

Franca lay there, listening without really comprehending, and blinking at the particles of dust which drifted in the long shafts of light shed by the high windows opposite the gallery.

'You are quite sure we are safe to talk up here, Cuono?'

'Of course, Archbishop. We purposely arranged to have the house full of Guido's friends. Do you realise that young della Sera has only just left? No one with any sense would think we were discussing such a plan in the midst of the young men's roistering.'

'And your son is with us?' a choleric voice demanded. Franca could imagine it belonged to a man who would fall into a rage for no reason.

'Naturally, my dear Francesco. Your idea is much to Guido's taste. We Cuonis, just like you Pazzis would sleep easier if the tyrant was removed. Then our hopes for the future will not be impeded: power will be where it rightly belongs – in noble hands … and the rabble won't be able to dictate to us any longer. What I require to know is, Archbishop Salviati, do we really have His Holiness's blessing for our venture?'

Franca stirred. She recollected these names.

The modulated priestly tones contained amusement.

'Blessing … ahem, old Sixtus is too cunning for that, Cuono. As the being closest to God on this earth of course he approves that the present order should be changed ... just so long as no one is killed...'

'But that's impossible!' Vanozzo di Cuono interrupted.

Salviati laughed gently. 'Quite. I told His Holiness that he must permit us to steer the boat ... my very words ... that way his papal conscience will be clear. That I was accompanied by Giralomo Riario naturally helped convince the Holy Father. The new lord of Imola and Forli is very anxious for our plan to succeed. At present I am not actually Archbishop of Pisa, but if Sixtus died then Riario would probably lose his newly-acquired territories. They lie right between Venice and Florence, so he would be crushed by the two allies ... therefore he wants to strike first and remove the chief enemy.'

'We all have good reasons.' Cosima's father's voice made Franca tremble. 'But I want to be sure that I do not commit my family to a band of hotheads who are unlikely to succeed, so I must know their names.'

Franca judged that the man who answered was old, and accustomed to being obeyed. In a dry, cracked tone he said: 'My dear Vanozzo, I would not approach you until I was sure of our numbers. Last week they swore their fealty to this cause at my Villa Montughi. As head of the Pazzis, I, Jacopo, guarantee my relatives' help. In fact, Francesco here was the first person to be approached by the lord of Imola, and Salviati the second.'

'Giralomo can hardly come here himself. He found us the gallant soldier, Count Gianbatista Montesecco, who went to the Pope with him and Salviati. Gianbatista is to be our instrument of justice. Then my priestly secretary, Antonio, is also one of us. He hails from Volterra and wants revenge for what the Medici's condottieri did to his city when they put down that uprising. There are two daredevils below with your son: Bandini and Francesi … and Bracciolini too: he'll do anything for gold in his impoverished state. Do you really want me to continue, Vanozzo? The list of noble names pledged to help us is very lengthy indeed.'

'An odd assortment,' Cuono commented.

'What the devil's the matter with it?' shouted the irascible Francesco Pazzi.

'Hush, Francesco,' the eldest Pazzi soothed. 'Cuoni is right to consider carefully. You know we can rely on his loyalty.'

'This is how we'll proceed then,' Francesco said belligerently, 'unless of course Vanozzo di Cuono has some objections: a detachment of soldiers will be placed at strategic points outside the city to secure our power once we are in control, and the brothers are removed.'

'Brothers?' Cuono questioned.

'Both must die at one time,' Jacopo Pazzi replied gently, 'to leave one alive even for an hour might give him a chance to rally support against us ... a clean kill is what we want.'

'Surely that'll be very difficult,' Cuono said meditatively, 'how do you intend to get them together at a suitable time?'

'Ah, there we have His Holiness's help,' the Archbishop explained. 'He has provided us with the perfect opportunity. The new young Cardinal Raffaello Riario is to be made Legate of Perugia. That means he must pass through Florence. Naturally he will be entertained as befits his station, and he must return his noble host's hospitality. Very graciously Messer Jacopo has offered to lend the Cardinal one of the Pazzi's splendid villas so that he can give a dinner in honour of the Medici brothers. Then we will have them both in our hands. You see: it's so simple.'

Franca pressed her fist against her mouth to prevent herself crying out. What had she overheard? That those four urbane gentlemen were planning to kill Lorenzo and Guiliano and seize the state? Did Andrea know, she wondered suddenly ... was he involved in this plot ... and what about her own father ... after all they too were magnati.

Terror held her in a manacle so she could not move. If they discovered her presence, it would be so easy to dispose of one small girl without asking even her name. She had no real right to be in the house anyway. Franca cowered there, sweating with her fear.

'I must depart,' Salviati said. 'I'll leave by the back entrance, if I may, Cuono. I did not bring servants or horse to your house. My men are waiting for me in the small wood to the north of the estate.'

'Francesco and I must leave separately,' Jacopo Pazzi added. 'No one would suspect me of anything, but it is well known that Francesco is no friend to the Magnificent, and people may already be wondering why he's not in Rome.'

'You'll inform your son,' Francesco said irritably.

'My dear Francesco,' Vanozzo di Cuono spoke calmly, 'why are you always so bad-tempered? You'll make yourself ill. Of course I shall tell Guido, and we'll hold ourselves in readiness. As soon as you know the day for the dinner party, I'll expect an invitation for my whole family.' He gave a soft laugh. 'The presence of my beautiful Cosima will ensure that the Magnificent attends even Riario's invitation. As you know, he has not been exactly subtle in his attentions to my daughter ... and she, the minx, encourages him...'

One by one the men left the bower. Franca counted the pairs of feet. At last, shaking uncontrollably, she crept downstairs, sidling along the wall … and then ran out into the courtyard to the horses. Andrea was waiting, but he failed to notice her agitation.

They rode away from Casa Cuono. Andrea's tired eyes and smiling lips spoke that his mind was still in Cosima's warm embrace. Franca found herself wondering if the beauty would make him a good wife. Somehow she could not imagine her visiting Castelfiore to discuss babies and servants with Isabetta and Madonna Ginevra. Yet, Andrea certainly deserved to marry a princess … and princesses could not be expected to lead mundane lives.

'Andrea,' she said insistently, 'I have overhead a dread plan. Please hear me.'

He listened abstractedly, and then waved his hand as if to dismiss a mayfly. 'Forget it, Franca. You've heard Papa say there are always such intrigues, and he's often been approached to join plots to overthrow the Medici's power. Believe me, nothing will come of this. It's just winecup talk.'

'Couldn't you warn the Magnificent?' she persisted.

'That would only involve our family for no purpose. Let's leave well alone, and not draw Lorenzo's attention to ourselves. Besides we mustn't do anything which might harm my dear love.'

Fontelucente

It was the first time she had visited Fontelucente that year, and the only time she'd been there without Berto. Even before her betrothal he had suddenly refused to go swimming there with her ever again, and would not listen to threats or cajolery.

Of course, it had always been a forbidden thing, yet so long as nobody knew that they threw off their clothes to plunge into the deep pool, there was no harm in it. No one ever came to the place, for it was widely claimed that male and female witches visited the spot to practise their diabolical arts.

Franca was disappointed that up till now she had never glimpsed one of those dreadful beings … but Berto had explained they only came there on moonless nights. Yet she had witnessed magic at Fontelucente – when Berto taught her to swim.

How magnificent to cut through icy water which made her gasp, and turned the cape of hair into fronds of dark red weed, and her pale body into an arrow of quicksilver as it flashed among the green depths.

'You're just like a little fish. I don't believe any girl can swim like that.' Berto had muttered doubtfully, crossing himself and staring down at the girl splashing beneath the tumbling waterfall which fed the pool.

His grudging approbation always made her shriek with glee. He was just like Ser Agnolo really. Though neither would have been flattered by the comparison. Both were always complaining she didn't listen to instructions, and then discovering with mortification that she did in fact know her lessons.

Under the canopy of new green leaves the pool was a stretch of chrysolite, fringed with tender ferns. In its depths pebbles shone like a hoard of precious gems. Franca had often dived for them, only to discover they were ordinary stones beyond the water's enchantment. Violets scented the fresh warm air. Ripples spread over the pool's surface as the fish rose. A blackbird trilled winsomely to his mate.

Franca's heart knew a great loneliness. The unsought-for knowledge isolated her from her loved ones. Since it would mean betraying Andrea's secret she dared not confide to her father the fragments she'd overheard. The burden made her unusually solemn, and she slept badly, awaking unrefreshed. Ser Agnolo had more reason than ever to scold her for inattentiveness. Vincenzo insisted Franca needed fresh air to restore her good spirits, so this expedition into the countryside was donated rather than filched.

Each day she waited in trepidation for dire news from the city. The young cardinal's visit had begun, and tales of the splendid entertainments given in his honour were widely discussed. Yet the Medici brothers continued to flourish … so much so that Florence had a new piece of gossip to relish: the lovesome Giuliano had got with child one of his mistresses: Gorini's young daughter. Sometimes it occurred to Franca she might have dreamed those voices, whose names and intentions could have been spun out of threads from her own memory, and she prayed to God that this was so.

To plunge once again into the clear green water would be to slough off winter for good, and perhaps rid herself of these terrors. Impulsively, Franca unhooked her gown, stretching her arms towards the warmth which stroked her skin. She sighed looking down at her body. She would never have those luxurious curves of Cosima di Cuono … like spoonfuls of thick cream.

She slid into the deeps, and splashed boisterously in an attempt to get warm … and laughed at the joy of the year's first swim. That was what she always relished: the year's turning, and the chance to be able to do and eat all the summer things for the first time. As she swam, she knew winter was really fled. The promise of summer stretched before her: an infinite golden road.

The sun climbing towards noon shone warm on bare shoulders and tangled wet curls, and Franca began to sing:

'A youngling maid am I and full of glee,
Am fain to carol in the new-blown May,
Love and sweet thoughts-a-mercy, blithe
and free…'

She did not hear the soft whinny of a horse being tethered, nor see the bushes parted by a stranger who came upon the pool, induced there by a sweet voice singing an old ballad. The man stared at the girl in the water, and half believed he had returned to the Golden Age and saw a naiad at play. He was unable to wrench his glance from the singing creature, as she hoisted herself out of the water by an overhanging willow branch … a shower of tiny drops put a rainbow halo around her slight form.

Like a deep echo another voice picked up her song:

I go about the meads, considering,
The vermeil flowers and golden and the
white,
Roses thorn-set and lilies snowy-bright…'

Franca's eyes grew large with terror. She

turned, but was dazzled by sunlight, and could only distinguish the dark outline of a tall man against the pale greenery as if he had been fashioned out of night and crept insidiously into the day. So now one of the devil's creatures had come to claim her soul for trespassing in the magic pool.

'Good day, little madonna,' the voice was gentle and human. The man stepped close.

Franca slithered back into the water, and remembered all Gostanza's grim warnings that she must not walk alone in solitary places, or talk with strangers. Now she was doing both, and naked as the day she was born. In this case, she felt sure men were more to be feared than demons.

'I do believe,' he continued, 'that last time we met you were clad, though somewhat simply. You still wear the topaz, I see … a great protection against amorous advances in lonely groves!'

Franca had not forgotten that soft voice, and he was wearing dark mulberry again, slashed with black and silver. 'Good day to you, Messer Ridolfo,' she said breathlessly. 'If you will kindly turn your back I may dress myself.'

'If I don't?' he spoke seriously, but his eyes were merry.

'Then I must stay here until I turn blue, but…' her eyes grew dark as sea beneath rolling storm clouds, 'when I manage to tell my Papa and brothers of your unchivalrous behaviour, you will have no eyes left to spy upon swimming maidens…'

Messer Ridolfo began to laugh gently. He drew aside his cloak, and fingered the hilt of a sword decorated with his lion emblem. 'Madonna Franca, did you never think that a man might chance upon you here, force you to accept his body's pleasure, then cut your throat and leave a young corpse for the crows to pick clean. Then no member of your loving family would be any the wiser of your fate…'

Franca shuddered. 'Is that your intention?'

He held out her gown. 'Madonna, I hope I am always a man of honour. I assure you I have no need to force ladies, besides my tastes is not for the bud but for the flower in full bloom.'

She climbed out of the pool, and reached for the gown, then held it before her, flushing brightly under eyes which refused to look away.

'One day though, Madonna, you will be in full and beautiful bloom. Already your breasts are burgeoning like the earliest spring buds, and the first golden hairs of modesty have grown on your body.'

Franca could not find a way to cover her chest and sex as she scrambled into her dress. She tried to pull away as the man hooked it together, and straightened her hair, but his hands were too strong. He turned her round to face him, and bent his head so that the black eyes were very close to hers.

'Yes, one day, little Franca, you will be a woman, and then you will belong to me.'

She said defiantly: 'You seem to forget that I am betrothed.'

'Oh yes, of course.' His eyes mocked the ring on her finger, 'You will find Daniello cares more for his beauty than yours…'

'And for my dowry more than anything,' she retorted with heat. 'I know, but he is to be my husband, and I shall love him, and bear his children.'

'No, Franca, I vow that when you are a woman you will belong to me and bear my children.'

Franca began to laugh. 'You are mad, Messer! What makes you believe these things?'

'It is written we cannot escape our destinies. Our paths are to run the same course, Franca. No matter what your intentions are now … or how far you wander from them, one day you will lie close to this heart. These lips and hands will teach you about love.'

She began to tremble. His words disturbed her thoughts, and stirred her untried senses. They stared at each other for a long minute. Finally Ridolfo smiled, and offered the girl his arm.

'May I escort you back to Castelfiore, just in case you encounter some less gallant fellow?'

Franca asked: 'What are you doing so far from Milan?'

'Attending some of the festivities in honour of Cardinal Riario.'

'You see Lorenzo de' Medici quite often?' she questioned anxiously.

'Obviously. He is Riario's host, even though he detests both cardinal and Pope. Rulers have to obey these tongue-in-cheek politenesses.'

'Messer Ridolfo, can I trust you with my secret?'

He looked amused. 'What? Have you another sweetheart beside your betrothed?'

Franca snatched her hand from his arm. Her eyes filled with angry tears. She would not weep before this prince of darkness who derided everything and disrupted her every hope. 'Yet I am so perplexed,' her voice broke with agitation, 'I have to tell someone I can trust.'

'Come then, Franca,' he said gravely, and kissed his ring with its carved ruby. 'This is my family crest, and I swear by it to take your secret seriously, and serve you if I can.'

When she had finished telling him about the fatal dinner party intended for the Medici brothers, Franca could not help realising it did sound an improbable story, and began to feel very foolish before this dignitary from Milan.

'Where did you hear these details?'

'At Casa Cuono.'

He looked baffled, then his eyes lightened with understanding. 'You went there with Andrea?'

Franca bit her lips, but would not answer. She was furious with herself for revealing so much.

'You are not really betraying his secret,' Ridolfo said gently. 'He is love-blinded if he thinks sharp eyes don't detect his feelings for the lovely Cosima.'

'So you know her?' Franca felt unaccountably jealous.

'All Florence sits at the feet of this beautiful creature.'

'But she loves Andrea,' Franca insisted proudly.

He gave a secret smile. 'Perhaps, but others may yet win her even from your glorious brother. Like a spoilt pet cat, Cosima tangles up men's hearts as if they were skeins of wool. Now for your plot, Franca – the dinner has already taken place without misadventure. Giuliano was unwell, and could not attend, but Lorenzo enjoyed himself mightily in Cosima's company, and scarcely spoke to Cardinal Riario, which is only natural.'

She began to perspire with relief. 'Then

there is nothing to worry about. Andrea was right as usual. It was just wild talk.'

'Probably. I shall make some enquiries in the city, and attempt to warn the Medici without revealing where I heard about this business. The Cardinal leaves Florence soon.'

'Don't ever tell Andrea,' Franca begged.

'You love him so very much?'

The smile that flooded her face spoke of complete adoration.

'Then don't fret any more.'

He lifted her into his saddle, and as if he was her groom took the reins and led the great black horse down the hillside towards Castelfiore. He left her near the house. 'I must ride on to the city, Franca. Remember all my words. We shall meet again very soon.'

'Thank you for your reassurance,' she said gratefully, and then in mocking tones, added: 'As for the other, Messer Ridolfo, you had best find yourself a wife before you grow too old, for my future is already sealed.'

Eastertide

All Florence rejoiced in Easter. Who could wear a dismal countenance when the sun shone on pretty ladies, carrying nosegays as bright and sweet as their faces and gowns? Multitudes decked in new finery made their way to the churches. Afterwards they would embrace family and friends with the joyful greeting: 'Christ is risen', and then go home to break their fast on good food and wine, amid song and laughter. People would feel, and celebrate, the Resurrection in their hearts and bodies after weeks of Lenten fare, and the agony of Friday's tenebrae.

The route between the cathedral and the Palazzo Medici was lined with crowds waiting to see Cardinal Riario pass by. The young Eminence had especially requested to hear High Mass in the beautiful Santa Maria Fiore. General opinion had it that not even in the Eternal City had he prayed in such perfect surroundings. Afterwards the Medici brothers would bring him to their house to dine with many of the important members of Florentine society.

Noon lacked little more than an hour as Giuliano de' Medici neared the cathedral.

Men and women called blessings on his handsome face. He was a universal favourite, the acknowledged leader of fashion, admired for his prowess in sport and love. The gods truly loved Giuliano, and had given him a trusting heart and guileless nature. Whenever he smiled Florentines felt rewarded as if with gold. He and Lorenzo were their darlings.

'Thank Heaven,' he said with endearing frankness to the men at each side of him, 'that you two were kind enough to call by and bring me to the service. The canon must already have begun. As usual I overslept. Lorenzo frequently tells me I'll be late for my own funeral, which isn't as impolite as being tardy for High Mass in the Cardinal's presence.'

His companions, Francesco Pazzi, and Bernardo Bandini displayed affection and friendship by embracing him whenever one of their sallies provoked too much laughter for them to continue walking. Many people were amazed to note that for once Pazzi's ill-temper had evaporated: the spirit of Easter must have softened his nature, or his squat figure rocked with mirth instead of the usual paroxysms of rage.

Fragments of these jests made maidens hide their blushes behind gloved hands, but men and matrons openly giggled. Nearly all featured the ever-popular theme of tired old men marrying hot young girls, and brisk lovers escaping through bedroom windows without their hose.

'And he knew all the time?' Giuliano demanded, wiping his eyes with a fringed silk handkerchief.

'Naturally,' Francesco's face shone red with glee. 'It saved him a job he really hadn't been able to complete for years. He just used to roll to the far side of their bed, and when he thought there'd been enough sport for one night, and wanted to get some sleep, he'd snore and snort as if about to wake up. Then, the young man would depart. There's no denying that the old boy achieved more satisfaction as the silent audience than he would have by being in the performance...'

'We really must compose ourselves,' Giuliano gasped. 'My sweet friends, we can't burst upon a pious congregation sniggering as if our drawers were lined with feathers...'

A vast crowd packed the cool interior of the cathedral. Incense and fresh flowers suffused the atmosphere with intoxicating fragrance. The murmur of prayer, behind-the-hand gossip, and the whisper of silks and taffetas played as soft background harmony to the melodious choir and the celebrant's reverent chanting.

Greenish gloom filled the soaring dome and resembled an evening sky. Against it the hosts of candle flames and massed lilies formed constellations of stars. The vivid-hued garments of the congregation completely hid the fine marble floor.

Lorenzo de' Medici raised his eyes, and noticed Guiliano standing on the opposite side of the choir between Bandini and Francesco Pazzi. He smiled warmly and nodded, then raised expressive dark brows in the direction of the cardinal apparently wrapped in devout prayer. Giuliano grinned. He understood. It would be a blessed relief when this particular Papal Legate went on his way to Perugia. Were they always to be inconvenienced by some Riario or other?

What a gaggle of Pazzis and Salviatis, Lorenzo thought, and wondered why old Jacopo Pazzi was absent from their numbers. His thin lips twisted ironically. We're all such good friends on the surface. We smile and dine together, while I watch their movements as sharply as my peregrine falcon searches for heron. Messer Ridolfo told me nothing new when he suggested I beware of their desire for power, but he's wrong in imagining they'd usurp our rule with violent methods. Oh no, they're too subtle for that. They'll try to outwit me through some political manoeuvre among the Signoria ... so I must take care none of their sympathy gets office in the Palazzo.

He noticed Ridolfo di Salvestro dressed in

his usual colour. A wily fellow, Lorenzo considered, I would he was a Florentine … but no, he's too able, which might eventually lead me to doubt his loyalty. Still I'm looking forward to see if the future brings his real patron into power – that would be of some help to Florence. Duchess Bona and her father-in-law's one time secretary, Cecco Simonetta, are impossible to rely upon in case of emergency. Milan is a burden not an ally.

Messer Ridolfo's eyes scanned the brilliantly clad young ladies, like so many exotic plumed birds … and Lorenzo's own gaze slid covertly among them too, guessing they both sought the same proud dark head. He sighed. The Cuono family must have chosen to attend High Mass elsewhere.

The recital of the canon ended. The celebrant spread his hands over the bread and wine. The air moved expectantly. Lorenzo's mind returned from contemplating politics and beauty to the Mass. He noted close beside him two priests, their pallid faces seemed to burn with the white fire of religious fervour.

Giuliano, who had been wondering about the sex of his unborn child, and just which political marriage his brother might inflict upon him, crossed himself devoutly, and smiled with genuine joy. His fine eyes embraced the men at his side. It was good to celebrate the Mass among friends – just what the Last Supper had been about.

Audible surprise stirred among people close to the main doors as Archbishop Salviati hurried from the cathedral with his brother, Jacopo, and a group of followers. He was overheard to whisper. 'We must make haste to visit our mother. She is unwell…'

The priest recited with supreme reverence: '…accipite et manducate ex hoc omnes… Hoc est enim corpus meum…' He genuflected deeply, then took the Host in both hands and elevated it to show the waiting worshippers.

The bell rang.

Those who had previously agreed that this most solemn moment should serve as a signal began to carry out their plan.

Giuliano de' Medici's features did not even have time to register shock. Bandini, standing so close, suddenly thrust the blade of a short dagger into his chest. Their demonstrations of affection had ascertained that the younger Medici concealed no weapons under his elegant clothes. The savage blow sent Giuliano tottering a few paces. He fell to the ground, his lips parted in an attempt to say a Paternoster. Men and women screamed in alarm. The Mass came to an abrupt horrified halt…

Francesco Pazzi flung himself on to the dying youth. In a frenzy of violence he struck again and again at the convulsed figure and once-beautiful face. The sight of spurting blood seemed to increase his fury ... and he failed even to feel the dagger plunge into his own thigh ... so that the blood of attack and victim mingled.

Lorenzo had no opportunity to see what had befallen his brother, for at the same time Bandini attacked, the two priests produced daggers from their cassocks' sleeves, and started towards him. One of the Medici's closest friends, Francesco Nofri, sprang in front of him, giving Lorenzo a chance to unsheath his sword.

The dagger thrust intended for him struck the human shield, and Francesco fell dead. Only one blow penetrated Lorenzo's neck. Blood poured on to his jewelled shoulders, as he fought off the priests with desperate strength. Poliziano and Cavalcanti, their swords drawn, strove to reach his side, cursing and yelling. The two priests fled, their daggers clattering on the marble.

Panic ravaged the congregation. The tumult and struggling figures before the Host must bring divine wrath on all of them. Surging shadows suggested that the cathedral walls were in fact collapsing. Wailing in terror, people rushed to escape, colliding with others fighting their way forward to see what was happening.

Cardinal Riario, his dark eyes wild as an

unbroken pony, clutched at a crucifix, and threw himself towards the altar, where the celebrant, deacon and archdeacon defended him against the incoming tide of fury.

Noting that the priests, Stefano and Antonio, had left their task undone, Bandini and Pazzi launched themselves at Lorenzo. He leapt over the choir, and across the cathedral, accompanied by Cavalcanti and Poliziano. They dashed into the sacristy. With the clangour of a giant gong, the enormous bronze doors slammed shut in the faces of their pursuers.

For the first time Lorenzo failed to admire Luca della Robbia's twenty exquisite panels framed in a damascene of gold and silver, and only thanked God for the strength of the bronze which stood between himself and his assassins. Screams of terror, anger and pain echoed horribly from without.

'My sweet Lorenzo,' Poliziano was pale and trembling, 'you must permit me to suck that wound in case those fiends used poison on their daggers.'

'I have loyal friends indeed,' Lorenzo's hoarse voice contained a sob, 'one has already died for me, and you do this. Dear Mother of God, what have they done to my brother?'

Afterwards they bound his neck with a silken scarf.

'What can be happening out there?'

Poliziano asked.

Lorenzo leaned on his sword, his face ashen with fury and pain. 'We shall not know until we leave here, and at present we dare not open those doors. We are caught like snared rabbits.'

After an hour, the sounds of turmoil subsided, and voices began chanting: 'Come out, Lorenzo. All is well.'

Through the bronze barrier, the calls were sepulchral and menacing.

'But who wants me?' Lorenzo turned to his companions. 'How can we know if this is also part of their accursed plot?'

'There is a way to find out.' Cavalcanti stripped off his crimson doublet with its ballooning upper sleeves which narrowed into tight cuffs. 'Ah, that's better…' he breathed, and began climbing upwards to the cantoria.

All Florence considered the perfect singing gallery of carved marble to be Luca della Robbia's finest achievement. Below it the tympaneum was also his work. The enamelled terra cotta reliefs depicting the Resurrection were a tragic reminder of this Sunday's true meaning.

'I can see them,' Cavalcanti yelled. 'Friends, God be praised. Let's open those doors, and get out and kill the treacherous bastards!'

'Lorenzo must be taken home and tended

by his physician Leoni.' Poliziano insisted, and the shabbily clad writer supported his friend and patron through the doorway.

Lorenzo looked at the Cardinal cowering beside the altar, and commanded: 'Escort His Eminence to the Palazzo, and keep him very safe. We must discover just what role he played in this piece of bloody theatre.'

'Believe me...' Riario pleaded as armed men led him away.

The Medici ignored him, and knelt beside the body of his brother, his hands and knees stippled by the pool of gore. He kissed the cold lips, and closed the unseeing eyes which would never charm the world again. When Lorenzo looked up, the flat features had become an unyielding mask of vengeance. No tears flowed.

'Fifteen wounds. Giuliano never harmed any man, may Heaven accept his sweet soul. No punishment is too terrible for those involved in this bloody deed. Our city will not fall into their inhuman hands...'

Somehow Francesco Pazzi managed to return to Messer Jacopo's mansion. He tried to mount the saddled horse, but faintness from loss of blood made this impossible. He stumbled indoors, threw off his sticky, gore-soaked garments, and sank on to a bed, grinding his teeth with pain and fury.

Old Jacopo Pazzi's eyes were distraught, but Francesco ignored his question and commanded. 'You must ride out and rally the citizens to arms. They will follow you for sure. Bandini, curse him, has fled with his usual swiftness. Part of our plan has gone awry. The tyrant still lives, and is safe within his palazzo. I would call the people myself, but for this accursed wound. Where are Vanozzo and Guido di Cuono? They should be here now to help gather our supporters. For the honour of our name, and the freedom of this city, Jacopo, you must take my place. There's not much to do: Salviati will by now have control of the Palazzo della Signoria. With the seat of government in our hands the people will flock to us, and Lorenzo's power will be at an end...'

Old age had unfitted Messer Jacopo for sudden desperate action, but he mounted Francesco's horse, and galloped towards the Piazza della Signoria at the head of a hundred armed men. Waving a sword above his head, he roared out the rallying cry: 'Liberty, and the people!'

His followers took up the call, but were dismayed to realise that Salviati had not succeeded with his part of the plan. Their own attack on the Palazzo's massive walls was beaten off by a savage hail of stones thrown down by the Signoria under the command of Cesar Petrucci, the Gonfalionere della Giustizia. The members of government also flourished spits and larding pins from their kitchen in case the supply of rocks did not fulfil the need.

'Liberty and the people!' drowned under another chant which swelled through the narrow streets to burst upon the Piazza. The people summoned by the urgent ringing of the Parlemento bell, in the Palazzo's tower, demonstrated their true loyalty and fury with the Medici's own emblem as their rallying call.

'Palle! Palle! Palle!' rang out from all quarters. The Medici's personal followers galloped into the tight-packed square, and the city seemed about to explode with the screams, the clanging bells, and the crash of arms.

Jacopo Pazzi understood their cause was lost. They had underestimated the Medici's popularity among the common herd. From the upper windows of the Palazzo della Signoria the bodies of the Archbishop of Pisa, his brother, and Bracciolini appeared hanging by ropes. Gradually their legs ceased to twitch. They swung back and forth like sides of butcher's meat in the Mercato Vecchio. The archbishop's costly robes were kirtled about his loins, and the purple silk stockings made a touch of macabre gaiety.

Messer Jacopo turned his horse, and crouching in the saddle, galloped from the city through the Porto alla Croce, in the direction of the Romagna.

As the news of Giuliano's murder spread, a frenzy of blood lust and revenge seized the populace. Men and youths, armed with every sort of weapon, hacked at the corpses of the archbishop's followers, which lay in a grisly tangled heap on the piazza's paving stones. They carried the bloody relics on staves through the streets, screaming: 'Death to the traitors!' while the Signoria's men-at-arms diced for the dead men's clothing.

Crowds milled before the Palazzo Medici to protest their allegiance. Lorenzo, his face gaunt above a swathe of bandages, showed himself to the citizens, acknowledging and encouraging their loyalty. His own followers led the search for more traitors. They ransacked each of the Pazzi mansions to bring to justice all holders of that name, and their minions. Many had already fled. Giugliamo Pazzi only survived because of the Magnificent's perfect knowledge of his brother-in-law's innocence.

The mob discovered Francesco Pazzi, and dragged him naked through the streets, spitting on him and throwing ordure. His round ugly head remained unbowed, and his eyes glowed with malevolent fury. In the Palazzo della Signoria fire and iron were agonisingly employed to wrest the names of the fellow-conspirators from his lips, but Francesco shrieked nothing save: 'Death to the Medici!'

They hung his mutilated body from the window beside the Archbishop. As Salviati and Pazzi knocked together the crowed below hurled obscenities. They returned again and again to disembowel the stiffening corpses ... like children never tiring of a new game. The air reeked with the excreted terror of the executed, their blood and guts.

When night spread across the city, torches flickered crimson on the ever-increasing necklace of human pendants strung across the Palazzo. All gates were closed to prevent the guilty from escaping.

The joy and flowers of Easter were stamped upon by fear and hatred...

Blood and Fire

Franca trudged down the path from the woods, whistling against the eeriness of thickening dusk. Somehow she'd failed to hear Castelfiore's bell. The family had all gathered for Easter in an effort to cheer Vincenzo de' Narni who brooded too much on Raffaello's death. It had been a happy day though. The adults' sleepiness after their sumptuous feast had enabled her to sneak away on a secret pilgrimage to the shrine of San Christofero at the lonely crossing south of Fiesole. There Franca had placed fresh flowers before the tremulous little light, and prayed fervently for Raffaello's miraculous return, trusting that this holiest of Sundays would make her prayers especially favoured by the saint who had such a fine reputation for aiding travellers in peril.

The breeze carried a faint acridity of smoke. They must have become anxious, she thought, and sent out searchers. That's the smell of torches.

Franca topped the rise from where she always surveyed Castelfiore on her way homeward. No torches, like a swarm of fireflies, starred the darkness, but pale smoke plumed from the farm buildings, yet she could not hear the shouts of men who must be beating out the fire. A sudden eruption of flame sent her running down the hillside.

Unreasoning terror blotted out the ability to think. She tripped over her skirts, unaware of the stones and brambles which tore at her hands and feet. The nearer Franca came to home, the emptier seemed the surrounding dark. Now she could hear the flames, and the fiery glow through a barn's open door threw the buildings into black relief.

Not even a dog barked.

Franca stumbled into the courtyard, her mouth dry, her eyes streaming, and her rasping breaths interspersed with attacks of coughing from the stinging smoke. A pain nagged in her side.

Then she saw the dog. Cassio lay before the open door, as he often did on sunny days. He didn't even thump his tail at her approach. Franca bent over him, then recoiled. The animal had been clubbed to death. She could not understand what she saw.

Beyond the silent unlit interior astonished rather than frightened. Familiarity allowed her to feel the way into the wainscotted chamber where the family must be awaiting her at the end of this feast day.

Once she called out: 'Andrea!'

There was no answer.

The big room was lit by that orange glow slowly encircling the house, and also by the last red ashes in the hearth. Overturned chairs … fallen hangings … a never-before-seen confusion … suggested the family had fled away without once thinking of her.

Then Franca saw them. Her beloved ones. Vincenzo de' Narni stared across the room at his daughter. She ran towards him, and stopped. He was transfixed to the wainscoting by his own sword. Franca backed away. Her foot touched something soft and heavy. She looked down. Nofri lay there, his head almost severed from his neck. Her bare feet knew a moist stickiness.

She did not cry out, or move. Her eyes roamed the scene like a sleeper unable to waken from a nightmare.

Domenico sprawled across the long table among the debris of broken china, scattered food, and spilt wine. His hands had been lopped from the wrists, and his head was an unrecognisable bloody mass. On the ground beside him lay his young wife. The matted long hair half concealed her face, and the plump throat garrotted by the gold chain from which hung the pearl crucifix – Domenico's gift on the birth of their first son. Isabetta was quite naked, and the white flesh tinged orange from the fire's light. Blood smeared the heavy breasts, the inner sides of the obscenely flung apart legs. The swollen stomach had been ripped open.

Franca understood what had happened to Isabetta before she was slain. She knew it with a primitive female instinct rather than the certainty of any taught knowledge, and her hand involuntarily pressed through her gown against the top of her own thighs.

'Mamma … Mamma…' Franca kept repeating the first word she had ever learned in a flat monotonous wail. 'Mamma … Mamma…'

Madonna Ginevra, her heavy skirts covering her face, had been as brutally assaulted as her daughter-in-law. This wasn't her mother … it couldn't be: for Franca could not associate the sweet virtuous lady with that grotesquely spread-eagled, blood-stained horror. Beside her, Gostanza had shared a similar fate.

Close to them lay the pathetic nakedness of Ser Agnolo. He had been obscenely mutilated, and the skin on the soles of his feet was charred away in strips like meat which has been grilled overlong. Beside one stiffening outstretched hand rested the knife he used to sharpen pens – a last futile and gallant attempt to protect his dear lady.

Both babes were dead. Their small rounded bodies hopelessly twisted like discarded toys from being flung against a wall … as if some wicked boys had been tormenting newborn kittens…

Jewels and precious ornaments were gone. The new clavichord Franca was just learning to play had been hacked into firewood. Torn leaves of the prized illuminated manuscripts littered the floor with an autumnal profligacy.

Someone was missing from this carnage.

Franca searched, dreading to find him. Andrea was nowhere to be seen. A tiny flame ignited in her heart. She was not quite alone. He would seek out the killers and bring them to justice even if this could not wipe out the hideous sin.

She did not cry. Grief could not encompass the feelings. She clasped and unclasped her hands, and could not understand. Her gentle, often mundane world had come to an abrupt end … erased with steel, fire and violence. No one had ever suggested such a thing could happen. Franca shut her eyes, re-opened them, believing it was all the enchantment within an evil dream … but the ghastly setting remained. An etching in darkness and blood filled with the odour of the shambles and burned flesh.

Footsteps slapped against the darkness. Terror and shock did not allow Franca to move. A fitting apparition for this red and black hell. Taddeo resembled a mis-shapen demon that had come to claim the souls for the devil's kingdom of agony.

He wandered the room, stopping before

each corpse. At last he stood over his mother, and with unsure fingers – in case she suddenly sprang up and started to berate him as was her wont – he pulled the skirts down over her belly and legs to reveal Gostanza's face curiously tranquil even above the gashed throat.

Taddeo stared for a long while at the girl frozen in the centre of that room. Then he tugged at her cold, clammy hand. She did not move or even react. He peered into the transparent face, as cold and gleaming as any marble sculpture, and listened to the shallow rapid breathing. The staring eyes conveyed a great void as if they could see nothing. The soul had flown, and the shell awaited its return or the entrance of another. Taddeo pulled at her arm fiercely, and began to drag her from that human abbatoir.

Once Franca screamed: the hopeless cry of a small animal swooped upon by a night-hallowed owl.

'You cannot stay,' he mumbled, the words as usual tumbling over his too large tongue. 'You will be killed too.'

The fire had increased. Despite the cool of night, the air held the intense heat of an August noon sun. The roar of flames belonged to an overhead thunderstorm. Now and then a violent crash sounded as a barn wall collapsed. Dense smoke filled their lungs and made breathing a painful, tearful process.

On the paving stones lay a limp silk banner: a scarlet ground with a trailing black flambeau woven into it. Some distant memory echoed that pattern. Franca picked it up as Taddeo dragged her across the painted court.

Once the girl looked back from the hilltop. The flames had encroached upon the house now. Sparks cascaded into the darkness. An enormous funeral pyre that reduced to dust not only the beloved characters in her life, but also all the beauty, comfort and civilisation she had ever known. With it went the greater part of her own self, for that belonged to Castelfiore.

And the night was written upon by death…

It was dark and stale within the cave, but untouched by the heavy dew. Franca crept to the very back, and cowered against the rock face. Taddeo handed her his one comfort: a stinking goat's skin peeled from some beast that had died of exposure, hunger and age. The girl ignored it, merely remaining crouched, staring and trembling.

He left her, to return shortly with a rough wooden bowl of fresh milk. The young goatherd was always easy to scare from his duty. Whenever Taddeo's terrible head peered at him over some bush, the boy would flee with the agility of one of his own creatures, as if the hounds of hell were snuffling at his heels.

'Drink,' Taddeo ordered, and pushed the rim against her mouth. Dutifully she sucked at the thick sweetish milk, but he had to wipe away the creamy outline from her lips with the back of his hand.

Vision seemed to return to her eyes, and concentrated itself upon Taddeo's belt. Before he could gauge her intentions, Franca darted forward and seized the knife.

'No ... no...' he protested, and tried to force her to drop the blade. She fought like a cornered animal, and he did not want to hurt her. He licked his scratched hands and arms, and blinked as she seized fistfuls of her own hair, and hacked at it until she had a shorn head as ragged as Taddeo's. A wealth of soft red gold carpeted the cave.

He picked up a strand and stroked it reverently.

'Beautiful,' he grunted. 'Why?'

She gave a wild laugh. 'Now I'm a boy. You must call me Franco. Do you understand? I'm Franco,' she insisted. 'Then they cannot do these things to me. I shall not have a baby to be destroyed...'

The mirth became sobbing. She cried without tears, rocking back and forth in an agony of memory which stayed fresh-painted on the canvas of her mind.

For two days Taddeo kept her in that cave.

He gave her milk at intervals, but she would not look at it, or touch the flesh of rabbits he snared and cooked. During daylight she sat holding the stained silken pennant. At night she curled up on the floor and stared into the darkness until sleep claimed her.

Taddeo would cover her with the goatskin, but he was always woken by her terrible screams. He could not know what she saw in those dreams, but vaguely recalled that when he was smaller he too used to waken in the lonely places, crying and trembling, from encountering some horrors which prowled the avenues of his sleep. Taddeo did not dare touch her, and knew no way to soothe ... for gentleness was something he had never experienced. When he lay down to sleep he closed his fist on a tress of that wonderful silken fire as if it was a talisman.

Sometimes Franca would question him with a wild intensity, and he tried to tell her his jumbled memories of how the destruction of Castelfiore came about.

'A man,' Taddeo mumbled thickly, wary of Franca's spurts of rage, 'a prince of night from afar, but when I crawled closer to the track I saw his clothes were of that dark red, like the fruit of the tree silkworms feed upon. He had many sparkling stones, even in his hat, and he rode on a great black horse.'

From the pointed beard and long dark

eyes Franca determined the man was Messer Ridolfo di Salvestro. Yet whether he had come to Castelfiore before or after the company of horsemen that had dropped the banner, Taddeo could not recollect.

She sat rubbing her hands in pitiful triumph. 'I know my enemy now. Andrea will find him out, and we will destroy him…'

Then she commanded: 'Fetch Berto to me. He will take us down to the city. My brother will be anxious about me and must be awaiting my news.'

The voice was wild with hysteria … as if the mind that proposed this plan was about to split asunder under an unbearable strain. Though Taddeo was unwilling to seek out a youth who loathed and tormented him, he could not ignore Franca's order. He left her alone for nearly the whole day, but Franca had ceased to notice time.

Taddeo returned alone.

'Berto?'

He sank down, tired and puzzled. Suddenly his familiar though grim world had turned a somersault, and he seemed to be the one person who had not altered.

'The night the house burned,' he grunted hoarsely, 'Berto hit his father and ran away. In the village they are saying he hurt a woman very badly so that she almost died.'

Taddeo's explanatory gesture was crudely direct.

'Berto too...' Franca shuddered.

She was not to know he had visited Castelfiore that night of violence, and seen enough to be convinced his playmate had suffered the same brutalities as the Narni ladies, and all their maidservants. When Berto returned to his father's hovel he had demanded they seek out the killers of their master's family.

'What, and get ourselves butchered!' his father shouted. 'Listen to me, you idle lout, let the noble folk fight and slay each other just so long as they leave us alone. We have no rights. Why should we look out for others?'

'You know what they did?'

Giovanni Spenozzi shrugged. 'They do as much to us and our women and children, for sport, and we are not allowed to defend ourselves. You've just had your head filled with madness by their fine daughter. All you wish is that she lives so you could have your chance with the strumpet...'

It was then Berto struck his father.

Franca was defiled and dead. Therefore life had tricked him monstrously. No such things existed as goodness and beauty ... or angels and music ... or glorious words and pictures. The devil ruled. The rest was just a sweet fantasy to incense man and then leave him arid and empty. From now on he was free to be as wicked as he chose. He would take what he wanted. That would be his revenge on a world that had duped him.

So the middle-aged countrywoman he encountered on the road, knocked senseless, and raped was his first act of rebellion ... by which he hoped to banish Franca's magic memory.

Franca curled up on the floor like one of the fox cubs which had long since departed for the woods. A terrible lassitude enmeshed her. Taddeo, ignorant in the ways of men and their artificial world, but cunning in the laws of nature, thought only of discovering some protection for the new foundling he succoured. In the night he listened to her calling desperately: 'Andrea ... Andrea...'

She awoke, feeling Taddeo's hand shaking her shoulder, and her voice contained accusation: 'You're not Andrea! You're a fiend!'

He ignored her harsh words just the way he ignored the bites and scratches of wounded wild creatures.

'We must go now.'

Her eyes dilated in terror. He was quick to reassure. 'There is no danger. You must come to them. They are waiting for you.'

He could not answer any questions as to who the 'they' were, and almost carried her out into the cold night. The air smelt thin and pure. It hurt her nostrils to inhale after the stuffiness of the cave.

Night was total, for it was that phase of the month when the moon presented her dark face to the earth, so that the oldest mysteries might be practised away from the eyes of men who wished to eradicate those deepest beliefs engraved upon the night before May's first day…

The chuckle of a waterfall told Franca they had reached Fontelucente. She longed to be clean. Taddeo's rough attempts at washing her face, hands and feet had been to remove the blood rather than due to any concept of cleanliness. Her skin itched from countless bites, and reeked as if it belonged to a stranger. She felt permeated to the marrow with the odour of the frowsy cave and the goat pelt.

Fully clothed, Franca waded into the icy pool, heedless of Taddeo's urgent call. She did not even flinch from the numbing cold, as if her senses were already frozen, and her nerve ends failed to respond to normal feelings. At last, she clambered on to the bank, where Taddeo grumbled: 'You'll die of cold.'

Her fierce bright look penetrated even the dark, and spoke of a total indifference for life, and he was scared. In the thicker darkness of the grove above the pool, Franca saw the figures, and tried to pull free, but Taddeo held her fast.

At first, she thought they were beasts standing on their hind legs, but then realised they were men and women, their bodies half concealed by animal pelts with swinging tails. She could not distinguish their faces, but from their varying miens could determine that some were young and others old.

A woman with wild grey locks approached. Pale eyes stared at Franca. She was conscious of her own lack of fear. Once, she would automatically have recited the prayers which had become part of herself. Since that night she had not even thought of saying an Ave or Paternoster.

The woman put thin knotted hands on the girl's shoulders.

'Not afeared then,' she muttered, reading the unwavering expression. 'They who have been through the fire, and known the worst either madden or die … or else they are made new. You are re-born, and so can be one of us. Take off that wet dress. Put on this cloak, and get warm.'

Franca did not stir. The woman pulled off the soaking gown, and bundled the frail body into rough wool which smelt of fresh air and grass.

'Who are you?' Franca demanded, gazing at the figures outlined in the flickering light of the fire behind them.

'We are members of La Vecchia – the oldest faith.'

'So you are streghe then.' Franca did not shy away. She had found the witches of Fontelucente … or rather they had sought her out to be among their numbers.

The different voices proclaimed their stations in the daylight world. Some accents were of peasant folk: the wise women who supplied villagers with philtres which procured love, abortion, the easing of labour, or fertility. When all went well, their arts were secretly and gladly solicited ... but if folk died, crops failed, or cattle sickened the blame was located on these streghe, who sometimes paid with their lives. Other accents belonged to the educated and priestly. These were the wizards of the city who tried to understand the universe, pored over the Cabala, and the Clavicle of Solomon ... attempted to conjure up spirits to unlock the secret wisdom. Their powers as astrologers, alchemists and necromancers were consulted by popes, princes and kings. Yet they too existed in jeopardy: for their experiments and beliefs could lead to torture and execution on the grounds of heresy and witchcraft.

'The world only knows what the Church tells it about us. To gain power the Christians have garlanded our faith with every abominable deed,' the wise woman explained. 'We do not pay homage to the Devil, for those who do merely practise the converse of Christianity, seeing rebellion against their baptised faith as a means to gain power. We worship the dark queen, Diana Aradia, who rides with us through the skies, and whose domain over men's minds belongs to the womb of time. Tonight is hallowed, and we hold a feast in honour of our lady. Sometimes she sends us a special envoy to take her place in our revels. All hail to you, child, for you are sent to be our lady.'

She drew Franca into the circle of thirteen. They did not touch her but bowed their heads in welcome.

'We shall invoke the spirits to guard you, little lady,' said a man's educated voice.

'I'm a boy,' Franca insisted wildly.

'Our goddess permits you to be both,' a young and pretty wench explained softly in the accents of the Mugello. 'You may serve her in whatever guise you choose. Whoever you are, little creature, you have nought to fear from us, who know what it is to be hunted down in the name of the god of love, or by the vagaries of power-greedy laws.'

They removed the cloak, and sat Franca upon a stone slab. It formed a natural throne in the midst of a dark clearing studded with the pale stars of Jack-by-the-hedge, which by day tempted butterflies of a similar appearance to linger on its stems. Sometimes Franca had brushed this garlic-scented plant, and laughed to see what looked like flowers flying up into the blue. Beside her was a lock of her own hair, and small silver axe with a dark bone handle. Upon her head they placed a crown of herbs and flowers interwoven with dried poppy heads.

'These are the flowers of forgetfulness,' the old woman said. 'You will learn that life is but a dark dream.'

Franca did not fear them … even when one of the men, an old and silvery-haired being, took the axe and gently touched the ten orifices of her body and her left breast with its blade. He recited words in a tongue she did not understand, and then placed the hair in a small box, which he buried at the base of the throne.

They danced around her in a solemn circle. Their complete nudity did not repel her, for in that flickering firelight they were not creatures of the world. Then each knelt and kissed the child's hand, laying their heads for a moment upon her knees in homage.

'Tonight we do you honour,' the man said. 'For you will sit in the place of our queen at this love feast. Ever after you will be among the elect, although you may not recall this ceremony until many years pass. It is written in your face and your hands that this event, like all others, will come to pass.

'You cannot but accept a strange destiny. Our powers will be transmitted into your own blood, for you have been brought to us, new born, neither man nor woman, without name or place, cut off from the world of men. You will never betray our secrets, and we shall not reveal yours until the death.'

Even as he spoke a star shot against the black heavens in a stream of silver spray, and its reflection touched the axe blade. Franca understood this was a special omen as if the queen of night welcomed her to La Vecchia.

'You must be marked with our sign,' the old woman said. 'It will not pain very much. By it, the chosen will always know you are one of us for we all bear such a sign. Our enemies call it the devil's mark, claiming that it is inflicted by the devil's kiss when a worshipper forfeits his Christian soul. We are not creatures of hell.'

Franca smiled. 'No, I have been to hell,' she said, and the low voice was not a child's. 'You are not the devil's minions.'

They anointed her upper left buttock with a herbal salve which deadened the flesh, and then marked her with fire. She felt the slightest discomfort. Later, the burn healed to leave a tiny star-shaped scar that could almost have been part of her flesh since birth.

They placed her at the head of their company, and gave her to eat and drink. A silver beaker was passed among them. Franca swallowed the liquid slowly. It was heady and sweet and made her feel warm for the first time since the fire. 'What is it?' she asked.

'Our enemies would say it contained all the vilest ingredients ... like human blood, fat of a murdered babe, our own excrement, and naturally the ashes of a toad which had been fed on the Host,' a girl replied cheerfully. 'It is just good Vernaccia laced with honey.'

They ate new white bread, fresh cheese, green herbs, roasted meats, and honey cakes. Taddeo sat in the deepest shadows, and partook wolfishly of the fine food they offered him. He played no part in the gathering, and was completely uninterested in their doings. He was content for he believed that whatever transpired in the future now the child would be protected.

They sang songs that Franca had never heard, in an old tongue: strange joyful chants which seemed to be echoed by the whispering springtime leaves ... as if the grove was impregnated with such music from the birth of all time.

Afterwards the women rubbed her body with a pungent smelling ointment, which stung a little when it touched broken skin; then they all anointed their flesh in a similar manner.

'As the leader of our revels,' they said, taking her hands, 'you must dance with us. You will learn how to fly, and begin to understand your own powers.'

The steps of La Volto were not difficult to learn. Franca found herself laughing, but it was not her old carefree laughter: this was the sharp-edged mirth of the defiant, who have lost everything, yet dare all. She felt as light as a sycamore butterfly caught in a gust of wind.

They formed a chain that danced among the trees. At its head leapt the figure they called the child of Aradia … sent to them as a sign … the chosen one. She felt safe, and that she belonged … belonged to those who were cast out from society by secret and forbidden beliefs, or through cruelty and ignorance.

So many stars shone in the heavens it seemed the dark backcloth had worn thin and began revealing its glittering hidden kingdom. Each leaping step carried Franca up towards the eyes of night, until she was flying amongst them … right above the trees. Even outcasts and vagrants could enjoy miracles impossible for ordinary safe-abed mortals if they performed the mysteries.

They set her reverently on the ancient throne. No one attempted to molest the child who witnessed their rites in a grove which was dedicated to such deeds. Firelight painted the flailing limbs red against the black shadows. Franca stared impassively, without once shutting her eyes or ears to the sight and sound of the witches slaking their unhallowed passions…

BOOK II

'The Red Lily'

The Outcast

No one paid any attention to the two beggar children who entered the city by the Porta della Fiesole. One was too repugnant to look upon for his hood failed to conceal the purple birthmark. His smaller companion was almost lost under a drab hooded jacket. The tiny pale face, so hollow and pointed, held none of the roundness of childhood … nor the onset of premature age as often seen among the derelict poor … but seemed to belong to some new remote age, which having been forged with the cleansing fire, stepped purified and incorruptible into the everyday world. The enormous amethyst eyes did not smile or weep. They had learned to mask thought and reaction so that an observer might conclude the pitiful creature did not feel.

A group of urchins ran, yelling and laughing, through the streets, dragging something on a long rope. A terrible stench of putrescence emanated from this plaything. The boys fixed one rope end to the door bell of an elegant palazzo, which bore the Signoria's seal forbidding anyone to enter. Each time they jerked the rope their grisly burden rose up as if to ring the bell. Convulsed with laughter, the boys kept screaming: 'Knock on the door, Messer Jacopo! Knock on the door!'

The beggars stood and watched without speaking. At last the smaller demanded of one of the urchins: 'What are you doing?'

'Don't you know anything?' he retorted. 'You two must come from well outside the city. We dug him up this morning – old Messer Jacopo Pazzi – the bloody traitor. The soldiers captured him escaping, so he joined his relations and pals hanging in the Piazza … and everyone had the sport of sticking him in the guts…'

'What did he do?' the small husky voice asked.

'The Pazzis, the Salviatis, and a host of other accursed magnati killed our marvellous Giuliano, attempted to murder the Magnificent, and seize our city. The Medici forced young Cardinal Riario to write to his uncle, the Pope, and inform him about the conspiracy. That's a real joke, for Count Montesecco has blurted out the whole truth. He was supposed to kill the brothers, but refused to perform such a deed during Mass, and he revealed that old Sixtus was at the bottom of all this villainy. For his confession Lorenzo allowed him to be honourably beheaded. The Pope keeps demanding Riario's release, but our Magnificent is making uncle and nephew sweat for their impudence. Wish they'd string up the Cardinal and the Pope ... that'd be worth watching...'

He returned to his game. After a long while the boys tired of their sport, and threw the toy from the Rubaconte Bridge. The swollen dreadful carcass floated on the surface of the Arno towards Pisa.

The Aquia's house stood just behind the Mercato Nuovo. Franco and Taddeo threaded their way among the bankers sitting at green-covered tables with purses and ledgers ready for transactions. They halted briefly to watch a bankrupt obtain discharge ... by publicly striking his bare buttocks three times on a black and white marble circle – the site of the symbolic chariot of the city.

'My father's sister is bound to help me,' the smaller child muttered, and tugged at the bell rope. 'Perhaps Andrea is already here.'

It was a long time before a linen-faced maidservant peered through the grille in the outside door, which she made no attempt to unlock.

'Go away!' she cried. 'My master won't have beggars hanging round his gates.'

'We aren't beggars.'

The maid laughed. 'Who are you then – princes? Clear off!'

Reaching into the neck of a filthy ragged shirt, the smaller child drew out a glistening yellow jewel. 'Show this topaz to Madonna Riccarda. Go on. It's not stolen, and won't bite off your nose. It belonged to someone who is dead.'

Reluctantly, the maid took it, and disappeared. They waited a long interval before Tommaso di Aquia appeared, his sour features like a streak of rancid fat.

'Whoever you are, you've no business here. Get away before I summon the Eight.'

Mention of the body of law enforcers did not send them packing. Instead the pale child pushed back its hood. 'Can't you see – I'm a Narni?'

'You!' his eyes slid fearfully along the street to make sure no one was watching. 'I'll not be linked to anyone who bears that name. I've had to bar my door for days because I'm married to one of them. The shame of it. The mother of my children. I'll never live it down. I always knew that alliance would ruin me. You get away from here, or I'll set my dogs on you.'

'Don't you know that the family have been slaughtered?'

'They deserved worse than death. Joining with the vicious Pazzis and Salviatis to murder our sweet Medici, and overthrow this wonderful state. They were traitors.'

'That's a lie.'

He laughed. His mirth had never been pleasant, now it was the raucous call of a carrion crow. 'Is it? We have to be grateful to Messer Vanozzo di Cuono and his brave son, who overheard part of the foul plot. When they learned that the villains had almost succeeded in the city, they went and exacted vengeance at Castelfiore. The law is that all who bear the name Narni are to be hunted down and destroyed like the vermin they are. Their name is to be erased totally from all records. Their estates and possessions are forfeit. Do you understand? The Narnis, like the Pazzis, do not exist any longer.'

'We are innocent,' the child stormed. 'We have been traduced by those who wish to conceal their own complicity. I shall go to my betrothed. His family will help me.'

'They would merely turn you over to the Eight,' he jeered. 'It is forbidden for anyone to marry with a Narni on pain of losing all rights and possessions. Luckily, the della Seras are such intimates of the Medici, else suspicion might have fallen on them too, and...' he gave a narrow unpleasant smile, 'Despite my accursed wife, everyone knows how loyal I am.'

'To whoever comes into power,' the child retorted. 'What will become of me?'

'You'll die on the streets of plague or hunger, and your body will be tossed into the river. Or else you can play the whore. I've already heard how you tried to corrupt my innocent Lionello. The Narnis were nought but brothel sweepings. You're nothing to me. Get away. Your presence is as contaminating as a plague spot.'

The door slammed in their faces. Franco picked up a handful of dirt and flung it at the wall. 'Weasel!' she shouted. Taddeo looked at the ground and shuffled his feet. He was quite accustomed to such treatment, and knew that in order to survive his companion would have to learn a similar lesson. Slowly they walked away, but the sound of hurrying footsteps made them halt.

Riccarda di Aquia, her face ghastly with grief and fatigue, and red eyes set within enormous violet shadows, ran after them. Her ill-combed, grey hair contained a few rusty streaks: the only sign of her Narni heritage.

'Francesca,' she sobbed.

'Franco,' the child countered.

'Whoever you are, may God and his blessed Son protect you. Here, I dare not give you more. He would beat me for this if he knew,' she thrust some hard dark bread, and the topaz, into the child's hand, and began retracing her steps, her shoulders heaving pitifully.

'Stop.' Franco called.

The woman half turned, hunched and fearful.

'Where is Andrea?'

'In the Piazza, but you must not…'

Franco refused to listen further. 'Her lot is worse than ours,' she commented, and threw the bread into a refuse channel. 'It'd be better to die than live imprisoned with the Weasel.'

Pained and hungry, Taddeo stared at the discarded crusts.

'It would choke us to eat something so unwillingly given,' Franco's tired voice could still ring with pride.

They wandered along the Calimala, which was unnaturally quiet for the centre of the thriving wool industry; but the city fearing new conspiracies and Papal reprisals, had not settled back into its normal trading rhythm. Each day fresh conspirators were rounded up, and joined the ranks of corpses. By day and night guards patrolled the streets, and no other citizen was permitted to carry weapons, or to be outdoors after dark. The very air smelt of treachery.

In the Piazza della Signoria Taddeo gazed up wonderingly at the soaring tower and crenellated roof of the Palazzo, and at the graceful Loggia dei Lanzi where on fine days government matters were debated in full view of the citizens. He had never thought to visit the city. The loud noise, strange odours, and sense of being enclosed terrified him, but Taddeo was also filled with awe at the spectacle of so many fine folk and beautiful objects. Occasionally he trembled to hear the lions roaring in the Palazzo's menagerie.

Franco was blind and deaf to all these wonders, although not very long ago every aspect of Florentine life entranced her. Now she only saw the festoons of remains hanging from the civil buildings. The air reeked of decomposing flesh, and hummed with innumerable flies, while packs of stray dogs barked and chased about the square, snapping hopefully each time a corpse swayed on its rope. Now and then irate citizens stopped to shake their fists and shout abuse … publicly and safely demonstrating their loyalty.

Only the brilliant hair made what had once been a lovesome young man distinguishable as Andrea de' Narni. The limbless trunk had an indistinct outline from the swarming flies.

Franco swayed, and Taddeo grabbed the thin arm. Yet, like someone who believes there is some solution to an impossible problem, she purposefully entered the Santa Maria Novella area.

The Narni palazzo and the great silk warehouse bore the Signoria's forbidding seal. All the emblems of Castelfiore – even Niccolo Grosso's elegant iron torch-holders and door-knockers, cunningly fashioned into the Narni crest – had been smashed or erased. There was no longer any sign to show that the building had up till recently belonged to a gay, handsome and noble family.

Franco led Taddeo down to the malodorous river. While he blinked at the goldsmiths' shops along the Ponte Vecchio, and the boats being unloaded beside the grain wharves, she gazed into the waters.

In the greasy depths Franco seemed to see a procession of faces of her father's and brothers' influential friends. No one would risk lives, reputations, safety and wealth to help the insignificant youngest child of a treacherous family … whether or not they believed in the Narnis' guilt. This was the law of the world. Religion had taught her God's own son had fared no better among his own friends.

Then Franco perceived that without name, possessions or rights, she did not really exist. Only death remained. She pointed at the river and said simply: 'That is my only destination.'

Taddeo thumped his stained forehead with an angry fist. 'No, there is another way. Your nurse once told me that if anything ever happened to your family Frate Sandro would be the one person for you to turn to … only I had forgotten. Forgive me.' He pawed at her hand like a dog that fears a whipping, but Franco managed a brief smile.

'I have not heard of Frate Sandro. Who is he?' she asked, at the same time thinking:

how strange he never calls Gostanza mother, and accepts that she belonged to me rather than to him.

It seemed that Paulo di Freddiano Lucca had begotten a bastard on a young peasant girl, Sandra. She had died giving birth, and Franco's maternal grandfather, ashamed of his brief amour, had sent the boy to San Marco to become a Dominican.

Darkness filled the alleys as they limped towards the monastery. Franco was exhausted and faint, for they had not eaten since the crust of bread they had begged and shared at daybreak just outside the city. Her feet hurt and bled, and her head ached and contained a dull buzzing.

'If he will not help us,' she murmured, 'the guard will throw us into the dread Stinche prison. Taddeo, you must leave me. You heard what my uncle said: no one will help me now, but you could manage alone. If they discover who I am you might suffer. Here…' she held out the topaz, 'take this, I have no need of it. Try to buy yourself food and comfort with the money it fetches. But go now…'

'I shall never leave you,' he said.

And if this Frate Sandro spurns me, what then? Franco kept asking herself.

As if in reply life displayed the alternatives in the poorest alleyways and courts. Among the piles of stinking rubbish, flung out by housewives and merchants, emaciated beggar brats rummaged for scraps, fighting for subsistence among the slinking rats, curs and shrieking cats. In the darkest corners girls of no more than Franco's age sold their immature bodies for the smallest coin to any sort of man. The briefly heaving and panting couples against the walls suggested a grotesque sideshow at a carnival.

It was the first time Franco had visited the city to find it anything but fair. The architecture of Michelozzi and Alberti: Ghiberti's heavenly doors to the Baptistry; gateways showing palatial courtyards with pretty fountains and graceful statues ... these meant nothing. All that counted were the immediacies of life and death. Beauty dwelt on another plane: to reach it there had to be time to pause in the midst of the struggle for existence.

The gaunt-visaged Dominican, who opened the grille in the gate, examined the beggars without hostility. 'Who wants Fra Sandro at this late hour when all honest folk should be in their own homes?'

'Franco.' The smaller child answered wearily.

Fra Sandro unlocked the monastery gate without question. He sent Taddeo to the kitchens with a young novice to ensure the cripple was given food and a straw mattress. Though starving, Taddeo left his companion with reluctance, fearing to lose what was familiar in this curious new country.

With a gentle hand Sandro piloted Franco among Michelozzi's cloisters, and into his own cell. Momentarily, the child forgot weariness. The heavy eyes flared with pleasure at the sight of the devotional picture of the Annunciation.

'How beautiful. So light and airy, like the first morning of the world.'

'So, you appreciate beauty. It is the work of the blessed Fra Angelico. God be praised for giving one man such talent, and sending him to San Marco to decorate our walls. He has gone to his Heavenly Father, but left behind for us a touch of paradise…'

The child recognised Madonna Ginevra's features set in masculine mould: melancholy brown eyes with heavy lids, the gentle smile, the sallow, tight-pulled skin, but there was an aura of peace and contentment about Fra Sandro. He fetched some thin beer, bread, olives and cheese.

'Sit down. You are famished and can hardly stand.'

Despite hunger, Franco could only sip the beer under the monk's solemn gaze. Staring round the tiny, sparsely furnished chamber, she thought: it seems a lifetime since I sat on a chair inside any house, and saw food on a plate. I had almost forgotten these things.

'Do you know who I am?' It was a struggle

for her to ask this question.

He pushed back the hood, and nodded. 'A supplicant fleeing from men's lust for power. An innocent caught up in events beyond any individual's control ... like the majority of mankind, alas, my child. Rest now. We shall decide what is to be done with you.'

'Then you won't help me,' Franco protested bitterly. 'I am truly cursed. Every man's hand is against me.'

'Hush. Be still. I must go to Compline, and then confer with our good prior. I fear you cannot remain here simply because you are a female.'

'No!' the anguished cry drowned that soothing voice. 'Look, my clothes and my hair. I am a boy. I won't be a girl.'

He flinched before the terror in her eyes as if it contained the dark images of all she had witnessed, then placed a tender hand on the ragged head. 'You have seen too much of man's inhumanity. Sleep now. Do not fear betrayal or hurt.'

The distant murmur of plainsong lulled her into sleep as deep as any swoon. Franco awoke to see Fra Sandro kneeling in thoughtful prayer. Without turning, he said: 'I have been asking for your protection, and that I might be shown the right way to help you. Will you pray with me?'

Franco shook her head vehemently.

'Never! There is no God! Not since that night. If he really knows everything and allows such evil to happen then he is not good … and if he could not save the innocents then he is not all-powerful. Man and the Devil rule this world. So what is the point in asking for God's help?'

Sandro did not chide her as she expected. 'God sent his Son to share our worst suffering, and to show whatever our earthly fate we shall be redeemed to a greater joy. If we dismiss all that is good because of man's wickedness, child, I should say we despair, and so allow the Devil his triumph. I have been praying for the souls of our dead in the complete faith that they will dwell in the company of saints. Tell me, if you could pray, what would you require?'

'That I may have vengeance on my enemies.' The torrent of words gushed with desperation. 'On the Medici who believed in the Narnis' treachery, and allowed my good brother to be hanged like a common felon… On Messer Ridolfo di Salvestro who betrayed my confidence, and warned the Cuono family… On *that* family who silenced my own dear ones to protect themselves. Perhaps Messer Ridolfo was jealous of their daughter's love for Andrea, and saw an opportunity to rid himself of so perfect a rival. I have reasoned it all out, and blame myself for ever admitting what I overheard. I, too, have blood upon me.' She spread the thin dirty hands and looked at them with anguish. 'But no one would believe my accusations. I should be rendered mute with a knife, poison, or the rope!'

'Have you reasoned rightly?'

'Yes and it seems to me I was appointed to be the instrument of revenge,' Franco insisted.

'You must shed these thoughts.' Fra Sandro's stern words sounded odd in that tiny room, which seemed a whole world away from violence and horror, and where the dark was just held at bay by the flickering glow of a solitary rushlight. 'They will embitter your soul, and stunt your mind. Hatred is a canker. Eventually it perverts and destroys only the hater. You must learn to love mankind and God. He alone knows what purpose your life will serve...'

He held the pointed white chin in a firm hand so that the blazing eyes were forced to look up at him. 'Think, Franco, what can a nameless pauper do against the mighty of this world. It would be best if you could resign yourself to fate. Why not seek out the solace of a convent? Your cousin Carlotta has entered the Carmelite order at Santa Maddalena.'

'Carlotta is too good for our world,' Franco said miserably. 'Andrea's death must have broken her sweet heart. Another lady suffers such torment too … a worse one if she realised the full truth. But I don't want to hide for the rest of my days. Is that all I was spared for? To triumph over my enemies I shall live. That, Fra Sandro, will be my revenge if I can have no other.'

'Then you must be very careful, for the Eight are more assiduous than ever in carrying out their policing duties, and there are spies everywhere in all sorts of guises seeking the Medici's enemies.'

An adult smile hovered on the fair young lips. 'This is a good moment for any ruler to investigate all those who have been against him in the past, and also to tighten his own control on the city.'

Fra Sandro was torn between admiring the world-wise head on the slight body, and wishing the child had no need to be tainted by such knowledge.

He sighed. 'Very well, you may stay here until we discover what is best for you. To be quite safe, and remain in this monastery you had better continue with your pretence as a boy…'

The Apprentice

Domenico Ghirlandajo had just begun a great painting of the Last Supper in the small refectory. He was content with his sketches yet anxious to find some way to make his picture different from those executed by fellow artists. Not just another Last Supper, the heavy features sagged in obstinate thought, but Ghirlandajo's Last Supper.

The monks irritated him too, always slipping in some pious suggestion about how they thought the apostles should look. Of course he contained his temper, but then shouted twice as loudly at his apprentices, who winked and nudged each other: 'Old Domenico hasn't his fine high society manners today ... what would some of the noble patrons he likes to flatter say to that language!'

It was not very long before the artist espied the silent red-curled lad with the beautiful almost unearthly pale face, who watched each movement, and listened to every command given to the apprentice.

Ghirlandajo's own smile lightened his face, and he became what he was: a young, enthusiastic and highly professional artist who could wonderfully fulfil any commission. 'Do you want to learn to paint?' he asked.

'I want to learn everything,' the child declared passionately.

The artist laughed. 'All of us die ignorant but striving after perfection. What can you do? Have you any spark to be fanned into genuine artistry?'

The child beckoned him to follow. On a worn white patch of a corner pillar was a sketch of a man with dark eyes ... even the rough drawing suggested that these were eyes not too ready to meet another man's gaze. The expression battened down some dread secret knowledge.

Ghirlandajo stared, and was openly astounded by the skill shown in such a rough drawing. 'You did that? Who taught you?'

'No one.' Franco backed away like a dog that expects to be kicked.

'Who is this fellow meant to be?'

'Judas,' she said with conviction. 'It is the likeness of a man I once saw who deserved the name. Behind him I think there should lurk some creature ... yes, a cat. It is a fiend in disguise.' The thin capable fingers drew in the animal, as the husky voice described the thought.

'A strange idea,' Ghirlandajo commented softly. 'If you will allow me to use it I shall take you as a pupil, and try to teach you all I know ... which of course is not everything.'

From that moment onwards the workshop in the cloisters saw little of Franco. The monks had been quick to notice her wild defiance and lack of religious vocation, but also the natural talent for sculpture … yet though she enjoyed learning to copy the draperies and muscles of antique statues, Franco was more interested in painting or sketching designs rather than chipping them out of stone. It had already been widely remarked and regretted that the powerful innate artistry leaned towards classical pagan subjects, and not the conventional religious ones.

Franco was so hungry for knowledge, she scarcely found time to eat. She could not learn enough, as if it was fresh air and sunlight after being long incarcerated in some stifling dark dungeon. The technicalities of the craft never ceased to intrigue her.

She rapidly became adept in mixing colours, laying on gold, sizing canvas, and painting on fabrics in such a way that the tints did not run. The optics of perspective enchanted her … so much so that the other pupils were often infuriated when this thin intense child examined their handiwork to declare that the perspective was quite wrong. 'You've merely copied what you see,' she would say, 'which doesn't completely convey that sight to another spectator.'

'Franco!' Ghirlandajo would shout in exasperation, 'you'll end up like poor old

Paulo Uccello – he can't pay his taxes because he never makes enough money ... he's so blessed taken up with his love of perspective!'

He was furious too when this brightest of all apprentices started to pursue the revolutionary invention of Leonardo. 'That dabbler, da Vinci'; Ghirlandajo cried, 'is not your master. You'd never learn anything from him. He spends all day looking at something without once applying his brush, and some of his ideas, God save us. You, Franco, can execute beautiful clear outlines. Why go for this what's it called "sfumato" – blurred mellow stuff which fades together?'

'To stir the imagination and make people see even greater depth in any picture.' Franco replied calmly, 'But no one will ever match Leonardo's use of this technique.'

Franco's own small areas of work on the master's large paintings could soon be distinguished from all other apprentices' attempts by its soft and airy contouring. As a baby's bone structure is the foundation for a man's strong muscled body, so the deepest memories of sun, shade, texture and colour among the Tuscan hills of childhood became the essence of Franco's painting.

Light and shadows were not just skilfully applied. The canvas seemed to radiate light from somewhere within, while the shadows held a disturbing depth which seemed to draw the onlooker down into their murk.

The master almost feared this fountain of talent had some divine or diabolical origin. Certainly, Franco was a troublesome pupil, but the others showed grudging respect rather than jealousy, which grew into rough comradeship. For the child was always up to some wild or amusing prank.

It had been Franco's idea to tie a mountebank's tame she-bear to the bell rope inside a small church. Bells chiming in the still of night had brought the priest out of bed, but he had been too scared to examine this nocturnal bell-ringer; for in the darkness he was convinced it was a demon … and sent for another priest to join him in a ceremony of exorcism.

The story had circulated widely, and provoked the mirth Florentines always enjoyed … and also shamed the congregation into spending money on locks for their church door.

Yes, Franco had a growing reputation, but Ghirlandajo felt only a little envious of his pupil's talent: the child's charm and beauty frequently erased the irritation that impudence inspired.

'This is an even rarer talent,' Domenico confided to his old friend Bernardo Gozzoli, over a jug of wine in the 'Buco'. 'Sometimes I lift my hand to wallop him for his sauce, then those great eyes mock me, and I feel foolish and begin to laugh at my own fury. God alone knows what will happen to a lad endowed with such craft, and that smile. I know he thinks I'm holding him back out of jealousy, but it's for his own sake. He must learn some discipline and patience. He always gives you the feeling he's gobbling up life, as if frightened it'll be wrested from him...'

So Franco lived in a new-found haven. It felt, sounded and felt so different from the violent tunnel through which she had been thrust to be re-born. In these complicated acts of creation and self-expression, beauty and happiness could be grasped however briefly. The grimmest memory could be incorporated into paintings, and so she could oust some of the personal terror and grief.

To create was to comprehend God just a little. But this god was wholly pagan: Dionysius and Apollo warred in Franco's spirit. Fra Sandro recognised that the child had discovered salvation ... for a while at least ... and though he thanked God, he trembled too ... apprehensive for the future.

At night Franco dreamed only of the intricacies of the art she pursued in daylight, and the paintings she longed to start. Taddeo who curled, upon the palliasse at her feet in the novices' cold and cheerless dormitory, was no longer woken by shrieks of horror.

By day he sat in the darkest corner of the refectory of Ghirlandajo's studio, and watched Franco's efforts and marvelled. He was content with the new order. He ate regularly, dwelt indoors, and had a reason to live: to watch over this magical changeling he would have followed into the mouth of Hell, and who allowed no one to torment him for his deformities.

The apprentices and urchins they consorted with in the squares and streets quickly learned this lesson, for Franco had acquired a reputation as the most reckless of fighters. She fought with an audacity which undermined far bigger opponents ... and anyway some had glimpsed the small dagger concealed in the shabby sleeve...

Even the excommunication slapped on the city by the Pope in retaliation for the execution of Archbishop Salviati did not turn the people against the Medici as had been intended. The Florentines openly mocked Sixtus and his interdict, and considered he was fortunate to get the wretched Cardinal Riario back alive.

The Pope's threat that he, Ferrante, King of Naples, and their allies would make war on Florence unless they rid themselves of the Medici tyrant, provoked only the citizens' contempt. The Signoria promptly announced that Lorenzo's life was bound up with the well-being of the very State, and allowed him a large bodyguard, and so many prerogatives that he was prince in all but name, and acted accordingly.

Anyway among humble folk, who cared if Lorenzo's power had somewhat altered the concept of government, so long as he continued to provide such clever lavish entertainments on public holidays? ... and the sculptors, writers and artists warmed themselves under the interest of this keen and sympathetic maecenas.

Because of the aftermath of the Pazzi conspiracy the celebrations for the feast of San Giovanni – the city's patron – had been postponed until early July. Pent-up gaiety after so much fear and tension exploded in the streets with the force and colour of the countless rockets and firewheels, constantly igniting to form brilliant brief pictures of houses, palaces, ships and animals.

Apprentices shoved their way in and out of the holiday-attired crowds, screaming, whistling and throwing melon rinds to incite the cat in the cage. Accompanying this wild shaggy beast was a shaven, half naked man, whose task it was to kill the near-demented cat with only his teeth.

The Cat and the Knight was one among many popular spectacles arranged to delight the revellers. Above their heads ruddy-faced, enormous giants and thin spectral figures, moved as if by magic, so that people forgot they were merely men borne on stilts. Their up-gazing wonder gave the cut-purses a happy day too.

The palazzi were hung with fine tapestries. Equally decorative were their crowded balconies. On velvet-upholstered chairs sat throngs of ladies throwing down flowers and smiles to their known and unknown gentlemen admirers. Sun caught on gems, rich brocades and ostrich plumes, so that the scene seemed a Gozzoli fresco inspired with breath.

In the Piazza della Signoria a hundred golden towers rotated on wagons to show the crowds every aspect of their relief designs ... beautifully fashioned dancing girl, soldiers, fruit or flowers. These were not merely charming fantasies to delight the eye, for they represented the tributary cities. On the ringhiera of the Palazzo multi-hued flags fluttered a proud echo of their allegiance to the city of the Red Lily.

All morning, processions made their colourful and cheerfully solemn way to San Giovanni with offerings. Members of guilds marched in twos under the banners of their crafts, and each citizen under one or another of the sixteen gonfalons – a subtle demonstration of the State's requirements for an individual to play some stipulated role. Franco could read the underlying message: find a way to belong here, or else forfeit rights and happiness.

'Come on, Taddeo!' she dragged him away from the Cat and the Knight, each now spattered with the other's blood. It was not the barbarity that affrighted Franco but she recognised the bulging-muscled Knight. Berto Spenozzi had also come to the city.

'If he's that desperate to make some money,' she muttered, 'he'd be glad of the reward for selling my identity to the Eight.'

'He wouldn't know you now,' Taddeo mumbled fearfully.

'I'm not going to give him the chance. Oh Berto, I never believed you would turn into such a savage beast.' She shuddered. 'How little I knew of human beings.'

Rather like a wizard who enchants people to follow in his wake, as soon as Franco moved off, the apprentices chased after, yelling: 'Hey, wait for us. We're coming with you, wherever you're going.'

Franco took full advantage of the situation to lead her wild cohorts to the Aquia residence. It wasn't too long before they were chanting: 'Tommaso di Aquia is a stinking old weasel…' and hurling every kind of missile, except flowers, at his house. Other boys attracted by such an enjoyable chorus swelled the numbers. Franco slipped outside the crowd.

From a discreet distance she saw Lionello emerge and with pompous indignation order the gathering to 'Be off!' All he succeeded in securing was a bloody nose and a torn doublet.

Franco's mocking joy merged with the apprentices' shrill hoots of triumph as they chased back into the Piazza which overflowed with a deafening pandemonium of screams, songs and laughter. The air was rich with the sulphurous fumes of fireworks and the sweet or savoury aromas of food temptingly displayed on street vendors' trays. The whole scene was a pageant of beauty and savagery ... a concert in tone and colour.

Franco ate it all up as greedily as she munched a fresh crumbling pie filled with soft curd cheese ... desiring to absorb the very ethos of Florence into her blood and bones.

In the late afternoon the buildings glowed a soft rose like the cheeks of the citizens over-replete from too much food and wine. Sleepily gay after the siesta they staggered into the streets to see the Palio run from the Porta alla Croce to the Porta al Prato.

Franco, Taddeo and some other boys stationed themselves near the finishing post close to the magistrates who judged the race. Fat belching merchants, their frisky flirting wives and daughters, and apprentices all held similar conversations: the horses' past performances, bets laid, and tips given.

Speculation ended as the bell in the Palazzo's tower rang three times. The Palio began…

The city began to swell with the murmur of mounting tension. The powerful horses decorated with their owners' emblems galloped through the streets. The moving roar of the crowds punctuated their progress.

A crescendo of applause, cheers, shouts and laughter clearly showed the Florentines' delight when the Palle just beat the Golden Acorn, and the Dark Torch. So the Palio – that highly prized length of crimson silk trimmed with gold and fur went to the Medici. Afterwards it was paraded through the city on a four-wheeled wagon, decorated with a carved, gilded lion at each corner.

Franco did not listen to the moans of the losers, or the gloats of the winners. She barely noticed the Medici. Her attention was concentrated on the golden smiling youth by his side. Daniello della Sera did not seem at all vexed that his own Arab horse had been beaten by less than a flick of its ears.

The hungry violet eyes softened. Her lips parted. Under her shirt the gimmal ring knocked against the topaz. It did not matter that now Daniello's own hand was bereft of that particular token … though he still wore the Narni's magnificent diamond. Just to gaze on his beauty inspired the frozen heart with hope. One day, one day, she vowed, like a true knight he will clear my name of all stigma.

As ever Daniello was surrounded by the dark nimbus, that group of young men who demonstrated their fidelity to the Medici by loving his handsome companion. They were finely dressed and elegantly educated: the brightest flowers of young Florentine society – yet a sharp eye might detect the faint pollen of the effete and vicious. Despite his ugliness Altoviti was a permanent member of this glittering retinue.

Franco's gentle expression vanished as she saw Guido di Cuono: strangely pale-skinned under the hot sun, it seemed no blood flowed in his veins ... indeed he looked cold to the touch.

The Medici placed his hands on Guido's and Daniello's shoulders. Onlookers gossiped that Lorenzo had found two brothers to replace sweet Giuliano, and were glad for him.

To Franco it was a symbol. She laughed aloud and unmusically at her own romantic notions of revenge and restoration. The di Cuonos were now as secure as the della Seras – any dream that the Medici's favourite would jeopardise such a position by fighting for her rights was beyond even the bounds of fairytales.

The gentlemen's attention shifted from the

panting, steaming horses and their riders to a young woman who drifted gracefully into their midst. Her loose gown was so heavily embroidered with precious stones, it looked as if it had been fashioned from a sunlit waterfall rather than any textile. Curls of black hair trailed over the gently vibrating upper globes of full white breasts like a blackamoor's caressing fingers.

Guido's fine lips twisted in evident amusement at the effect his sister had on Lorenzo and Daniello. Cosima seemed plumper than Franco recalled and even more beautiful. The Medici's gaze never left her face, but her great dark eyes smiled at Daniello who seemed almost ill-at-ease.

They made a perfect couple… Adonis and Venus. The way Cosima turned her neck and laughed suggested a flower that bloomed in the sunshine of male adulation. It would be unreasonable to imagine her retiring to any convent, Franco reflected. Perhaps there was now even a scheme for her to wed Daniello. That way the Narni's wealth, possessions and future plans would be neatly re-settled. Although some small items were sold when all the Pazzi conspirators' possessions were publicly auctioned, it was an open secret that the Medici had permitted the della Seras to receive most of what had been promised in the Narni girl's dowry … and the di Cuono family had been rewarded for their zealous loyalty with a vast amount of property from the same source.

With a bitter mouth Franco smiled. Probably Messer Ridolfo received some political favour for his valuable services. The Medici's helping arm could stretch as far as Milan … or Pisa…

A cloud had shifted for an instant to reveal Olympus, and Franco knew that mere mortals could not topple the gods...

The threatening storm of turmoil broke in chaos and suffering. Rome, Naples and Siena declared war on Florence, Milan and Venice. It soon became obvious, however, that Pope Sixtus and King Ferrante – like skilful puppeteers with long wires attached to their marionettes – had cunningly contrived to stage this bloody performance well away from their own territories. While Siena and Florence shouldered the burden of war, both armies reaped its spoils.

Franco and Taddeo could no longer wander the streets without confronting the human misery created by the war. Refugees from Florentine subject cities, toting sad little bundles which contained all their worldly possessions, flocked in vast numbers to the security within the city's walls. The looting raids of allied and hostile soldiers alike had forced them to flee their homes as much as the actual skirmishes.

There were other grim sights too … each day becoming more frequent. Men, women and children of every degree might be seen falling dead in churches, markets, and streets. For the increase in population helped produce ripe conditions for a virulent outbreak of the Moria, which was ever simmering in the humid atmosphere and frequently bubbled over into an epidemic whose hunger was only appeased by gorging itself upon countless citizens.

As many were decimated by plague in Florence as by violence in the battle areas. Franco grew almost accustomed to losing familiar faces among her apprentice acquaintances. The comfortable folk who owned country retreats fled to escape the disease, but no one could avoid the steep rise in taxes needed to finance the ever-increasing hostilities.

War ruined trade. The Florentines cursed their enemies and their own Commander with equal fervour. The law required the Capitano – who received a generous remuneration for his services – to be a noble non-resident. Ercole d'Este, duke of Ferrara, had a fine military reputation. Despite this and all the Florentine gold he rarely gained a victory, or pressed home an advantage.

With ironic humour, the Florentines concluded his curious failures might be traced to his marriage: after all, he was the King of Naples' son-in-law. Meanwhile all soldiers relished a continual looting spree, and it was claimed with some truth that both armies went to considerable pains to avoid conflict!

One other ludicrous aspect of this war was the French king's personal intervention. It did no good whatsoever, except cause the Florentines to slap their sides in bitter mirth. Louis XI sent ambassadors to all rulers concerned in the fight with the hasty suggestion that they join forces in a crusade against the Infidel in Constantinople. Christian leaders, he claimed, and especially the head of their faith, should not be seen squabbling amongst themselves. Citizens even contributed funds to this cause which never came to anything…

To forget death and hardship Franco chose to lose herself in a painting. When voices of strangers could be heard approaching along the cloisters, she hunched over the canvas, determined to be left in peace.

'One interruption after another,' she muttered, 'if it isn't Maestro Ghirlandajo sending me on some fool's errand then it's visitors coming to examine and admire his handiwork…'

Of course, this was the best way of securing wealthy men's patronage: whether they were prominent members of the major guilds – wool, silk, bankers, and furriers – wanting their churches, warehouses or halls beautified … or some noble gentlemen interested in decorating their palaces and chapels … and seeking to be tastefully represented for the eyes of posterity as a character in some religious or historical fresco.

Sometimes it was more than irksome to listen politely to uninformed criticism or praise, although Maestro Ghirlandajo could be relied upon to be charming to any noble patron. Like the other apprentices Franco found it difficult not to laugh aloud as their master suddenly oozed amiability to those who came a-visiting his workshop. He had many satisfied clients though, for he always managed to depict their wives, daughters or selves as handsome and hallowed!

The sudden shadow darkening the ground at her feet roused Franco from the painting – at this rate she would never complete it while the vision was fresh in her mind. She glanced up unsmiling. The man who leaned over the incomplete canvas was simply dressed, and the way he screwed up his eyes suggested he was very short-sighted. The dark flattish features seemed vaguely familiar. She noticed a crowd of other men, all finely clad, who stayed at a respectful distance.

'Do you know who it is you paint with so much care?' his harsh accents contrasted oddly with the gentle smile.

'A face in the crowd.' Franco said brusquely, 'Beautiful but dangerous.'

There was a low murmur of consternation, but one or two men stifled their laughter in kid-gloved fingers.

'If I say she is a dear friend to me and my wife, won't you then change your remark, and describe her as beautiful as an angel with the features of the Virgin, or Santa Caterina?'

'No,' Franco replied coldly. 'Why should I? Lovely certainly, but she would serve as a model for one of the maenads, or Leda, or even Helen who caused the Trojan war. Hers is hardly saintly beauty.'

Domenico Ghirlandajo rushed forward, his fat cheeks flaming with embarrassed fury. 'Sir, sir, I implore you to ignore my pupil's churlish manners. He's always this rude, and only cares for what he's doing. He regards any interruption as an intrusion upon his muse. Also he's far too young to know about ladies.'

'That's not bad manners,' the hoarse voice contained humour. 'Rather honesty and dedication. He doesn't believe in flattery, yet recognises beauty. Maestro Verrocchio and others have described this lad to me. He's the one who's forever running in and out of their workshops like a bee in a honeycomb. They say he can be devastating in his criticism for one so young. Therefore I sought an opportunity to see if his own talent merited such self-confidence ... and, of course,' he added hastily, reading Ghirlandajo's injured expression, 'I longed to examine your own great work, which is as superb as ever. Yet, this boy's painting though unfinished has captured the radiance of Madonna Cosima di Cuono. Tell me, boy, what's your name?'

'Franco … of Florence.'

'You have no kin then?'

Franco shook her head ferociously.

'Then you are right to adopt the city of the Red Lily as your family. I am also of Florence.' The man spoke simply, 'My name is Lorenzo de' Medici. I like this painting Franco.'

Rare colour stained the pale face, but the purplish eyes boldly examined the Magnificent's undistinguished features. He gazed down at Franco in puzzlement, creasing his forehead thoughtfully. 'You recall someone I've known,' he murmured at last, 'yet you are no one I've ever seen, I swear that. Tell me, Domenico, is he a good pupil?'

Ghirlandajo nodded grudgingly, and then added: 'He thinks there's little more I can teach him…'

'That's a lie!' Franco flashed. 'You just won't show me all I want to know. You prefer to send me back to fetch paints or sketches you've forgotten…'

'Franco, be silent!' the cloisters had rarely heard Fra Sandro's rebuke. 'Remember before whom you speak. Learn a little humility.'

Lorenzo grinned down at the indignant small face. 'I like your spirit, Franco of

Florence. In future, I vow your master will allow you to learn all you can, while I invite you to my palazzo in the Via Larga. Bring me this painting when it's finished.' He produced a handful of golden florins. 'Here's payment in advance. I want to give your picture to a friend.'

The monks and Ghirlandajo's helpers clustered between the carved pillars to stare at the child, the painting and the Magnificent. Only Fra Sandro shook his head doubtfully.

Domenico Ghirlandajo's face expressed mingled fury and delight, as he roared: 'The sooner you know all you need, you rascal, the sooner I can rid myself of your presence. I can't believe I'll ever have such a troublesome apprentice. If I do I swear I'll send him to another master. Remember though, Franco, you've begun to acquire a reputation. You'd better live up to it. Or I shall put these hands to more forceful work than painting… I'll enjoy turning your scrawny backside the very fashionable shade of scarlatto d'oricello!'

Lorenzo's large dark eyes, ever eloquent ahead of his tongue, were highly amused by the excitement he'd caused, and also by the impassive child who had returned to the painting.

'Come, gentlemen.' He sighed and turned to his friends. 'We mustn't spend all day in pleasure. We can never forget we're at war…'

'And your revenge?' Fra Sandro asked, when later that evening Franco sketched his gentle features.

She did not look up. 'The Medici has given me my chance to live as a Florentine, and I must seize it. I cannot think of destroying him, but perhaps through this I'll find a way to clear the dear name that can never be uttered.' Her voice became sombre. 'Yet I shall never forget that he can have me removed as simply as I wipe out this charcoal line which displeases my eye…'

The finished painting met with enthusiastic approval when Franco presented it at the Palazzo Medici, especially since the fair subject had denied the city her presence because of the plague.

'Now at least you can see her whenever you wish.' Lorenzo chaffed when he presented the likeness to Daniello della Sera. 'You can even take that face into your bedchamber and set it on your pillow without risking a dagger thrust from brother Guido.'

Daniello sincerely admired the painting, and bestowed one of his golden smiles on the artist whose own expression transfigured a silent skinny boy, growing out of ill-fitting rags, into an ethereal and beautiful creature of fire and ice. That the picture pleased him erased Franco's jealousy of his interest in Cosima.

'If only you and she would wed,' the Medici continued.

'Why so? You know I have no mind to marry at present.'

Franco's heart surged with relief, yet her mind mocked the ridiculous dreams for stirring once again.

'Then I could see her every day,' Lorenzo explained merrily.

'And crown me with horns, which I'd have to wear in silence, or else look a fool, as is the custom with complacent Florentine husbands, eh?'

Lorenzo winked. 'That's not my style with friends.'

Franco thought: yet he is only half jesting.

Guido too was delighted with his sister's picture, and took special pains to be pleasant to the silent young painter who had earned the Medici's interest, but his smile shed cold winter light and made Franco shudder.

'Perhaps you will visit us soon,' Guido's voice sounded as sharp as thin ice cracking underfoot, 'and paint Cosima from life.'

Fierce emotions racked Franco's body and mind, and she was unable to cope with the strange paradoxes. The sight of Daniello still inspired a mixture of hero-worship and girlish adoration, while Guido's presence induced unreasoning terror more than thoughts of revenge. Now that she was actually within the Medici's magic circle her overwhelming desire to become an artist with a place in Florentine society superseded the wish to destroy her enemies: for she could see with perfect logic this would involve self-annihilation...

So Franco was permitted to enter that glittering company, who met to talk, to sing, to feast in one or another of the Medici palazzi in Florence or the countryside. Her talent alone ensured membership to the most select Florentine guild, and she rapidly became one of those to be pointed at, whispered about, even fawned upon for her friendship with the powerful and famous.

The Magnificent quickly perceived Franco's wide education, and encouraged her to use the Medici's superb library. He permitted her to begin a study of his little daughters, Maddalena and Lucrezia, holding Giuliano's natural baby son on their laps.

It was a joyous relief to escape the rigid monastic routine of San Marco to stroll among the palazzo arcades studded with Donatello's best plaques ... almost to visit another world ... or return to the memory of Castelfiore.

Lorenzo's intimates – the poets, philosophers and artists – who formed an informal Platonic academy, welcomed Franco's sharp questioning brain and quick wit. They would discuss for hours anything from the nature of the soul to the current war. Ideas were merry and serious, but never solemn or constrained by doctrinal rules. The teachings of Christ, Plato and Socrates were argued with equal vigour, and nothing was too sacred to be probed or ridiculed by the sceptical minds.

With sad and reminiscent amusement Franco noted that Lorenzo's wife, Madonna Clarice, was openly shocked by her husband's frivolous friends. Pious and haughty, this daughter of the Orsinis, an aristocratic Roman family, disapproved in vain of her children's classical education. None of her stern glances could quell the turbulent happy river of concepts, jokes and songs which flowed unceasingly from the Magnificent's brilliant coterie.

Franco's own life glowed with a set of bright new tints from this palette of fresh experiences. She listened with delight to Gigi Pulci recite his fascinating Morgante Maggiore about the absurd exploits of a dwarf and a giant ... and the ever-shabby Angelo Poliziano discourse upon St Augustine, or relate stories from Herodotus as if they were his own ... and Marsilio Ficini stammer: 'My very dear ones in Plato,' before expounding Platonic teachings ... and the Medici himself display his craft as a poet in bawdy, humorous and delicate verses.

The Magnificent's hospitality, easygoing manners and simplicity of dress sustained the idea of equality among men, but Franco was swift to realise that this gave him superiority over them. Yet it spoke much for the belief in such equality that a nameless young painter could join the Medici and his friends when they rode through the evening streets in vivid masks and costumes. They all carried torches or musical instruments and sang to the delight of the citizens leaning from their windows to listen.

Lorenzo's own unmusical tones ceased, and he motioned to his more tuneful companions to be silent, so that the youth with the red-gold locks and violet eyes could sing alone those verses the Magnificent had written for Lucrezia Donati.

'Was the sky bright or clouded when we
met?
No matter, summer dwells beneath those
eyes
And that fair face creates a paradise…'

Franco accompanied her melodious voice upon a lute. The full moon shed soft light on the city and the pale lovely face ... and the eyes of Guido di Cuono and Daniello della Sera rested almost spellbound upon the perfect features of the singer who rode between them…

Across this newly-won horizon drifted a cloud. Despondency settled heavily on Franco's heart. Her head often ached, and she found concentration difficult. Maestro Ghirlandajo had frequent cause to scold this unusual absent-mindedness and clumsiness.

'Losing your great talent, eh?' he yelled, 'and wasting my paints into the bargain! Pull yourself together, Franco ... or is all that night-time revelling with the Magnificent's fine friends going to your head? Perhaps you're deep in love with some little wench who is sapping your brain by draining your spindly loins with her hungry white thighs. When I asked you to dip your brush, I meant...' and he roared with laughter.

The coarse suggestiveness appealed to the other apprentices but Franco could ignore it.

Taddeo watched with anxiety. Only the day before they had passed close to the cathedral, and a woman had dropped down dead of plague within a few paces of them. It was now impossible for anyone to disregard the Moria that visited rich and poor, palazzo and hovel.

Even Ghirlandajo showed real concern when this brilliant and mercurial apprentice fainted in the refectory while they were clearing up after the light had grown too dim for any more painting that day.

Taddeo leapt forward, and would permit no

one to touch Franco. 'No, no,' he grunted ferociously, pushing them all away with his elbows. He lifted the slight figure reverently, and carried Franco into Fra Sandro's cell.

'Can it be the plague?' the monk demanded anxiously. 'Shall I call for a doctor … though there's nothing he could do…'

Taddeo shook his head, and pointed at Franco's shrunken working clothes, which always made the slender wrists and ankles appear lank and awkward. Fra Sandro flushed deeply, and he clasped his hands in agitation.

'Dear Mother of God, I had forgotten this. But it is woman's business.' He spoke with horror. 'What can we do? We have ignored nature, but nature will have its way. No doubt, terror postponed this event…'

When Franco swam back to consciousness, she could smell the sharp vinegar on the damp cloth Taddeo had placed on her forehead.

'What has happened?' she demanded, staring up at the monk.

'You must go into a convent,' Fra Sandro murmured, and then added with acute embarrassment. 'You are now a woman, my child. You cannot deny it any longer.'

When Franco realised the truth, a terrible rage engulfed her. The frail body shuddered with fury, nausea and self-disgust.

'This cannot be,' she kept repeating. 'I

shall not let it happen again,' and she pressed flat the small breasts her jacket concealed.

Fra Sandro took hold of the strong fine fingers that had lost their childishness. 'I cannot talk about these matters to you, Franco … you see that is the name I know you by … but whatever you are called your body now belongs to womanhood, and is subject to that same cycle which rules all female kind. This is not something to resent, but rather welcome … and once…' he sighed, and shook his head. 'If life had only run its proper course, you would have been glad, for it means that your body is prepared for childbearing.

'My daughter, I have seen enough outside these walls to know what the world expects of a lone woman without family or fortune. In the simplest female raiment you would be an incomparable beauty. If you sought honest menial work in a household or inn you would be pursued by men, and eventually forced to play the harlot. Whatever you did … wherever you went … your very beauty would ensnare you and most men. That must not happen to one of your name, even if that name no longer exists. For your honour and happiness I beg you to enter a convent. There, your secret will be forever safe.'

'And my hope for vengeance?'

'Can a woman seek revenge? It is against

her very nature.'

'And my painting?'

'Women do not paint...' Sandro suddenly laughed, and seemed young and foolish. 'No, you have proved they can. But, Franco, nobody will accept a female artist ... you would not be allowed to work on religious paintings in churches or monasteries, and again not be safe in this world of men. I doubt if there will ever be women artists ... it seems shamefully unfeminine.'

Franco began to chuckle, and ignored the pains raking her stomach. 'Then I must stay as I am.'

The priest thumped his high yellow forehead with a bony fist. 'You cannot. You know that. You are dominated by all that women must feel and can never deny this.'

'I shall not deny it.' Franco returned quietly, 'I recognise it, but no man will ever discover my true nature unless I choose to reveal it. I shall become what the world thinks I am.'

'Child ... child.' Fra Sandro remonstrated, 'What will befall such arrogance? Surely it is a sin to deceive mankind.'

'As to that,' she retorted, 'I am the one who was deceived about life.'

Franco developed a boldness and self-assurance to disguise the seal of femininity, and bound her small hard breasts with linen strips to prevent them revealing her true sex. She wore the new fine clothes purchased with money earned with the air of a prince. Men and women turned in the streets to admire the tall slim youth whose swaggering walk and fearless eyes epitomised the ideal young Florentine.

'You're becoming a handsome devil, Franco,' Lorenzo remarked to his protégé, and put a hand briefly on the green velvet-encased shoulder. Franco shook it away, and the Magnificent smiled. It had been widely remarked that this youth aggressively disliked physical contact, so much so that people dared not slap him on the back in case it was greeted with a sword cut.

'Daniello will have to look out,' the Medici continued, 'for long he's been the most perfect man in our city. Beware the ladies who will cast languishing eyes on your bold beauty, and try to steal your freedom with their sweetest wiles. By the time I return I suppose you will have lost your heart and any gold you've been paid to some scheming little goddess, who is in reality a fat merchant's philandering young wife!'

Lorenzo left for Naples accompanied by the prayers of the Florentines for his safe return. It was an act of personal bravery … and clever gambling … in an attempt to bring the protracted pointless war to some conclusion by cajoling or bribing the crafty Ferrante to sever his alliance with Sixtus. It meant that the Magnificent must walk right into the enemy's camp though, and no one could trust the King of Naples…

'And if he never comes back?' Taddeo asked after Franco had explained Lorenzo's departure.

'I do not know,' she said soberly, 'chaos most likely leading to the Pope's triumph. There is nothing we can do.'

They were passing by the small house in which Dante's Beatrice had dwelt so long ago and making for the Duomo when a single rose fell at Franco's feet. She picked it up, smelt the faint perfume, and then looked around. On a narrow wrought-iron balcony sat a young girl wrapped in a deep red woollen cloak against winter's chill. She had the softest brown hair and eyes that contained a gentle wistfulness. When Franco bowed and smiled towards her, the very pale cheeks took on the wool's tint, and the eyes glazed with swift happiness.

‘Thank you, madonna,’ Franco called, and kissed an elegant, green-gloved hand towards the young lady.

Each time they passed that house, the girl was sitting up there.

‘Do you sing, little lady?’ Franco demanded one day with a merry turn of heart.

‘Sometimes.’ The voice was sweetly pitched. ‘Why do you ask?’

‘You remind me of a caged song bird that Leonardo likes to buy in order to set free. How I wish I knew a way to let you fly from your little prison.’ Franco feigned a lover’s sigh: for it was a game that all young gallants and maidens enjoyed playing.

‘Leonardo who?’ came the serious question.

‘Da Vinci of course. Don’t you know what wonders our city possesses, Madonna? He is more than an artist. I swear he is a god among men. His brilliance confounds us all, and there is nothing that doesn’t excite his interest.’ Franco spoke with reverent enthusiasm. ‘He is also the handsomest of men.’

‘No. He can’t be.’ The high voice rose in confusion. ‘You are.’

Franco laughed gaily. ‘Oh, you’ve been taking lessons in how to flatter your future husband,’ she teased, ‘so that he will never deny you a new gown or pearl necklace just like his neighbour’s wife wears. What’s your name, honey-tongued madonna?’

'Fiametta.'

'I am Franco, a poor wretch of a painter. Won't you come and walk with me, Madonna Fiametta?'

'No,' the girl replied sharply, and her eyes brightened with tears.

'Even though I am so handsome.' Franco laughed. 'Perhaps your sweetheart will be jealous, eh?'

'I have no sweetheart,' she sighed.

'I don't believe you. If this is the way you reward one who treasures the rose you threw him I shall away and drown my sorrows...'

Franco went off to attend a meeting of the Company of the Cauldron – a group of artists who met regularly to eat, drink, sing and jest. The centre piece of the entertainment were the dishes of food fashioned to represent scenes from Dante ... capon legs and tripe became marvellous buildings ... marzipan horrifically depicted the gates of Hell. As they demolished these models, they declaimed their favourite lines from Purgatoria or Paradiso. Franco frequently chose: 'There is no greater grief than to recall a time of happiness when in misery...'

She enjoyed these evenings, achieving sly pleasure that this all male province had been penetrated by a mere girl ... and that if any of them had known they would have been utterly mortified. It was an accolade of some success to sit down with Botticelli,

Gozzoli, Ghirlandajo, Cosimo Rosselli and the rest … and it was also amusing to realise that none of them who had visited Castelfiore in the old days associated young Franco's appearance with the daughter of the unmentionable Vincenzo de' Narni.

Franco never drank as much as the others, and always held herself aloof in the midst of horseplay. Afterwards, when many of them rolled into the evening to pursue further pleasures with compliant ladies – their own personal property or merely borrowed from someone else for a few hours – Franco left them to return to San Marco.

'Spending your substance on boys then?' Ghirlandajo jeered. 'You beware, Franco, you don't want to be accused publicly of sodomy like Leonardo. Did him a lot of harm. Many still cast accusing eyes. You don't want to be thrown into the Stinche as a reward for your Italian appetite…'

Botticelli encouraged the young artist to go along with him to a mammazuole. 'You can play cards, read, write letters, talk and drink in humble but fair comfort, Franco. The little ladies are supposed to be available for hire as serving wenches. To perform their particular sweet services many of them never leave the house.

'Sometimes though one of 'em takes your fancy as a model, and you bring her home for your very own. I'm not suggesting you smuggle one of these little pets into San Marco, Franco … though it's probably been done … but just pay a quick visit. It's not expensive like visiting the great courtesans. After all such as they are not for the likes of us … they're frequently our patrons, and the friends of great men rather than bed-partners. We don't want to rise to such dizzy intellectual heights for a bit of fun…'

'From the way you're always out of funds,' Franco retorted laughing, 'it'd be cheaper for you to get married. You spend so much on that particular pastime.'

She felt a secret sense of relief that at least she had escaped life in a mammazuole.

Rosselli urged with earnest argument. 'Franco, you must join your fair body to a woman's some time. I swear it's only a brief arrangement. Do you want to keep what you've got brand new until your wedding day? Your bride won't thank you for bringing to bed an enormous appetite and no manners. It's like going to table after starving for years. You can't be an artist only in paint and not in bed. You've learned one craft. Come on, learn another. It doesn't take so long, and it's easier to get pleasurable results from a soft moist bit of flesh than a bad canvas…'

But, Franco was always deaf to these suggestions…

At her balcony little Fiametta was pale and listless.

'You've not come by for two whole days,' she complained when Franco and Taddeo passed that way.

'I thought you had no wish to see me,' Franco said lightly.

'No, you forgot all about me,' Fiametta reproached. 'I know about you young man ... you've been enjoying yourself in the company of lots of laughing girls.'

'Of course,' Franco agreed nonchalantly. 'Tell me, Fiametta, what does your Papa do to leave you all alone like this forever sitting at your window?'

'He's a wool stapler in the Calimala. I'm his only child. My mother died when I was born.' She smiled dolefully. 'So I sit at home and wait for Papa to return for his meals...' and added with some pride, 'I take charge of the household, and my pleasure is to watch the world pass by below my window.'

'Would your Papa allow me to take you for a walk around the Piazza with a maidservant, so that you may join the world at least for a brief while?' Franco asked, feeling sorry for the practically imprisoned girl.

'No, I can't do that.' The anguished cry pierced Franco's mind and heart.

'What is wrong?'

'You have a gentle voice, Franco,' Fiametta whispered, 'but you would not talk with me if you knew I am a cripple.' Tears poured down her pale cheeks like rain on snow, and began to thaw the ice in Franco's own heart. 'I can't walk or dance with light steps. I stumble and limp like your servant. Now you will leave me, won't you?'

'No, Fiametta, I shall ask your Papa if I may visit you to paint your portrait.'

When Matteo Panetti learned that the strange young fellow with the gentle manners was one of the Medici's favoured companions he made no objection.

'Indeed if you can cheer Fiametta and make her smile,' he confided to Franco, 'I shall pay handsomely for this painting. She should be away from infection at this time,' he sighed, 'but my poor little girl hates to be out of the familiar world she knows ... and I would miss her so.'

It became the custom for Franco to sit each afternoon for a few hours with Fiametta. The servants left the young people together, and Panetti seeing his child flushed and laughing praised God for the young man's kindness. It would be worth half his fortune at least to see her happy, and he had dreams of an artist becoming his son-in-law, even though it wasn't what he called a steady trade ... but if this Franco would love and care for Fiametta then a grateful father could provide the rest.

'Do you still keep my rose, Franco?' Fiametta asked. 'You may have a fresh one.'

Beside her chair a small potted rose tree

bloomed unseasonally in its indoor surroundings.

'However many you give me,' Franco said, 'I shall hold the first one dear, because you gave it with spontaneous affection. That is something no one has shown me for a long while.'

'Do you need affection, Franco?' Fiametta asked shyly. 'I'd have thought you were pelted with love tokens.'

Franco's face grew serious. 'I had hoped to live without feeling, Fiametta. You are crippled in your legs, yet can offer affection, but I am deformed in my heart yet can run and jump. I have learned it costs too dear when you lose what you love, so I'm determined not to suffer again.'

Fiametta thought for a while and then said: 'Why are you always accompanied by that hideous servant?'

'We with fair faces must remember that those who are disfigured carry a terrible burden in this world which worships beauty to the extent of being cruel to those without it...'

Her eyes filled with tears. 'You are wise to chide me, Franco. If Taddeo is loyal to you then he is good. I'm sure he loves you ... and I ... oh Franco, from the first moment I saw you smile I fell in love.'

Fiametta hid her face, and the blush flowed over her long white neck. Franco looked at the soft bloom on the innocent profile, and put a paint-stained hand on the frail pale one. Fiametta trembled like a captive bird, but she did not pull away.

'I feel so safe with you, Franco.'

'You are quite safe, I vow.'

'You're laughing,' Fiametta pulled away her hand.

'Only at myself, dear Fiametta.'

'Can't you ever love me, Franco?' the voice was muffled and the brown eyes beseeched affection above the tumble of white fingers covering her mouth.

'I love you as if you were my dear sister.'

She grew angry. 'Because I'm plain and crippled,' Fiametta stormed. 'You will paint beautiful amorous ladies with shapely dancing legs, and slender feet, and you will love them in ways other than you would a sister.'

She stumbled from her chair, and defiantly and inexpertly flung herself into Franco's arms, and kissed the laughing lips.

It is the first time, Franco thought with shock, that I have been embraced these two years.

They gazed at each other in surprise and embarrassment, and then Franco kissed the smooth forehead. 'No, Fiametta, you must not play at love with your painter.'

'I am not playing,' she whispered, as Franco helped her back to the chair. 'My heart seems about to burst whenever I hear your voice.'

'Your father would send me away,' Franco said, 'I cannot ever love you other than as a sister, believe me.'

'Because you love someone else?'

Franco sighed. It was a rare cruel joke. The kind the boys of the Cauldron would relish, but it could never be recounted. Oh yes, playwrights might enjoy the comedy of their situation but living it was to share a tragedy. 'No, Fiametta, my dove, I have sworn never to love a woman.'

Before Franco left, she kissed the girl's cheek, and felt the young full bosom heave against her own bound breasts.

When she came to the Panetti house two days later, Franco found one distraught serving woman.

'What is wrong, Nencia?'

'The master left for Fiesole yesterday, but this morning our little lady became sick. We fear it is the plague...'

Franco ran upstairs. Fiametta lay on the bed, her hair wet and tangled, her eyes and cheeks bright with fever, her white limbs knotted around the sheets, her lips frothed with vomit.

'Get me clothes and vinegar and cold water.' Franco cried, 'We must tend her.'

'But the infection?' Nencia began, 'and a man should not see a maid in such a state...'

The violet eyes scorned her protests.

Franco bathed Fiametta's face and body, and then tucked her between clean linen sheets.

'Oh Franco, Franco, I'm glad to see you once more before I die,' the girl whimpered, 'alas we shall have no more lovely afternoons together...'

'No, no,' Franco insisted. 'We shall make you well.'

Fiametta lapsed into another wave of delirium, and Franco stood helplessly watching the fever ravage the fragile young body it had captured.

At last she wrapped Fiametta in blankets and her own cloak, and carried her downstairs.

'If Maestro Panetti returns tell him I have taken his daughter to La Scala Hospital. Pray God he will come quickly, but I cannot leave the child to die without seeking some help.'

Franco held the light little figure as reverently as if she had been entrusted with the Grail. Taddeo followed close behind, mumbling to himself, anxious about Franco's own health. Groups of citizens fanned away from their progress. It was no unusual sight to see a plague victim borne to a hospital by a bravely obstinate relative.

Once Fiametta opened her eyes and smiled. 'So you are taking me for a walk, dearest Franco.'

'Yes, my dove, and the beauty of the city smiles on your sweet face.'

'I love you very much, Franco, and am not afraid, if you only care for me.'

'I love you, my dearest Fiametta,' Franco's voice broke.

'Oh I knew you would,' she smiled at the unsteady husky voice, and closed her eyes. Franco felt the soul fly from her like a bird ... free and winging away from disease, pain, and misshapen limbs.

Franco stumbled but did not let the burden fall. Dear God, it cost dear to love. She shed her first tears for many months...

Benedetto

Lorenzo de' Medici returned in triumph from the Kingdom of Naples. Not only had Ferrante permitted his departure, but also signed a peace treaty with Florence. Without his chief ally Sixtus found it impossible to continue the war. The interdict was lifted, and the papal account returned to the Medici bank. Praise to God – if not Lorenzo – the plague too began to abate. Once more the sun of fortune shone on the City of the Red Lily.

The Magnificent's personal popularity had never stood so high, and he ruthlessly capitalised on it. Florentines looked the other way when he raised taxes to subsidise the Medici banking concerns ... and grumbled quietly when the Signoria devalued the currency thus leading to a further increase in taxation ... although the crafty government valued its receipts at the old rate!

Lorenzo's bold astuteness virtually gave him a mandate to rule. The pretty glove that concealed his power was fashioned from the finest Florentine silk, but the hand beneath had the cruel sureness of the keenest dagger. No suspicion of a plot against his rule escaped violent reprisal. Yet, most citizens preferred to live and prosper in a secure state, and so were prepared to pay the price the Medici exacted.

He was quick to notice the change in Franco when the leaders of Florentine art, learning and pleasure assembled in the Via Larga Palazzo.

'There's a suffering and a gladness on your handsome face,' Lorenzo remarked. 'You are suddenly very adult. Can you have fallen in love, young Franco?'

The company crowded close, curious as ever about their chaste Franco, who shook her head smiling.

Guido di Cuono spoke with cold amusements. 'Lorenzo, the lad's still a virgin. Can't you read it in those eyes. None of our citizens' wives appeal to his fastidious taste; no smiling slut tempts him to her bed, and no brother artist's model inspires a lickerish desire. Yet now he has left the monastery, perhaps he'll shed his monkish ways, and begin the hot chase. Whoever knows that body first will be fortunate indeed.'

'You follow my movements closely, Guido,' Franco observed.

'Naturally, dear Franco, everyone is interested in our fascinating young artist. We don't want another city to tempt your talent from us, isn't that so, Daniello?'

Della Sera nodded. 'We do want you to be

happy among us, Franco.'

It was pleasant to know Daniello looked so kindly on her, but as ever Franco felt the brush of fear at having attracted Guido's attention.

She had not wanted to accept Matteo Panetti's payment for Fiametta's unfinished portrait, but the merchant had been heart-brokenly grateful for this memorial. It would have been churlish, even unkind, to refuse.

'Pray God you are not infected, Franco.' Panetti examined the pale face.

'Pray God I am infected with her gentleness and love.' Franco spoke fervently, 'But the Moria seems to have left me alone…'

The solid merchant voice contained shyness: 'Franco, would you not alter your life to become my son? They say you have no family. Now, nor have I. If things had been otherwise I should have welcomed you for a son.'

'It's impossible, dear friend.' Franco found it hard to disguise the emotion this offer inspired, 'Let me thank you with a full heart. Circumstances have made it so that I can belong to no one but myself.'

'Then, promise me that if ever you are in dire trouble, you won't hesitate to ask for my help. For Fiametta's sake, and also yours, I shall do anything I can.'

With this money, Franco took humble

lodgings above a candlemaker's shop in the Camaldoli near Porto Sand Freddiano. It was a poor district, and a strange address: for such rooms were usually taken by a cortigiana di candela. The candlemaker and his garrulous slattern of a wife found it an amusing change to have a young artist and his servant as tenants rather than a pretty little strumpet.

Taddeo was delighted by the different surroundings. He capered about like an excited dog, and set to cleaning the shabby apartment with great zest. One room served as a studio where they took their meals, and he would sleep. The other was solely for Franco, and she revelled in this new luxury of possessing a whole room to herself. A magnificent vista across the rooftops and the Arno compensated for the sparse furnishings; and the flood of light through the open shutters was ideal for Franco's purposes.

'It was bound to happen,' Fra Sandro sighed. 'But you will visit us sometimes? Thank God for that creature Taddeo. Guardian angels come in many strange guises. I need not be over-anxious about your safety while he lives.'

Indeed Taddeo was servant, watchdog, and confidant, grateful for the slightest attention Franco bestowed on him.

'I'll visit you … my dear uncle,' she whispered. The monk's thin face glowed for a second. 'And I'll never cease to thank you for my life.'

'The other brothers will miss you, despite your wild ways.' He smiled. 'They've grown fond of their changeling artist. One day perhaps you will eschew pagan subjects and use your art to add beauty to our monastery.'

'I doubt Fra Giralamo will miss me.' Franco grinned. 'He's certainly a holy man, but those black eyes like burning coals, and that great eagle nose projecting from haggard features the colour of a shroud speak that the Day of Judgment is already here ... and I'm to be cast into the pit!'

'He's a good man. I believe one day his voice will awaken the Florentines' faith. At present we are almost a pagan people. The merchants spend vast sums beautifying the churches, but if a voice in the pulpit speaks out against their doubtful business ethics they begin to grumble, and say religion has no right to meddle in trade. Everyone sees the holy days as occasions for new clothes, feast and merriment. The young men and maidens attend church to flirt, the older ones to gossip. If we do not mend our ways, then we must expect God's wrath...'

Giralamo Savanarola's eyes took on fanatical fire whenever he encountered Franco singing in the cloisters, and wearing some bright new raiment.

'Vanity! Vanity!' the monk mocked. 'Don't you know that all fleshly things end in dust? It is your soul you should clothe: in the fierce white light of godliness. Like the rest of them you are only concerned with life here and now. One day you and they will repent for your idle lascivious lives. You care only for what feeds and clothes your body, you waste your talent by not putting it to the glory of God, and you spill your manhood on those lumps of flesh with eyes...'

An echo of the Pazzi plot sounded in the city when the Sultan of Constantinople returned the murderer Bandino who had sought refuge among the infidels.

How long ago it seems now, Franco mused, mingling with the crowds which had turned out to see Giuliano's murderer hanging from the Palazzo del Capitano ... a whole lifetime of learning to live again, and discovering that some things are still sweet to savour despite the agony of memory.

'I don't envy you your commission,' Franco remarked to the handsome man in deep rose silks, who stood sketching Bandini, and making notes about the hanged man's clothes in curious mirror-writing.

'...tan coloured cap ... a black lined tunic ... a blue cloak...' Leonardo muttered as he wrote. 'Good day, sweet Franco. I too shall be glad when the task is over, for I have been commissioned by the monks of San Donato a Scopeto to paint an altar piece, and I am not allowed more than thirty months for it.' He sighed thoughtfully, 'Do you think out art is ever great enough to describe the evil mankind perpetrates? Yet what can we expect: we worship beauty, but live from cradle to grave in the midst of filth and degradation…'

Franco accompanied him to his frugal lodgings for supper. 'I am sorry,' Leonardo apologised, 'this will be a scant meal, for I believe it a sin to kill a living creature, so cannot offer you meat.'

'Dearest Hermes,' Franco addressed Da Vinci by the nickname his admirers used to describe him, 'it does not matter what we eat so long as I can hear you talk.'

Indeed, she thought with wonder, his lips must either be touched by God or madness. For idea jostled idea until her head spun from listening, and there was no possibility of ever understanding more than a fraction of his words. Da Vinci was forever rising from table to find sketches to illustrate his theories.

There were water pumps … devices for repelling scaling ladders … for breathing under water … a canal with locks and weirs … a portable bridge to use in warfare … and also a fantastic machine in which he insisted a man could fly through the air.

'I cannot argue with your wisdom,' Franco

said impatiently. 'Though some of the ideas sound demented, but I do wish you would cease all this experimenting, dreaming and drawing ... and only complete some of your wonderful works. Just look at all those unfinished sketches. If you dissipate your talent, dear friend, nobody will know what to take you for. Are you an anatomist, magician or artist...'

'I dream of one great patron,' Leonardo explained, 'who will give me freedom to put some of my ideas into practice. Don't tell anyone yet, Franco, but I'm about to write to Lodovico Sforza and offer him my services. God alone knows how he managed to seize the reins of power. He's exiled Duchess Bona, had Cecco Simonetta executed, and sent away his own brother Cardinal Ascanio – the sensible action of a man who knows he can't trust some relative of similar calibre... Although Il Moro is regent for young Duke Gian Galeazzo, I have the feeling he may yet prove to be one of the greatest princes of our age. As such he might find a use for my talents in his own court...'

Franco's heart seemed to leap into her throat. She did not doubt that Milan's new ruler must partly owe his change of fortune to the secret machinations of Messer Ridolfo, who would now stand high in the new order...

'Yet you are right, Franco,' Da Vinci continued gravely, 'sometimes I fear I'm doomed to die without creating anything wonderful. I am like a grasshopper, leaping here, there and everywhere.' Even as he spoke he began to sketch Franco's face, and suddenly added: 'You are one of the mysteries which beguile Florentine gossips. Being seen in my company won't enhance your name with the narrow-minded, but one thing I do realise about you that others seem to miss is that you haven't a man's face…'

Franco tried to control the flush that surged into her cheeks. 'Because I grow no beard,' she jested quickly. 'I'm fair-skinned, and many young men of my complexion had hairless faces.'

Leonardo observed the sudden agitation, and spoke reassuringly. 'I keep my thoughts to myself, and though I don't know who or what you are, Franco of Florence, I recognise that you are the most beautiful living creature in a city which abounds with inanimate beauty…'

Sometimes the city suffocated Franco. Then she and Taddeo would hire horses and ride out through the Porta al Prato, past the boys and young men playing football, running races, and testing their agility in jumps of great distance. Thence to the fresh fields and woodlands, where the only sounds were the splash of streams, birdsong, the trill of shepherds piping to their flocks, and cattle lowing on the breeze.

During these expeditions, Franco would send Taddeo away with their horses, so she could seek out an isolated pool and plunge into its chill flow and bathe herself. It was not possible for her to visit either the men's or women's public baths, and washing in the cramped lodgings was possible and necessary but hardly pleasurable. To swim naked in the open air brought back snatches of childhood … which had begun to seem like a remote dream in someone else's existence.

Franco never looked at her reflection in glass or water … even when she trimmed or combed her hair into a burnished helmet. Someone who minutely observed people, objects and nature had chosen to remain blind to the reality of herself.

On one such warm drowsy afternoon, Taddeo wandered off to find fruit for their journey back to the city. Franco lay on the grass, drying her body in the sunlight, listening to the hum of insects, and planning the painting commissioned by a furrier acquaintance of Matteo Penetti, who obviously wanted to be depicted as wealthy, worldly, proud, but also saintly and wise … and could see no contradictions in his demands. She had not dared to suggest 'Saint Croesus', although the Cauldron members had roared at her sly wit when she explained the problem of the furrier.

Suddenly aware of the crackle of twigs underfoot, Franco reached for the cloak, but was too late to prevent the young man glimpsing her body as he stepped from among the trees.

He was dressed as a priest, and asked in a hushed voice: 'Are you real, or are you a nymph? I have never seen such a beautiful girl.'

Franco held the cloak tight against herself, and drew out the small dagger.

'I shan't harm you,' he said earnestly. 'You have no need of that weapon. What is your name?'

'I am no one,' she insisted, 'I am not even beautiful.'

'But you are,' he declared ardently, and dropped to his knees in an attitude of admiration. 'You are the very spirit of love. I believe I have discovered Venus in this little forest. Madonna, I vow I love you.'

'Fine words,' Franco retorted acidly. 'And easily spoken, but ill-suited to someone of your cloth.'

'Until today I never minded being a monk. It was all arranged long ago by my parents who are dead. I was content with my fate until I saw you.' He rose and came towards her, smiling.

'No. No…' Franco recoiled. Her face contorted with horror.

The young man stopped. 'I swear I shall

not harm you.' He held up the crucifix at his belt. 'By the blessed Corpus, you have nothing to fear. My name is Benedetto, lady. Promise me that you will return here some time and let me talk with you, and I will go away now. I shall come to this same place every day.'

'My servant will be here in one minute,' Franco whispered. 'Perhaps I will come back, but don't depend upon it, Benedetto.' Even as she spoke, Franco wondered why she chose to part-promise anything so foolish.

When he had gone, Franco pulled on her clothes, and rode back to the city without once speaking to Taddeo.

That night before she went to bed, Franco examined her nakedness by guttering rush-light.

'Too slender for the present fashion,' she murmured as if talking of someone else, 'but still a woman.'

She ran her hands over the small firm breasts, and down the long waist and curved but tight-muscled hips. The skin was milk white and silk fine, and the hair of modesty a blaze of gold. Without male attire beneath it, the face in the small mirror did belong to a very beautiful girl, although the thick curling hair was worn too short for women's styles.

Franco knew a pride in herself, and a fear.

She chose to ride out to the trysting place alone, and Taddeo stayed behind, puzzled and worried. There was a sudden gentleness in Franco, and she seemed to be concealing some elation ... like someone who wants to laugh but dare not.

Within the screen of foliage, Franco slipped off the male garments, and donned a plain pale gown she had borrowed from one of Botticelli's models on the pretext that she required it for one of her own.

Benedetto appeared, and stared at the girl.

'I have come here every day since I saw you,' he reproached, 'but you were never here.'

'It is hard for me to get away.'

'Where do you live?'

'In the city.'

'You are a...' he examined the simple gown, 'no, not a servant. Your voice and manners belong to a lady.'

'Perhaps I am a nun,' Franco smiled, and the man's eyes filled with tears.

'When you smile,' he whispered, 'my heart breaks. Have you taken your vows already?'

'Perhaps I am about to,' she countered, 'and sometimes to escape the restrictions of my life I flee into the greenwood...'

'How could your family let you become a nun?'

'I have no family.'

'And you are to hide that beauty behind a

veil?' he said sadly. 'It should be crowned with jewels brighter than your hair or eyes. You should be the wife of a prince ... or do you shun love?'

'I don't know,' Franco said simply.

'What a terrible thing to say.' Benedetto stepped towards her, and Franco tried to flee, but his restraining hands were so gentle that she understood she was imprisoned by her own feelings.

'I never thought of love until now,' he said.

Franco tensed, but the young man clasped her to him until she ceased to feel fear. They remained thus until her arms stole around him. Benedetto kissed her forehead, her eyes, and her cheeks ... and then very softly her lips.

Franco could not respond, but the heart stirred, and when the young man looked down into her face, she pressed her head against his shoulder ... suddenly content and safe in his gentle affection.

'You really must learn how to kiss, little nun.' He said with mock severity. 'Come, perhaps the lesson will make you forget your vows.'

He pressed her mouth tenderly with his own, and Franco's cold lips grew warm and moist until at last they opened. His arms tightened about her, and though she tried to pull away when first she felt his tongue caress her own, Franco slowly grew accustomed to his touch and sweet breath. They stood linked by their mouths for a long while, and above them the leafy boughs whispered endearments.

'This is the first time I have ever kissed a man.'

'And will it be the last?'

'Who can say?'

'Oh, lady, lady, without a name, let me call you Venus... Venus and Madonna, flee with me and we could be wed. I shall take care of you, and you will never wear that wild frightened look in your great eyes.'

Franco remembered many things. 'I would bring you misfortune,' she said. 'Besides we must not snatch each other from our vows. Let us be to each other a dear dream, so that there will be nothing to regret in the future, and much beauty to remember if our world grows dark...'

She asked him to call her Lauretta, and that name seemed to belong to some other person.

They met nearly every afternoon. Though Benedetto always pleaded she would never permit him to accompany her to the city. When she was sure he'd ridden away Franco donned her man's clothing. Taddeo watched her broodingly in the evenings, blinking without understanding. Franco spoke but little, for she was engrossed with a new painting, that neither he nor anyone else was allowed to glimpse. It was kept covered with a cloth, and Taddeo knew better than to pry.

Franco's love was a little flower. It opened and bloomed, and soon she was the first to offer kisses. Benedetto grew delighted that her shyness had vanished, and she could show such trust in him.

They lay beneath the trees on the warm grass, tightly embraced.

'Lauretta … Lauretta…' Benedetto spoke the words as religiously as any Ave. 'I love you … I love you…' He kissed her face with a gentle passion, always frightened of scaring her … and also frightened of the feelings surging within himself.

His fingers stroked her throat just where the pulse fluttered, and then slipped down into the bodice. Although Franco's eyes widened with a tiny fear and she protested a little, his hand found her left breast. His soft sigh of ecstacy was echoed by her own, as he gently squeezed and stroked the perfect globe he had discovered.

Benedetto unbuttoned the gown, and buried his face against the soft breasts, closing his mouth on the hardening pink nipples with almost reverent passion.

Franco looked down at the dark head with wonder. He was so gentle and loving, and the stolen adventure so idyllic.

'I must strew your lovely breasts with flowers,' he breathed, and garnered bunches of wild iris to garland Franco's pale flesh.

Benedetto gazed for a long time at the girl lying before him in such charming disarray. At last, he sighed and began to re-button the gown.

'Ah, my Lauretta, I long to kiss every one of your secrets, but if we explore all the beauty in one day,' he whispered, 'we shall have nothing left for the morrow.'

'Tomorrow is something else,' Franco returned gently.

He touched the chain at her throat. 'You wear a betrothal ring, but you did not tell me you were promised to some other man.'

'Dearest Benedetto, there is no betrothal, but I still keep this ring as a memento of another time.'

And Franco thought of lying beneath the trees in Daniello's arms, yet she could not imagine sharing embraces with him. Benedetto made her feel young and girlish ... while Daniello was very much the companion of her pretended manhood.

'I am sure you will marry me,' Benedetto insisted, kissing her lips with determination, 'even if I first get you with child...'

Franco's face flamed, and she pulled herself from his embrace. 'No... No...'

'Hush, Madonna mine,' he whispered, 'it was but a coarse ungallant jest, and I am ashamed. Is that what you fear: to be seduced and deserted? My dear one, I would leave you no more than I would leave life itself. And I am sure you would love a little babe to dandle on your knee, to suck at those sweet breasts…'

But the terror stayed in her eyes, and he could not understand its fountainhead.

'Is it the act you fear?' Benedetto persisted. 'They say all modest maidens have such fears, and yet most take to it as happily as birds to flying. I am sure it is not so bad…' It was his turn to blush. 'Not that I know, for you will be my first and only lady, and we shall explore this great mystery together.'

'No… No…'

'Not now, of course.' He was disturbed by her vehement terror. 'When we are wed, and I shall be so gentle, my Lauretta, I swear, and never, never leave you…'

Franco rode back to the city in starlight. The dreams that Benedetto stirred in her were impossible, and she understood she would break his gentle heart if she allowed him to hope.

Why not run away with him, her mind prompted?

'Because it would blight his life,' she whispered, 'and I could not … could not…' Her cheeks burned in the cool night but she was unable to put into exact thoughts what it was she feared…

Venus Revealed

When Franco reached the lodgings, Taddeo seemed unusually glum. He had prepared her favourite broth of beans and pasta for the evening meal. Only after they had eaten did she discover that the painting was no longer beneath its covering.

'Where is it?' Franco shouted. She seized Taddeo by the arms, and shook him violently.

He had never seen her in an uncontrolled rage. The huge eyes turned almost black, and the white teeth grinding against the lower lip belonged to a wild creature. For once Franco could not show patience as Taddeo stumbled and stuttered over the words, and she raised her hands in fury, so that he crouched behind his arms to shield himself from the torrent of blows. Franco was immediately horrified by her loss of self-control, and she put her arms about the stunted youth.

'Oh, dear Taddeo, what have I done? Can you ever forgive me for striking you, my poor friend?'

He could not bear to see her so upset, and kept mumbling: 'It's all right, it's all right.'

At last she heard the story. Sandro Botticelli and Leonardo da Vinci had dropped by to wait for her. They had sent Taddeo for some wine, helped themselves to cheese, and begun in their usual inquisitive way to explore the contents of the studio.

'Then they uncovered the beautiful painting,' Taddeo explained. 'And asked me who it was.'

'What did you say?'

'Nothing.' In the stained flesh the small eyes grew cunning. 'But I know. It's you, Franco.'

Her face set in a cold white mask as if it had been chipped from a glacier. 'Why do you say that?'

'I have watched you bathing,' Taddeo replied slyly, 'before you chose to go out alone. This lady's hair is long and curling. That's the only difference.'

'And they took it?'

He nodded. 'They want to show it to someone.'

'It's not for show.' Franco clutched her hair as if she would tear it from her scalp.

She had to wait until morning to seek out the culprits. Sandro Botticelli was in his studio, as usual roaring furious insults at the weaver who lived below.

'He shakes everything with his accursed loom, so I can't concentrate,' he explained when Franco burst in.

'Where's my canvas?' she demanded without preamble.

Botticelli was astounded. He'd never seen the young artist so distraught. 'My dear Franco, calm yourself. First, let me tell you we've never seen anything to equal your painting. My Primavera and Venus do not have that magic...' He smacked his lips with appreciative relish. 'But who's the glorious female, my boy?'

Franco dismissed the compliments. 'I want my painting back, Sandro. If I don't get it, I swear you and Leonardo won't live to hold a brush. Where is it? Damn your eyes!'

Botticelli's full mouth slackened, and his round eyes opened so wide they looked as if they might fall out. 'We took it to the Magnificent. We wanted to help you...'

Franco dashed downstairs, and the weaver yelled up to Botticelli: 'As for you, you fornicating, wine-bibbing paint-splasher, I've had enough of your rowdy visitors...'

At the Via Larga Palazzo they told Franco that the Medici could not be disturbed as he was in conference with an important personage. She ignored the polite servants, and pushed through the aghast bodyguard to enter the long gallery exquisitely ornamented with the Magnificent's collection of pietra dura vases and cups in lapis and jasper.

The Medici's dark eyes registered anger at the noisy intrusion, but when he recognised Franco, he began to laugh, and slapped his knee.

'By San Giovanni, this is wonderful! Here is the artist, my friend. Franco, I always knew you could paint, but this surpasses anything I thought you capable of creating...'

'I want it back.' Franco did not attempt polite phrases. 'They had no right to bring it here.'

'Yes they had,' Lorenzo interrupted. 'Such a thing of beauty must not be hidden away. Of course you have to finish it, but...'

'It's not for sale. No, not for any money in the world,' Franco said defiantly. 'That painting is for me.'

'The lady is your mistress, or your sister?' a soft voice asked.

Franco's eyes moved from the Medici to examine his visitor. She did not listen to the introduction, but recognised Messer Ridolfo di Salvestro, as ever debonair in darkest mulberry.

'I have no sister.'

'Then you have fallen in love with someone of your own colouring,' the Medici returned gaily. 'As you are a prince among handsome young men, Franco, this lady is the queen of women. Who is she?'

Messer Ridolfo's expression put the same question. 'Once I knew a young girl,' he explained gravely, 'who I believed would grow into such a beauty, but she is dead, and...'

'So he seeks a replacement,' Lorenzo quipped. 'Come, my dear Franco, we shall not compete – and probably could not do so – for your mistress's favours, but at least sell your completed painting to beautify some gentleman's palazzo...'

'Lodovico wouldn't desire it,' Messer Rodolfo stated. 'But I fear in this matter I cannot be loyal, for I want that painting for myself.'

'And so do I,' Lorenzo exclaimed. 'Daniello della Sera also wants it, and Guido di Cuono has wagered that he will buy the picture for his own collection.'

'Don't you understand what this clamour means, Franco? For it will spring commissions from all the most influential patrons, not just in Florence, but wherever beauty is feted...'

Franco anxiously examined her canvas to ensure it had received no hurt. Venus reclined unclothed beneath some trees, and held a red lily against her fair breasts. In the shadows beyond a silvery stream stood the dark, bearded goat god. The painting palpitated with desire and the promise of fulfilment. Although the subject was classical, the figures appeared alive, and the Tuscan landscape was recorded in faithful and minute detail.

'You have won Leonardo's praise,' the Medici remarked softly. 'You know he always says that merely to copy other artists produces but mediocre work. Only a painter who studies nature, and transmits what he sees and feels on to the canvas has the divine creative spark. You, Franco, have that.

'I would call this painting "The Red Lily".' His harsh voice softened. 'It is the symbol of our beautiful city ... perfection amid the Tuscan hills, yet overshadowed by external dark desires. Franco, your work personifies Florence. That alone means it cannot be hidden away.'

'And I should like to meet the Red Lily.' Ridolfo appeared much older than she remembered. The lines had deepened to give him a saturnine countenance.

Lorenzo grinned. 'Franco, you really must introduce your lady to Messer Ridolfo. He has come here to ascertain that we are allies now Lodovico Sforza is Regent of Milan. To prove we love this new arrangement we should at least let him see the Red Lily.'

'Is that something you desire so much, Messer Ridolfo?' Franco asked quietly.

'More than anything now.'

Franco smiled without opening her mouth. I have no power to destroy any of them, she thought grimly, only to withhold what they all want.

'It's impossible,' she said at last. 'This lady

will show herself to no man.'

Rumours concerning the identity of the Red Lily ran wild throughout Florence. Since no one knew very much about the painting or the lady they were free to speculate ... until Franco began to see the funny side of all these incredible tales. For some whispered the model was a Carmelite abbess, while others insisted she was Lorenzo de' Medici's own wife.

Artists and patrons assailed her with demands for the lady's identity. Although Franco had suddenly acquired a reputation as a secret rake-hell, her name was firmly established in the Florentine calendar of painters by this curious throw of fate...

From every quarter of the city dogs began to bay. Their chorus grew until night itself seemed to be howling. Franco awoke. Her nerve ends responded to the animal fear. She lay shivering. The latch lifted. Taddeo stumbled in.

'The end of the world,' he mumbled, his eyes showing much white in terror, 'the dogs are all fleeing from the city...'

'Go to bed, poor fool,' Franco commanded. 'We are quite safe.'

He obeyed instantly, reassured by the tone of her voice. Franco wished she could convince herself, and began to recite a Paternoster.

The darkness became ominously silent.

Then a murmur of thunder expanded into a huge dull roar. It rolled about her until she felt contained within a rapidly beaten drum. Yet it was not the air that moved, but the earth.

For a few seconds the room rocked, tilted, and then settled down. Franco leapt from bed to prevent paints, knives and brushes sliding from the table. Next door Taddeo rescued plates and dishes, and straightened tumbled chairs. Shutters rattled. Doors banged … as if the night was full of invisible intruders. From the squeeze of dwellings came screams, curses, prayers, and children crying.

The shock subsided. In the moment of silence the city held its breath awaiting the tremor that did not come. The slight quake did little damage, but seemed an omen of impending change. Florentines rushed into the open to gaze up at the heavens, expecting some imminent supernatural event. Tomorrow the priests could rely on the fact that their churches would be full of penitent worshippers.

Franco's flesh crept against her spine. She lit the rushlight, and examined the completed painting. The 'Red Lily' was unharmed. In the faltering light the pearly body seemed as vibrant as the artist standing before it.

'Until I created you,' she whispered, 'I had

felt in control of my new life.'

It was to ride forth on a powerful horse which needed skilful handling, yet she had understood how to master the animal and follow the winding road. Suddenly the horse had broken into a crazed gallop. It veered from the path into a strange perilous country. The familiar reins flew from the rider's grasp. She felt bound to crouch low, cling to the trailing mane, and grip the heaving sweating flanks with her knees. Whip and spurs were pretty toys for which the wild steed cared nothing.

Franco pushed open the shutters. The oppressive warmth slid into the room, and touched her nakedness with moist hands. It brought with it the foul stench of the alleys and the river. Now and then a torch flared in its iron bracket on some outside wall, and the shadows of people wandering the maze of courts and turnings resembled an army of phantoms. Across the river a misty red glare showed where a group of buildings had caught on fire.

The candlemaker's wife began screaming: 'The end of the world is upon us…' Franco hardly blamed the drunken husband who hurled abuse to quell that monotonous dirge. A child cried out in unhappiness. The night was a sad, fearful time. Those terrors held at bay during the daylight returned to stalk in men's minds, and Franco kept recalling the man who personified for her the prince of darkness, and Judas the betrayer.

If the city survived, then she would have to face Messer Ridolfo with the 'Red Lily' at the Palazzo Medici. Half of her dreaded the confrontation; and half warmed to its challenge: the gamble of outwitting this powerful enemy, who no doubt felt he had an unknown painter upon the hip because the Medici would wish to secure Il Moro's friendship by all possible means.

She leaned on the window ledge, and watched the storm rip open the belly of night bulging low over the city as if about to flatten all the proud buildings. Under sheet lightning the river glowed blue-white. Against this swift fading curtain of light, towers and cupolas were as unreal as any marzipan confection.

Then the rain poured from the wounded dark. It lashed the Arno into a boiling liquid serpent. The alleys streamed and refuse poured down to the river. Raindrops pelted roofs with the fury of an attacking army.

The heavy air began to sweeten. Franco's body was sheened with a refreshing coolness. People running through the heavy mud, scarcely bothered to look up at the faintly lit room. Only one man noticed the pale shoulders and breasts, and copper hair of a girl at the window. He stopped among the shadows, oblivious of the rain, and watched until the little light drowned in darkness, and the white form closed the shutters…

'You seducing dog! You cub of evil!' the insults rang through the court where deep puddles reflected the pale morning light. Franco spun round. Standing in the shelter of a doorway was a young man with a worn face, and eyes reddened from weeping and lack of sleep. In an unsteady hand he held an unsheathed sword.

Franco's voice was as chill as the mist rising above the river. 'How have I offended you?'

Then she recognised Benedetto. It took all her self-control not to laugh, and doff her elegant hat, with its fall of purple silk which folded about her throat and concealed the brilliant hair.

'I see you are a priest,' she added. 'Your rage hardly becomes your garb.'

'And you are the artist called Franco: a fawning beardless demon, the Medici's favourite, and the creator of the "Red Lily". Now there are three of us who know her name. You, she and myself…' Tears stood out in his eyes, and Franco felt sorry for him.

'What is her name then?' she enquired, keeping her voice even lower than usual.

'Lauretta, my Lauretta.' It was an anguished cry. 'By ill-chance I have found out about you and her. The first time I saw her … on that sweet day which is engraved upon my memory with sunlight and green leaves, I chanced to glimpse the misshapen repulsive creature who I thought to be her servant… Now I know he's a ruffiano – her pimp. Yesterday in the Mercato Vecchio I saw him buying eggs, and followed him to see where my Lauretta lived. We came to this abode. How happy I was: I had discovered my treasure's hiding place. It meant I could come here each day and wait to see her fair face. Last night when I feared the city would be destroyed, I came to die with my Lauretta – if that was God's will.

'When I saw her at the window, I feared to go up. It was so late, and I had no wish to harm her sweet reputation. This morning I asked the candlemaker the name of the lady living above. He told me the rooms belonged to Franco … and that artists lead very loose lives, so that the lady I'd glimpsed was probably his elusive mistress. Lauretta is well placed beneath a candlemaker's roof … the strumpet! Is she still up there?'

'No, she left at daybreak.' It was the time Franco always dressed.

'Why didn't God destroy us all?' Benedetto cried. 'This wicked city corrupts the pure and beautiful. So all last night you kept her in your bed, and took pleasure in what she would never yield to me … or perhaps,' and his face was ashen with pain, 'she only feigned virtue to play my foolishness. I did not offer the bawd money. That's what is required to prime their passions, isn't it?'

'She is not a whore.' Franco insisted, knowing it to be foolish to feel indignation.

Benedetto snatched at the canvas she carried, uncovered it, and then cried out as if he'd fallen on his own blade. 'Not a whore? When she has unclothed her very beauty for you to display to all the lewdest men in the city. This way she and you will receive much gold from their dissolute desires…'

He flung the painting to the ground, and lunged desperately and inexpertly at Franco's throat. Hers was a reflex action: she loosed the dagger concealed in her right sleeve, and turned it to deflect the sword blade. The force of this deft pass caused Benedetto to stumble and fall. His sword slid from his hand, and he looked up blankly when Franco did not bother to take advantage of the reversed situation.

'Come on, kill me,' he begged, leaning against the damp-stained wall, panting with fear, anger and misery.

'Let's stop brawling,' she urged. 'We don't want to be thrown in the Stinche for causing an affray, and the Eight are ever patrolling this area for thieves and cutpurses. Believe me when I say your Lauretta met no hurt in my bed…' A small smile darted to her lips. 'Indeed she seemed as comfortable there as in her own.'

Franco suddenly remembered Andrea. It was long since she dared think of him for the pain memory brought. God, how he would have loved this ridiculous tragic scene.

Benedetto slumped forward utterly exhausted. The skin on his face sagged as if he'd lived many years in one short night. 'Dear Mother of God, then she is a harlot. Tell me, at least, that you love her, Franco.'

'No.' She replaced the dagger. 'But I shall guard her, good priest. She'll always have food to eat and a place to sleep so long as I live.'

'But I offered her love. Did she never mention me?'

'You're Benedetto. In her own words: the sweetest fool. But she could never be your wife any more than she can be mine.'

'One dark night I shall slit your liver with that sword.' Benedetto threatened with greater bitterness than conviction. 'And gouge out those mocking eyes to give as a gift to the faithless Lauretta who probably loves them well.'

Franco retrieved the painting, and asked seriously: 'Would you like this in memory?'

'And have half the gentlemen of Florence seeking my blood for it? No, you sell it and Lauretta for gold.'

He slunk away, bent as if carrying some unbearable burden. Franco sighed and straightened the short purple cloak, edged with silver fox. Perhaps it was better to let him believe what he chose, rather than risk betraying her own secret with the truth. She had needed his love: it had been to bask in brief summer sunshine, and learn she was truly feminine. She understood she did not love Benedetto enough. Even if she played again at Lauretta and fled with him, it was too late for her to be the sweet amenable maiden he dreamed of. To have ever been such a creature, Franco understood clearly, would have meant she died long ago … in fact Franco could never have come into existence…

'You did not need my help then?' a low voice chased her from thought. Ridolfo di Salvestro emerged from the gloom at the end of the courtyard. 'You were late,' he explained his presence, 'so I sought your address from Da Vinci, who had a letter for me to give Lodovico Sforza. I came to ensure you had not forgotten our appointment. Standing here I waited to see if you needed my aid, but Franco is evidently as adroit with a weapon as a brush.'

'He was but a poor priest, who knows more about good than evil,' Franco said soberly. 'As such he would not be much of an opponent, but, Messer, you should not walk these alleys. You are a glittering temptation.'

Di Salvestro shook back his cloak to reveal

even more splendid gems. He said nothing only smiled with thin amusement, and stroked the sword hilt with the hands of a lover.

'Perhaps you had best come up,' she said, 'we cannot talk here. Look at the folk crowding to their windows.'

Indeed the overhanging walls seemed to have sprouted sudden live gargoyles. Nothing could occur in this neighbourhood without countless curious eyes watching.

She sent Taddeo out of the studio, for his terrified expression showed he recalled their visitor from another time. Franco poured wine.

'I hope you will excuse these humble lodgings.' She apologised, and felt the warm red power set her blood racing, and begin to inspire her with a mad courage. This morning had turned into a dangerous game ... as if she played at dice with the Devil, and so had to win every throw. Once more with gentle pain she recalled Andrea.

'I don't doubt you have been accustomed to better surroundings.' Ridolfo looked round the cluttered room with distaste, and wrinkled his nose against the odours rising from the alley. The rainstorm's good work was fading under the stinking onslaught of daily life.

Franco's sharp mirth drew those dark watchful eyes to her face. 'What! A nameless youth know better than this! You jest indeed.'

'Then why are you so unwilling to sell your painting? Think of all you could buy with the gold.'

'It is not for sale.'

'Because Lauretta is your mistress?'

'You overheard that?'

Franco shivered. This man was not a love-blinded, unworldly priest. How much might his observant eye discover, and his clever mind discern? She became very calm.

'Why do you want to purchase the "Red Lily" so much?'

Ridolfo looked through the windows at the clouds which dissolved and re-formed as they sped across the city. 'I lost the maid I should have loved. My own belief in the astrology, which showed we should belong to each other, has foundered. Since then I have little faith in what the stars and planets foretell ... although my noble friend, Lodovic, does not share this scepticism. He is ruled by the science. His own astrologer and I read that he would return to Milan ... even greater triumphs await him.'

'What was the name of this girl you lost?'

'It no longer exists,' Ridolfo said harshly. 'Her family was involved in a conspiracy against the Medici, as far as popular opinion and law are concerned. One does not meddle in the political intrigues of another city, unless one is armed with great power.'

Franco poured more wine, and handed the pewter beaker to the man. As he received it, his fingers inadvertently brushed her cold hand. His dark eyes flared. 'Who, in the Devil's name, are you, Franco?'

The blood withdrew from her face, but she replied in a steady tone: 'You have answered your own question by naming me, surely.'

Ridolfo looked from his hand to hers, and Franco felt the unease which heralds a storm. They continued to stare at each other for a long moment. At last, Ridolfo re-examined the painting.

'I must seek out this Lauretta,' he announced flatly, 'for she is the mirror image of my fate.'

'She would have nought to do with you, Messer, so you would be wasting your dreams.' Franco's lips lifted in a grim smile.

'As you don't wish to sell me the painting it would be ill-mannered of me to bargain further. In future, I shall watch with the keenest attention the career of the young Florentine, Franco.'

Messer Ridolfo's words suggested a threat, and Franco thought: he suspects something about me without knowing precisely what it is. I must endeavour to guard the past, present and future from his eyes...

Cosima

How strange to ride again into the courtyard of Casa Cuono on a spring afternoon. Franco tried to banish memory. This time her companions were Guido di Cuono and Daniello della Sera, and they were followed by a company of mounted servants in the two distinctive liveries, with Taddeo riding a mule in their brilliant midst.

'It's a hideous old place,' Guido apologised. 'One day, Franco, you must visit my charming villa at Poggio, a more fitting environment for your artistic taste.'

'And you have never seen Buonventura.' Daniello's reproach was accompanied by such a sincere smile that Franco felt he really regretted this omission.

'My sweet friends, what would the city merchants say if I was forever leaving commissions unfinished to visit you?'

'You will attend Daniello's wedding,' Guido said, 'and you can paint the newly-weds.'

'You are to be married!' Franco exclaimed. Her heart grew heavy. It was to lose something she could never have, but the loss was nonetheless painful.

'It is still secret,' Daniello explained diffidently, 'but you are our confidant. The Medici approves. Now I have only to ask the lady's consent.'

'Of course she'll marry you,' Guido insisted.

'Any lady would,' Franco said. 'The golden god of our city smiles, and the maidens tremble and pale. Who is this fortunate lady?'

'My sister, Cosima, of course,' Guido replied instantly.

'May I wish you all happiness and many children.' Franco spoke sombrely.

Daniello sighed. 'Even in front of Guido I must admit I don't relish this marriage … not that Cosima isn't the finest girl in Florence … saving your mistress, the Red Lily … but women are such unaccountable creatures. Though the della Sera name must be continued, I don't enjoy the sight of babies. They're worse than any fountain … squirting and spewing from every aperture, and not caring who they dampen.'

'I thought you were already betrothed,' Franco ventured.

'That was long ago, and the maid's dead.'

She had heard him use a less unconcerned tone about a missing glove.

Franco entered the great house like someone visiting a place for the first time … yet feeling all the while she had been there in some distant dream, or other life. Certain objects were shockingly familiar: the large golden dish supported by tritons … a small painting of the Judgement of Paris by an unnamed Tuscan artist … a splendid ivory and silver crucifix … they had once graced the interior of Castelfiore.

The closer I am with my enemies, Franco mused, the less power I feel. This must be the frailty of my sex. A man would not hesitate to use sword, poison or hired assassin to accomplish his vengeance. I require something other than destruction: that the past could be unwritten. Revenge now seems strangely pointless.

When Cosima di Cuono appeared time ebbed away. Franco was a child again, gazing in wonder at Madonna Ginevra on feast days: around Guido's sister's throat, and in the cascades of dark hair, were the amethysts set in gold her mother had been so proud of, for Vincenzo de' Narni had given them her on Andrea's birth.

The present returned. Franco saw only Cosima. She had altered to slender maturity, and grown even lovelier. The dark eyes seemed troubled, and the soft colour faded to leave a lily paleness as she gazed on the young artist. Guido caught her arm.

'We were just saying Daniello sets all the ladies a-swooning … and now you demonstrate that truth, sister.'

'Who is this youth?' Cosima asked tremulously without looking at Daniello.

Guido laughed. 'This is Franco of Florence come to paint your beauty from life.'

Cosima became gay to the point of wildness. Franco had only seen little cocottes in the taverns tease and smile with such abandon to attract custom.

'So Maestro Franco, you are the faithful lover who will not sell his mistress's likeness to Lorenzo, or the Regent of Milan's special emissary. My brother will buy it yet, for he can be very convincing when he sets his mind on some desire. Now, tell me true, am I less beautiful than your Red Lily!'

'No.' Franco spoke emphatically. 'You are the most lovely woman I have ever seen.'

Cosima clapped her hands with delight. 'He speaks so ardently. I must believe him. That is the kind of man I most admire.' She smiled brightly at Daniello who failed to respond, and Franco knew a swift secret pleasure.

Franco found it difficult to sleep in that house, although the chamber, with its curtained bed, tapestries and carpet, carved chest and chairs, was the most luxurious she had ever stayed in. Despite Guido's and Daniello's expostulations she insisted on Taddeo sharing it.

'How can you have that vile abortion of nature near your couch?' di Cuono demanded. He loathed Taddeo, and delighted in striking the ground with a riding whip so that the poor creature leaped and snarled with terror.

'Because neither of us are accustomed to living in such palatial splendour,' Franco explained humbly, 'and he is used to my ways. I fear your servants might find me uncouth.'

Taddeo slept fully clothed before the door, waking and snuffing the darkness at the faintest footfall. He too felt uneasy within Casa Cuono.

To be a guest in her enemy's house seemed to Franco a crazed dream, but it was amusing to be waited upon by Gianni who had grown into a stout and solemn fellow, and offered the cook's famous cake not in exchange for kisses but with deference and a silver goblet of the house's finest wine.

Franco took a long draught of Orvieto to steady herself, for this cup with the large beryl set in its base had belonged to Andrea. Indeed she could still recall him holding it to her baby lips so that she might taste his wine. Gianni stared at the artist in some perplexity.

'You stir a memory, Maestro, but I can't pin it to a time.'

It proved difficult to wrest some daylight to work, for Daniello and Guido constantly required her company on hunting expeditions. Cosima chose to be painted in her bedchamber. 'Otherwise my brother and Daniello will keep distracting your attention,' she pouted. 'You are a target of much admiration, Franco.'

'I expect, madonna, it is rather like having a new hawk or greyhound … after the novelty wears thin I shall cease to seem interesting.'

Entering Cosima's room for the first time, Franco's heart twisted with a scimitar of memory. She could not look at the bed … the ornaments … or the lovely woman whose nurse, Bianca, was as ever fussing over the unbound tresses.

Franco's eyes sought the long window. A chamois still curvetted among the fantastically clipped bushes in the garden below. She half expected to glimpse a girl with a shabby dress and cape of red hair peering into the room. But she wasn't there or anywhere else any more.

The angry wail of a child drew Franco close to the window. Lying in a large wicker basket was a boy child of about two or three … plump and pink, his fine hair a field of corn at sunset.

She knelt down, and tickled the necklaces of fat. The eyelids flew open. The eyes were green. Franco understood. This was the reason Cosima had not visited the city during a long interval. Andrea was not quite dead. She picked up the damp child who smelt of warm sleep and soured milk. It was the first baby she had held in an age, and he was a Narni.

Oh Andrea, Andrea, Franco said silently, you should have lived to know your son.

He began to squall furiously, punching the green taffeta doublet with fat little crumped fists. Tears that had started in her own eyes became laughter. She had almost expected this love child to sense their kinship and be content in her arms. The nurse took charge of him, and the howl became a dimpled roguish smile.

'He's a real boy,' Bianca explained. 'A man's hands anger him, but he smiles at a woman's touch.'

Spirit of Andrea, Franco looked ruefully at her own hands, you can't tell if I'm your uncle or your aunt.

'What a beautiful child, Madonna Cosima, what is his name?'

'Mario. He belonged to the Caucasian slave my father purchased for me. Anna was young and foolish. Some unknown gentleman got her with child, as is the way of this wicked world, and then deserted her without paying us the customary fine for such an offence. Anna died when the boy was born. He was so beautiful it seemed heartless to send him to the foundling hospital in the city, so I keep him by me instead of a pet. Each day he grows more adorable. When he is of an age to learn, Guido will send him to a monastery to be a priest. It is the best way with bastards. Perhaps he will rise high enough for a cardinal's hat, and bring glory on our family.'

'Wouldn't his father acknowledge him? He's a fine child, and many a marriage bed does not beget such a son.'

'No. Mario is very well as he is. Besides he keeps Bianca occupied, and she stops treating me as if I was but five-years-old…'

'You are a gentle-hearted lady, Madonna Cosima. I had intended to depict you as a proud pagan goddess, but now you shall be Our Lady with the Blessed Babe…'

Franco knelt to drape the gown against Cosima's feet, and felt the knees quiver as if in fear.

'Don't be alarmed, Madonna. Here is Mario. Give him…' She stared around the room, saw a dish of fruit, and handed a golden-rinded pomegranate to Cosima.

The baby crawled at his mother's feet, and then reached for the fruit. The bright curls and dimpled profile etched against the dark blue drapery of the skirt made an irresistible picture, and Cosima's own attitude suggested gentleness as she leaned towards the child…

The painting grew, and Franco began to know Cosima: know her for her beauty, vanity, and foolishness. She had a babbling tongue that any clear mind could trip into revealing all sorts of closely-kept secrets. Franco was not very surprised when she said. 'Do you know why I nearly fainted when I first saw you? You recall someone else, though your eyes are very different. His were as green as sea water.'

Or as Mario's, Franco amended silently. 'Who was this gentleman?'

'Someone I thought I loved.'

'Alas, poor man. To be loved by you is Paradise upon earth,' Franco complimented. 'But that you only thought you loved him must have cast him into Purgatory. If you should begin to hate him then he will be thrown into the fires of Hell...'

'He is dead and already there,' Cosima said, and her eyes were grieved and baffled.

Guido rarely visited his sister while Franco worked. He loathed Mario, who began to scream immediately he appeared. Franco noticed that Cosima, who paid scarce attention to the child when they were alone, would hold him to her breast and smother him with kisses in a frenzy of defiance as soon as her brother entered.

Daniello never came near the chamber. Although Franco missed his gentle company, it delighted her that he found Cosima so irksome. As soon as the lovely creature appeared his handsome face dulled, and he withdrew into strained and polite monosyllables. Yet in Franco's presence Daniello waxed merry and talkative, delighting to exchange jokes, anecdotes, sing songs, and play tarocchi, chess or dice. He does not like her, Franco thought, and marries merely to please the Medici.

It appeared that Daniello disliked physical contact with women, and Franco began to fashion an impossible dream of one day being united with him in a spiritual marriage…

When the painting was all but complete, she discovered Bianca and Mario absent from the bedchamber. Cosima reclined on her couch, wearing a white camisia, trimmed with spangled ribbons and fine lace, but the material was so filmy that the voluptuous body might just as well have been naked. She lay as one unable to sleep on a sweltering summer's night … her cheeks flushed ... her hair tangled … and her ankles and calves uncovered. Each time her full breasts heaved their dark nipples peeped over the lace.

'Are you unwell, madonna?' Franco enquired politely. 'You seem feverish. Shall I call your nurse, and leave you alone?'

'No,' the beautiful mouth wore swollen discontent. 'Do stay with me. Tell me, Franco, why are you so distressingly faithful to your Red Lily? You never treat me as anything except the model for your wretched painting.'

'Why do you berate me, madonna? Since

that is the reason I was brought to your house.'

'I thought you found me beautiful, Franco.' Cosima's voice was warm and sweet as fruit plucked in sunshine. 'And I find you a most lovesome youth...'

Franco tried to stifle mirth, but it bubbled forth. The wench certainly had a taste for Narnis.

'Only because I resemble a man you thought you loved,' she returned gaily.

'Don't mock me,' Cosima reproved. 'I like you because you are Franco. Feel how hot my head is.' She caught the strong slender hand and held it against her temples. 'Can't you feel the pulse throbbing?'

'Indeed, madonna, I think your nurse might make some herbal infusion to soothe this fever.'

'There is no infusion that will do that,' Cosima whispered. She dragged the hand against her left breast. 'How my heart beats because of your proximity.' The dark eyes with the golden lamps in their depths examined Franco's burning cheeks. 'I do believe Guido is right, and you have never lain with a woman.'

'That is quite true.' Franco's husky voice contained an indignant edge.

With swift supple arms Cosima reached out and pulled the slim figure on to her bed. Franco fell forward, aware of the scents of orris root, bergamot and warm armpits. Cosima drew the red head towards her, and began to kiss Franco's mouth.

Benedetto's kisses had not prepared her for this embrace. Cosima's hands and mouth contained a terrible hunger, as if she wanted to draw the breath and blood from whoever she held captive in her arms.

I have heard men speak of such females, Franco thought fearfully. They are ever hot for a man's body, yet cannot be satisfied, so must go from lover to lover without care for their honour or modesty in the pursuit of some unattainable pleasure. It is a sickness not a loving spirit. She is merely inflamed by the belief that I possess an instrument of a magnitude to satisfy her.

'How cold you are.' Cosima stroked the red hair, and passed the tip of her tongue over the white neck. With alarm Franco realised that very soon this amorous creature would discover the total absence of the instrument she so desired.

'You should learn about love,' Cosima urged breathlessly, and she took Franco's hand and pressed it between her moist thighs.

Franco pulled away, and cried out: 'Nay, madonna, your brother would slay me ... and rightly so ... if he found a worthless artist touching his sister's body.'

She felt sick and unhappy. The disguise was

no defence against certain situations she had not even envisaged. She knew such practices existed between women in convents … and many preferred to satisfy their appetites that way rather than endure some brutish drunken fellow in their beds. Although she feared the complete embraces of any man, Franco spurned the idea of indulging in carnal games with another female.

Cosima entwined her legs around Franco's thigh, and her body shuddered with desperate spasms. Franco sprang free. Horror and disgust were written across her eyes and mouth.

Cosima's own eyes grew wild and furious. 'Shall I tell Guido you forced your attentions upon me?' she hissed, 'I can tear off this shift and swear that you raped me. Then he and Daniello would castrate you like the worthless animal you are. After that, see if your Red Lily wants the body you refuse to cede to me…'

The more fear Franco knew the more controlled she became. It had always seemed that when other men's eyes clouded with hot blood the one who saw with cold clarity must outwit their fury.

'Would your brother really believe your accusation, Madonna?' she asked.

'What do you mean?' Cosima reared up, and her face and eyes belonged to the ferocious tigress in the Signorias menagerie.

Franco threw the reckless statement like a pair of dice. 'Because I know the name of Mario's father, and also his real mother. Would the gentle Daniello della Sera agree to, or Lorenzo de' Medici countenance a marriage with Cosima di Cuono, however fair, if they knew that the so-called traitor, Andrea de' Vincenzo Narni had given her a child?'

Cosima's feverish brightness faded, and the lamps in her eyes dimmed. 'How do you know?' she whispered. 'You must be possessed with the devil's own knowledge.'

Franco smiled. The power was with her, and she felt it. 'Through magic, fair Madonna, through magic. Why did you keep the babe?'

'I tried to lose it, God knows!' Cosima muttered, and her face took on lines of pain at the recollection. 'No matter what vile potions I drank, or what my nurse did to me, I could not miscarry. When my brother discovered he wanted to kill me…' She clutched at her throat in agitation. 'They say the shock killed our father: he worked himself into one of his terrible rages and then died. But, Guido is a cold reasoning man. To slay me, or lock me away from the world would have provoked curiosity and the Medici's disfavour. I kept to these apartments for many months so that no one could observe my condition. When my time came I was tended by my nurse and Anna. I made Bianca take the child away as soon as he was born: he was so pretty even at birth, and my very own. Guido would have strangled him then. I think he vented his fury on my slave.'

'And she is dead?'

'I don't know. For all his passionless appearance my brother has a temper more violent than a volcano … yet he can be so kind…' Cosima smiled at some reminiscence, and softly fingered her own bare breasts. Franco looked away, and detested her imaginings.

'When I grew stronger I made a bargain with him: I should keep my Mario or else enter a convent – then I would not be available to charm the Medici and foster our family's fortune. Guido gave in…'

Cosima's voice faltered. She twisted her fingers, and added helplessly: 'I did love the child's father, Franco. You are like him somehow, but much harder … a diamond, whereas my sweet loving Andrea was soft gold. Yet he and his whole family were traitors and my brother said I had endangered our safety and reputation by allowing him to visit me in the city and here. I didn't understand…'

It would be easy for Guido to weave the threads of intrigue to enmesh this sensual sister who wanted nothing but admiration and gratification, Franco thought dispassionately, and she must have been terrified, and no older than I am now…

'Are you going to tell your brother how I ravished you?'

The soft dark eyes Andrea had worshipped flinched before that implacable gaze. 'No.'

For the first time Franco was glad her brother was dead. Better that than he should have discovered his goddess's true value…

The Medici brought a crowd of friends, including Ridolfo di Salvestro, to admire the completed painting at Casa Cuono. No one failed to noticed that Madonna Cosima's eyes followed the young artist everywhere with a beseeching expression … even while the Magnificent announced her betrothal to Daniello della Sera…

The Bride

In the Panico the Company of the Cauldron caroused until late. So much wine was consumed no one could recall whose saint's day they had gathered to celebrate. There was nothing for it but to toast each of the members all over again to round off a jolly evening. With arms linked they swung through the streets, singing lustily:

'How fat you are, my girl!
May Heaven blast you, churl!...'

Now and then they would stop to yell abuse at the linen-capped merchants who opened their shutters to hurl imprecations and nightsoil upon the disturbers of rest. Franco dubbed these would-be-abeds 'the companions of the pisspot' which added to the merriment, and encouraged further catcalls.

Gradually the party broke up as individuals sought their lodgings. Taddeo was not in his usual spot behind the Duomo, where he always waited to light Franco back to the Camaldoli when she was out at night.

'Lazy vagabond must have drunk himself

to sleep!' she grumbled, 'I'll give him such a drubbing...'

Franco whistled as she stepped out. Her head began to clear from wine fumes. This is an odd life for any father's daughter, she mused, but better than that rich unwholesome existence within Casa Cuono.

For a few minutes she relished her complete if somewhat precious freedom, then a gradual awareness of being followed in the darkness quickened her senses. Franco did not increase her pace, or glance back. It might only be another nocturnal reveller ... not necessarily a footpad. The small court some way ahead with two alleys leading from it would give her an opportunity to ascertain innocent or malign intent.

A sliver of moon was emerging above one of the roofs. By its uncertain glimmer Franco saw that both narrow passages were blocked by men, and the one she had entered through would at any second frame her pursuer. Moonlight caught on drawn swords.

She stood in the middle of that small piazza, and grasped her dagger, aware of its coldness in her hot palm. 'Do you want my purse?' she called. 'I've but two florins in it.'

'You're Franco the artist?' one of the men demanded. His face was concealed by the shadow of a hood.

'What of it?'

'I have to deliver a message from a noble

gentleman who regrets your interest in a certain fair lady. Here it is.'

Franco had no time to ask the identity of man or lady, for a sword point pierced her padded sleeve. She began to fight for her life but it was to duel with shadows where only eyes and blades gleamed.

This is the finish, she thought grimly, wheeling and dodging their lunges, I cannot hope to defend myself against two, even if darkness gives us the same disadvantage and protection.

Franco noticed the third blade.

It was useless to fight any longer. The noble gentleman would get his wish.

Then the new sword flickered against her two attackers. Obviously they had not expected this second opponent, and fled through an alleyway, leaving Franco alone with the swordsman. She had never known sweat could feel so chill, as she leaned panting against a wall. 'Who is my protector?' she gasped.

The tall figure did not reply. He turned and walked away in the direction from which they had both come. There were sudden shouts, running feet, and the flare of distant lanterns. Franco knew better than to tarry. The Eight were on the prowl. She dashed into the warren of alleys.

In the studio, Taddeo was curled up on the palliasse. Franco kicked him in the side.

'What in the name of Creation are you doing here?' she raged. 'I've just missed being murdered, not that you'd have proved much protection.'

Half asleep and bemused by Franco's fury, Taddeo began to stammer: 'But you sent me a message. You are to stay overnight with Maestro Botticelli...'

'I sent no such message,' Franco shouted scornfully. 'Sandro's room's so packed with drabs there'd be nowhere to stand, let alone sleep. Who told you this nonsense? Or is it a figment of the wine barrel?'

'No, Franco,' Taddeo insisted. 'The messenger was a lad in dark red with gold embroidery on his sleeves ... a great beast holding a man in its jaws...'

She smiled bitterly. So Messer Ridolfo wanted her dead. Whether to secure the 'Red Lily' or because he suspected the artist to be a Narni who would accuse him of being involved in that never-forgotten plot, did not matter...

The rumour that Franco had escaped murder travelled through the city, and fellow artists advised her to leave Florence.

'I may as well suspect one of you,' she retorted when Leonardo, Sandro and Domenico visited her studio. 'What, isn't there enough work for us all?'

Ghirlandajo put a restraining hand on Franco's arm, and said earnestly: 'Listen to me, just this once. It would appear you have offended a noble patron, either by your stiff-necked refusal to sell him the "Red Lily", or mayhap you've been creeping into the scented bed of his mistress or wife. Such things are always happening to us. Go away, and let the air clear. When you return the matter will be forgotten, or some new problem will occupy your enemy's mind.'

'I refuse to be driven from my home,' Franco cried defiantly. 'Either by you fellows, or some autocrat…'

At the Palazzo Medici, Lorenzo's close friends and family gathered around the artist, enquiring who the attacker could be. The Magnificent's eyes showed concern, as he drew Franco into the shade of the arcade.

'Thank God, you are quite safe. It would appear that the climate outside Florence might be healthier for you at this time,' and his voice brooked no alternative.

Ridolfo di Salvestro joined them, followed at a discreet distance by a page. Franco did not need to examine the embroidery design on the mulberry livery.

'An excellent idea, Lorenzo,' he interposed swiftly. 'I'm to return to Milan. Franco can come with me. Lodovico would welcome his talent…'

'I have no thought to visit Milan,' Franco said coldly. She was scared ... trapped between these two powerful men, both apparently determined to send her from the city.

'Of course not.' Lorenzo agreed, and his dark gaze triumphed over di Salvestro. 'I had thought of dispatching you to Rome,' he added confidentially, and Franco knew this was no rash decision. The Ruler of Florence had planned each move well in advance. 'Here is a letter to His Holiness, recommending your talent, of which I'm sure he will avail himself. By going there, you will be rendering me a great service. I should like you to discover in subtle fashion what is in Sixtus's mind regarding our State now he's started this new war with Ferrara. That would give us useful information, my dear Ridolfo. No one would suspect our charming Franco of gathering such snippets.'

Franco took the letter reluctantly. She understood this was a command, and could not fathom the real reason behind it. Yet to disobey the Medici would be to forfeit his patronage…

'I must finish Guido di Cuono's portrait,' she said unhappily, 'then I shall go to Rome if that is your wish. Messer Ridolfo,' she added, 'your page gets into odd company…'

Di Salvestro's eyes were narrow bars of jet as he answered. 'Sometimes a lad with willing manners does services for those other than his master.'

Lorenzo looked at them in turn, but said

nothing. For once Franco found his eyes inscrutable…

Completing Guido's portrait was not an unpleasant task, and it was very well paid. His palazzo on the Via Larga held no agonising memories, and Cosima rarely intruded in her brother's apartments. Daniello often dropped by to watch the picture's progress, gossip and drink wine … and wherever he was Franco knew soft contentment.

Guido never ceased to demand what the artist would accept for the 'Red Lily'.

'It's not for sale,' she insisted. 'Perhaps I shall give it away, but never for gain.'

'Take my advice, and give it to Lorenzo. It might sweeten his attitude towards you. I fear he means you harm, and finds certain acts of yours disloyal…'

Franco laid down a brush to stare at the sitter with astonishment. 'You jest. He is sending me to Rome on a special mission.'

'Of course, that will take you far away from Cosima.'

'What does this signify?' her smooth brow lined in puzzlement.

Guido smiled. 'Deny all you will, but I fear Cosima tried to seduce you from your virtue. I realise that you are immune to such dalliance. However, Lorenzo could never believe that any man my sister looks upon so ardently as she does on you would not immediately fall into her arms, and bed…

To win her interest is an act of disloyalty to our ruler.'

'Surely, our sweet Daniello warrants the Medici's displeasure more than an unimportant painter?'

Guido shrugged with austere amusement. 'As a loyal citizen, he would not hinder his ruler's desires. To share your wife with the Magnificent is not to be cuckolded by a groom...'

Franco looked appalled. 'We are not discussing a courtesan. How can you speak thus of your own sister?'

'Your solicitude speaks of rare good breeding – strange in a vagabond artist – but you already know Cosima quite well enough to be aware my words are not misplaced.'

'What has she said about me?'

'That you have a well-informed and beautiful head.' Guido still smiled. 'Be careful not to lose it. Knowledge can be very dangerous.'

'Is that a threat?'

'I have no need to threaten you,' he replied reasonably. 'I can crush a worthless young painter as easily as this.' Guido tore a petal from a crimson carnation, and squeezed it until colour, texture, and clove scent were lost. 'Besides, Messer Ridolfo may well remove you from this world for reasons of his own. I hear he shows an over-keen interest in all your doings. Perhaps he has some personal grudge, or merely wants the original Red Lily for his bed. He has the devil's own temper, they say, when he is roused…'

'Why did you commission me to paint your picture?'

'Because you do my features much justice, and I like to have you under my roof and eye so I can determine the amount of your knowledge. What do you really know about my family, Franco?'

She gathered together the brushes and palette to show the day's sitting was at an end. 'Enough to turn the Magnificent's friendship into suspicion and hatred.'

'I doubt he would choose to believe *you*, for that would mean he had to forego Cosima's passionate charms. Besides I can silence you before you begin to chatter. See this ring I always wear…'

He held up a finger with a golden orb set in a jewelled shank. 'I can press a minute pin, which releases perfume into the atmosphere … or poison in a wine cup. No one would be a whit the wiser whatever they suspected. Yet I admire your courage, Franco, you're like fire and steel. Because of that your very boldness I offer you my personal protection.'

Guido rose and placed a hand on her arm. 'You're a curious youth, and damnably handsome. Are you as cold as you pretend?' He put an arm around her shoulders, and casually kissed the soft cheek.

Franco pushed him away. 'That is a sin,' she cried in horror.

'A very pleasant one,' he countered levelly. 'Do you know Daniello and I have made a wager that I shall melt your ice. He says you are too pure and innocent, and I contend that all purity can be corrupted and innocence learn knowledge. I am tired of vicious knowing boys who perform their tricks for anyone who gives them fine gifts.' Intensity filled his voice. 'I want someone with a mind and a soul as well as a beautiful face and body for my intimate.'

He smiled at her disgust. 'Why are you so shocked, Franco? Half the men who are married have a boy they can turn to when women's wiles and temperaments become too much to stand … even if it is both a sin and a crime in this city … men can have much pleasure with each other and there is no chance of begetting a bastard to maintain…'

Franco produced the dagger. Guido began to laugh. It was not an unpleasant sound. 'My dear boy, I can summon my servants immediately. They will drag you before the Podesta, and I shall swear you tried to rob and murder me. And my word would be accepted. Put away that little toy.'

He drew near, Franco's terror overwhelmed and weakened her. Casually Guido pushed the dagger from her inert fingers. Their eyes looked down to where it rested on the ground between them. He had gentle hands, and his lips were cold and hard on her closed mouth.

'There,' he exclaimed gaily, 'that was not so terrible. I trust we have sealed our friendship. You may count on my protection against men like di Salvestro, and I can rely on you not revealing whatever trifling secret you believe you possess which could ruin my family's good name.'

'And Cosima's bastard?' Franco spat the words with contempt and repugnance for herself and her companion.

His hands tightened on her shoulders. 'One person who dared taunt me with that still bears the scars and can no longer speak. It would be a pity, Franco, for me to mark your beauty in a similar fashion, or...' and he smiled, 'maim those clever hands so that you would have to put your body to a calling you eschew to earn your bread. As for the child, I can destroy all trace of him...'

'No! Not that!' Franco's plea pierced the shadows.

Guido stared at her. 'There is some mystery in all this. Before either of us are much older I shall know the truth.'

He drew Franco hard against him, and then gasped. 'By Christ's Passion, you're no male.' Guido pressed one hand to her doublet, and muttered. 'Woman's breasts by Heaven.' She tried to struggle free as his hands travelled down her body. Tears overbrimmed the cold dark eyes in an extravagance of laughter. 'My sweet friend, you have been gelded, or else are indeed a girl. This makes rarer sport. Either way it is a pleasure to embrace you.'

He began to kiss her mouth with growing passion. Franco broke free. She was less frightened by his insolent touch than the fact he had discovered her secret.

'Do you know who I am, Guido di Cuono?' she panted.

He raised his shoulders to express unconcern.

'I am a Narni,' she whispered.

'They are all dead.'

'Your butchers did not find the girl who overheard the Pazzi plot brewed at Casa Cuono.'

Guido grew very still, and his dark eyes took on understanding. 'Della Sera's betrothed: Francesca Lauretta. So you came to our house with your seducing brother.' He examined her face minutely. 'By all the saints, you are the Red Lily…' He began to laugh again. 'So the men who desire her must turn sodomite to discover her hiding-place. Now I have the Red Lily in my palm.'

'I am going to destroy the di Cuono family,' she whispered backing from him.

'You have too much spirit and talent for a

mere woman not to realise your words are folly. By doing as you threaten you will reveal your own identity, and be forced to flee to the sanctuary of some nunnery. After your accustomed liberty, life would seem unbearably restricted and tedious. Besides, I seriously doubt the Medici will take notice of your accusations…'

'Your father was…'

'He is dead. Lorenzo will not want to pick scabs from old sores without excellent reason, if that means relinquishing Cosima.' Guido smiled gently. 'Life is not as simple as you wish: self-interest governs most things. You should understand something, Franco: I was not involved in that plot, and had no particular wish to bring down the Medici. I won't deny I wanted your brother's blood for dishonouring my sister.

'When my father had wrung from her that the day the conspirators gathered at Cosa Cuono she had Andrea de' Narni in her bed, he swore to have the whole family silenced, lest Cosima's seducer spoke out against him. I don't dispute our sire was a vicious man, or that his servants were over-zealous in their acts of slaughter and plunder. He claimed that since Vincenzo de' Narni had acquired his riches through the devil's art of alchemy it was not stealing to bring part of them away…'

Franco shuddered. With sudden vehemence Guido demanded: 'Do you suppose I enjoy this blood guilt on my own head? Perhaps that is why I allow Cosima to keep her brat. And would you have betrayed your own father in my position?... I doubt that.'

She was shaken by the confession. 'Are you going to reveal who I am?'

'If I do,' he said quietly, 'your career will be ended. As it is your life is in hazard. You cannot always rely on a saviour with a sword. You need permanent protection and comfort…'

'They were snatched from me on a certain Easter Sunday,' she retorted bitterly, 'so I have to shift for myself.'

'I offer you a bargain, Red Lily,' Guido's eyes shone with a strange hunger. 'To atone for my father's misdeeds I shall marry a nameless girl without fortune. As my wife you will be safe, and able to take your proper place in our golden society. Surely that is to be preferred to a convent…'

'Don't be ridiculous,' Franco cried.

'Your sacrifice is far less than mine. The Medici has it in mind for me to marry into his own family…'

'Then you do fear my knowledge?'

Guido's smile held no warmth. 'No, but I am a collector, and should like to withhold the Red Lily from all others…' His tone was grimly detached. 'If you don't accept my generous offer I vow you will not escape me:

one day I shall be tempted to rid myself of the slight anxiety of your sudden wild disclosures. Death will snatch you in some dark alley … or a wine cup … or as you eat…'

Franco gazed at him, and perceived she had little chance to avoid agreeing. 'Guido…' she did not know how to speak her thoughts, and stammered: 'I am unused to a woman's role … and I fear…'

He took her hand and kissed it formally. 'You will be the most exquisite lady in the whole of Florence. People will say Guido di Cuono found the Red Lily, and Franco the painter fled away brokenhearted. So what is there to fear?'

She held her head very high, but could not prevent the colour flooding her cheeks. 'I dread the embraces of a husband.'

Franco expected some lewd jest, but instead Guido nodded gravely. 'Very well – I shall not treat you like a woman until you give me leave. I daresay you will change your mind.' He smiled. 'I am not as handsome as Daniello, my dear, but ladies have never found my attention displeasing.'

Franco wandered by the river, followed at a troubled distance by Taddeo. It was an impossible decision to make. 'Either marriage', she muttered, 'or destruction … and life is so sweet sometimes. I can't bear to yield it to death…' And then Franco remembered that there was an alternative. 'Very well, I shall go to Rome, and not return. It means re-making my life, but that is better than losing it…'

When they reached their lodgings, the candlemaker called out: 'Oy Franco, there's a young priest awaiting you,' he leered and winked. 'Think he's after your mistress.'

When she opened the door of the studio, Franco uttered a faint cry. Slumped across the table was the slight figure of Benedetto. A dagger very like the one she left at Guido's … or similar to most carried by ordinary folk … protruded from his back. A splash of his blood had touched the 'Red Lily' which lay close to him. She rubbed it off with her sleeve, and rolled up the painting.

'Come on, Taddeo,' Franco called, 'we must leave for Rome now…'

Taddeo eyed the unmoving body. 'But…'

'If I stay … or ever return to Florence … I shall be executed for a murder I did not commit. Whoever attacked sweet Benedetto must have intended that…'

They had not ridden a league beyond the Porta al Croce before a mounted company of armed men surrounded them.

'You are to come with us, Maestro Franco,' the leader commanded.

'No.' Her clear cry rang with defiance, and she drew her sword. 'I shall kill anyone who impedes my journey, for I ride to Rome with the Magnificent's permission. I have his letter to prove it.'

'You will accompany us to Milan.' Franco noted the mulberry beneath the riding cloaks. 'We have orders not to use force, but if you resist, we must…'

The thunder of other riders attracted their notice. Franco recognised the scarlet and black of the di Cuono's banner.

The two factions milled around her. Franco strove desperately but could not prevent Messer Ridolfo's men from carrying off Taddeo, who was knocked unconscious and flung across a saddle. A Milanese grabbed her horse's bridle, and had his hand hacked off by a di Cuono servitor.

'Ride with me now, Maestro Franco,' he urged, 'I have instructions to conduct you to safety. It reached my master's ear that these villains intend to abduct and murder you. Let us leave them to fight. For Christ's own sake, come…'

She could not recall much of the journey. The insistent pounding of galloping hooves drove out all thought except a faint memory of a crumpled pennant lying in a burning courtyard … now she rode under its protection. They came to Guido's house near Poggio: Villa Hermes so called because an antique figure of the gods' messenger had been unearthed in the grounds. The charming retreat was set amid gardens, and Franco felt calmed by the scent of flowers, the murmur of water, and the evening song of the nightingale.

An unspeaking woman with a coronet of flaxen braids above a hideously disfigured face led her to a moonlit bedchamber. Franco drank deeply from the proffered wine cup, and fell into immediate sleep on a soft couch…

She was woken by a man's hand. 'Taddeo,' she mumbled, 'Taddeo, what the devil…' Franco opened her eyes to see Guido marvellously attired in night-blue and silver.

'For your safety's sake,' he smiled calmly, 'I have arranged that our marriage take place today. It is given out that Franco the artist was attacked on the road to Rome, and has either been abducted or slain.'

'The authorities will soon be seeking my blood for a murder I did not do,' she remembered fearfully.

'I know nothing about that. I left the city as soon as I learned of Ridolfo's intention. Once you are my wife you will have nothing to fear. Allow me to thank you for bringing me a priceless dowry: the "Red Lily" painting.'

'Is there any way to rescue my dear Taddeo?'

Guido's expression showed revulsion. 'If di Salvestro has him I wish them joy of each other. I cannot have my bride tended by a monster. Come, my dear, a woman will help you dress. It is to be a secret ceremony, and no one will suspect the transformation of Franco into my wife.'

'If there is no other way,' she said heavily, 'then I must accept your offer.'

The silent maidservant remained impassive when the youth was transformed into a girl. She helped Franco bathe, and with the aid of pearled nets skilfully concealed the shortness of her curls.

The cloth of gold gown was beautiful but old-fashioned: it had belonged to Guido's mother, and the maid stitched the seams to fit Franco's slenderness. Only when a casket was set before her did she begin to feel emotion ... for she could not but recognise this jewellery: they were the pearl ornaments her mother had once worn, and which had been lent to Isabetta on her wedding.

'No... No...' Franco threw them aside. 'They are blood tainted...'

The servant left the room and returned with Guido, who stared amazed at Franco's appearance.

'Madonna, you are the most ravishing creature I have ever seen ... you put the stars to flight,' he whispered. 'I mean you no insult with these jewels. I am merely returning what is yours.'

With shaking fingers Franco fastened them about her throat and wrists. She felt as if she had entered some dream. How strange to walk in that heavy trailing gown

... the swaggering stride had to be replaced by small gliding footsteps...

The ceremony was brief and lonely and performed by a palsy-ridden priest.

'What day is this?' Franco asked her husband when he had given her his ring.

'The 10th August in the year of the incarnation 1482.'

She sighed. 'I am eighteen this day, and it was destined to be the date of my marriage.'

They dined alone and in great splendour. Guido was silent. He drank glass after glass of red wine, and never took his eyes from the girl opposite him. It began to grow dark, and the servants lit many candles.

Franco ate nothing. She felt like a wild animal suddenly put into a cage, and stared around the fine room, twisting the unfamiliar ornaments at her wrists. Her dream was all awry. If only the man sitting there could be Daniello, everything would seem right.

Guido spoke at last. 'Now I must show you to our chamber.' He laughed at Franco's alarmed eyes. 'Come, Madonna Francesca, I have given you my word.'

The silent woman helped Franco to disrobe. When her husband entered she was clad in a white silken shift.

'No,' he said to the woman. 'That is wrong. Get out!'

She fled, and Guido drew from a chest young man's raiment of gold and white.

'Come Franco,' he said with amusement. 'You must wear these.'

She could not understand, but allowed him to help her re-dress and tie the points of her hose. At last, Franco was arrayed as a gilded youth, all trace of femininity had vanished. Guido's eyes shone with pleasure.

'That is how I know you, Franco,' he murmured, 'that is what I want.' And he pinioned her against the tapestried wall, and began to kiss her face with monstrous passion.

Franco tried to pull away. Once her mouth was free, and she screamed until she thought her lungs must burst.

'There is no point.' Guido's pale face was unusually flushed with laughter. 'The servants have heard far worse sounds coming from this room, and would be more frightened to enter and disturb me at my play than to journey into hell. This whole villa is dedicated to my pleasure…'

The mystery of men's and women's embraces was not as secret as this. Franco's disgust and horror were boundless. Her husband ignored all the femaleness of her body, and forced her to play the catamite, as he had compelled all the boys who had visited his house.

Afterwards Franco lay weeping with shame and pain. Guido's voice came from a smiling mouth in the darkness. 'Why mourn? You are still a virgin, my sweet bride.'

‘Why did you marry me?’ she pleaded, stifling the frenzy of sobs with the heel of her hand.

‘It’s a rare joke,’ he explained, ‘as I said I wanted the Red Lily. Now I have painting, artist and model ... and know a secret that no one else does. You wanted revenge, Franco, and so did I. You will personally pay each day of your life for what Andrea de’ Narni did to my sister.’

‘He only wanted to wed her. They loved each other.’

‘At that time my father and I did not want Cosima to marry.’

‘Why not?’

Guido laughed, and Franco closed her ears to his abominable explanation.

‘Aren’t you afraid I shall betray all these ungodly secrets?’ she whispered.

‘You are my wife, Franco, and I have complete power over you. I can lock you away as a mad or wanton creature, or kill you if you are going to prove more problem than delight.

‘At present though it satisfies me to have you at my side...’ He touched her nakedness, and did not withdraw his fingers when she winced. ‘Soon I shall send word to the Medici that I have wed the Red Lily, and beg his forgiveness for not revealing my secret before. When you have suitable finery, we shall ride to Florence and be feted as the most lovesome young couple. Now I have nothing to fear from you, and Franco has nothing to fear from the outside world.'

While Guido slept, her mind searched for an escape from this terrible gilded trap. Occasionally in the past she had day-dreamed of how pleasant it might be to live as a woman dependent upon some powerful man … now she only sought for a way back to the freedom of life as Franco of Florence … and to unknow the vileness her husband had inflicted upon her…

The publishers hope that this book has given you enjoyable reading. Large Print Books are especially designed to be as easy to see and hold as possible. If you wish a complete list of our books please ask at your local library or write directly to:

This Large Print Book, for people
who cannot read normal print,
is published under the auspices of

THE ULVERSCROFT FOUNDATION

... we hope you have enjoyed this book.
Please think for a moment about those
who have worse eyesight than you ...
and are unable to even read or enjoy
Large Print without great difficulty.

You can help them by sending a
donation, large or small, to:

The Ulverscroft Foundation,
1, The Green, Bradgate Road,
Anstey, Leicestershire, LE7 7FU,
England.
or request a copy of our brochure for
more details.

The Foundation will use all donations
to assist those people who are visually
impaired and need special attention
with medical research, diagnosis
and treatment.

Thank you very much for your help.

to survive Francesca masks her true identity and sets out to revenge herself on the powerful men who destroyed her former happiness.

FRANCESCA THE FLORENTINE

A major historical love story...

The time is the Renaissance in Italy; the place Florence and the heroine, Francesca de Narni, a beautiful and courageous girl. While her destiny becomes inextricably entwined with the deadly intrigues of the Medici family the city is plunged into an abyss of destruction and slaughter. In order